THORNHILL

THORN

❦ ALSO BY KATHLEEN PEACOCK ❦

Hemlock

FOR MY FRIENDS—

I'M NOT ALWAYS SURE WHY YOU PUT UP WITH ME, BUT
I'M SO GRATEFUL YOU DO.

1

Some rooms looked better in the dark. This was definitely one of them.

Neon light slipped around the curtains, muted flashes of red as the vacancy sign blinked on and off. I shifted my weight and the mattress protested with a chorus of groans and squeaks.

"Are you okay?" Kyle's voice was still rough around the edges as he tightened his arm around me. "Was it okay?" He had done this before; I hadn't.

I pressed my lips to his bare shoulder. "It was perfect."

The muffled sounds of a fistfight drifted in from the parking lot, and Kyle made a skeptical noise in the back of his throat.

"Okay," I admitted, a sleepy smile tugging at the corners of my mouth, "so it's not the most romantic place to deflower a girl."

"Deflower?"

My cheeks flushed. I shrugged and my skin brushed his, sending a wave of sparks racing down my spine. "That's what Tess calls it. Anytime she tries to give me a serious sex talk, she turns into the mom from a sixties sitcom."

"Bet none of her talks covered werewolves." A somber note crept into his voice, one that hinted at the reasons he had left.

"No," I said, struggling to keep my voice light, "but she did say all teenage boys were ravenous beasts. Plus, her last boyfriend was a mass murderer. Compared to that . . ." I shivered and cursed myself. I didn't want to ruin what we had just done with thoughts of Ben and everything that had happened in Hemlock.

Silence filled the spaces where our bodies didn't quite meet.

"You shouldn't have come after me," he said, finally.

"I had to." I couldn't remember finding him or how we had gotten here or who had kissed who first, but I knew there had never been a choice. We were inevitable. "You know I did."

"I know."

"You can't just run away."

More silence.

"Kyle?"

"Yeah?"

"It's still kind of perfect."

He pushed the hair back from my face and traced the line of my cheek with the pad of his thumb. "I love you, Mackenzie."

I opened my mouth to tell him that I loved him, too, but a particularly loud thud from the parking lot made me jump. "Okay, the setting could be a *lot* more romantic," I said, looking over my shoulder. "The back of your car would at least be quiet."

I turned to kiss him, but he wasn't there.

"Kyle?" My throat was sandpaper dry, my voice thick with sleep. Soft snores came from across the room, and Jason's shape—a tangle of blankets and skin—shifted in the dark. Outside, the fight in the parking lot was going strong.

I skimmed my fingers over the other side of my bed. The sheets were cold. Reality sank in: I hadn't found Kyle; he had never been here; we had never done . . . that.

It had all been a dream.

For a moment, it was like losing him all over again, and I put a hand over my mouth to smother the small, strangled sound that lodged in my throat and fought to get free. I wouldn't cry. I *couldn't* cry.

Jason was sleeping seven feet away. If he woke, he'd put his arms around me and whisper that everything was going to be all right.

Part of me wanted the comfort and the lie—wanted it badly—but it wouldn't be fair. Not to Kyle, who had walked away from everything to keep us safe. And not to Jason, who thought he loved me and who belonged to my best friend even in her death.

Burying the desire for comfort, I stood and made my way to the bathroom, ignoring the way the carpet crunched under my feet. The North Star Motor Inn—cash up front and no questions asked—was a step above a total dive, but it wasn't a very big step.

I should know.

Home isn't a permanent address—not for people like us. My father's words drifted back to me as I flicked on the bathroom light. Hank had seen motels as the way stations between cons and as dumping grounds for things he no longer wanted. Things like me.

I ran the water in the sink and scooped up a drink in my palm. It tasted of chlorine and brine and did nothing to dislodge the lump in my throat.

Rat-tat-tap.

Three glistening drops of red hit the porcelain. They mixed with the water, tingeing it pink.

My heart jackhammered as I glanced up.

Amy—my best friend and one of Ben's victims—stared at me from the other side of the bathroom mirror.

I scrambled away so quickly that I tripped and had to grab the towel rack to keep from falling.

"Easy, tiger." Amy leaned forward. Her ink-black hair fell around her like a curtain and her eyes were shadows that shifted and swirled like smoke.

I hadn't seen her in days—not since the night Jason and I had left Hemlock. Foolishly, I'd begun to think maybe I had left her behind.

"Just because you didn't see me didn't mean I wasn't here," she said, reading my mind in the unsettling way she sometimes did. "Don't you remember what I told you?"

I shook my head. Amy had said a lot of things—both before and after death.

She pressed her fingertips to the glass, her manicured

nails making the same rat-tat-tap sound the blood had made when it hit the sink. With each tap, fault lines spread across the mirror. "Something's coming, Mac." She sounded oddly sad. Almost apologetic. "It's not over."

A large crack split her face in two and the mirror exploded outward.

I woke—really woke—gasping. Soft yellow light filled the motel room, and I was lying, fully clothed, on top of my bed.

I struggled to shake away the fog of sleep.

Jason and I had come back to regroup. I remembered lying down—just for a second—and . . . nothing. I must have passed out.

A ball of lead settled in my stomach as I realized I was alone.

I checked the bathroom—empty—and then pulled my phone from my pocket. Ten p.m. I'd been asleep for over three hours. Pacing, I dialed Jason's number. The call went straight to voice mail.

"Where are you? I woke up and—"

My foot hit something smooth and solid. I glanced at the floor and then crouched down.

"GoddamnitJason." I breathed the words in a rush as I straightened, one hand still pressing the phone to my ear, the other holding a half-empty bottle of Jack Daniel's.

2

THERE WERE FIVE BARS WITHIN STUMBLING DISTANCE OF the motel, but in the end, I found Jason right back where I had started.

More or less.

We were in room eleven. He had made it as far as number seven before slumping to the pavement, bloody and battered, beer and whiskey riding his breath. He'd forgotten the room number. And his key.

That had been thirty minutes ago.

Now he leaned against the bathroom door frame, shirtless, blond hair still dripping from a dunk in the sink. Two cuts crossed his chest—just over his heart—like the X on a pirate's map. There was a third gash on his upper arm. *A broken bottle*, he had promised. *All three. Not claw marks.*

I thought he needed stitches, but he had refused to go to the hospital.

He reached past me and set a bloodstained washcloth on the edge of the sink. "You can't give me the silent treatment indefinitely." The slur had left his words, but his voice was slow and cautious.

I stared at his tattoo in the mirror—the black dagger on his neck that marked him as an initiate in the largest anti-werewolf group in the country—before dragging my eyes upward.

Jason's gaze was brilliant green and bloodshot.

"Are you hurt anywhere else?" The words—the first I had spoken since he told me where he had gone—sliced my throat like razor blades.

"No."

I glanced at the floor where his shirt lay in a crumpled heap. Torn and stained red, it was beyond saving. The cuts were bad, but they weren't *that* bad. I'd had enough practice patching people up—my father and, more recently, Jason—to know that much.

"Not all of the blood is yours." I closed my eyes and gripped the edge of the sink.

"It's Tracker blood." There was an undercurrent to Jason's voice that was as dark as the stains on his shirt. "All of it. We ran into a fleabag and his reg girlfriend. He tried to throw a guy through a wall while she came at me with a busted bottle. Tiny, but fast."

I tightened my hold on the sink, clutching it so hard that I cut off the circulation in my fingertips. "You could have been killed." Another thought occurred to me. A group of Trackers didn't just happen onto a werewolf by chance.

"They were hunting." Hunting wolves. Hunting people

like Kyle. "They went on a hunt and you went with them. Did you . . . did they . . ." I sucked in a deep breath. "What happened to the reg and the werewolf?"

"They got away. Both of them." There was a faint rustle of denim and then Jason was behind me. I could feel the air he displaced and the heat radiating off his skin. If I turned my head, I'd smell the alcohol on his breath. "I wouldn't have let them hurt her. The reg."

"And the wolf?"

He hesitated. "I don't know," he admitted. "It almost killed a man. . . ."

"A man who was hunting him." Jason didn't deny it. "What if it had been Kyle?"

"What if . . . ? Jesus, Mac. Kyle's my best friend."

I opened my eyes. I wanted to say I was sorry and I knew; instead, what came out was, "You promised to stay away from them."

Jason held my gaze in the mirror. "The local Trackers are the best way to figure out where a wolf in Denver might go. You know that."

I did know, but if Jason got sucked back into the Trackers, if they ever discovered the part he had played the night their leader had been killed . . .

I had almost lost him to them once.

"I didn't have a choice, Mac. My father's going to report the car stolen and Tess is going to report you missing— sooner rather than later. We're running out of time to find him."

"And the drinking?"

Jason was standing close enough that I felt him flinch. He reached for me, but I pushed past him and out of the bathroom.

I stopped when I was halfway to the motel room door. I wanted to storm off, but I'd have to come back here eventually. Jason was all I had. I crossed my arms and waited, half hoping, half dreading he would try to talk to me.

He didn't.

The bathroom door clicked shut. A moment later, the shower clanked to life.

Kyle had once told me that I needed to have faith in people instead of expecting them to let me down. But putting my faith in Jason's promises had almost gotten him killed.

I couldn't lose anyone else. Not after Amy.

I pulled my phone from my pocket and punched in a number. A familiar, melodic voice answered on the third ring.

"I need a favor."

The Denver Bus Center wasn't hard to find. My hands tightened on the wheel as I pulled off the street and up a ramp marked Public Parking. After today, I would well and truly be on my own.

"I thought we were getting breakfast." Jason flipped open the glove compartment and dug through a rat's nest of paper and plastic.

"Lunch," I corrected as I turned off the ramp. "It's past noon. And we are."

He paused his search just long enough to shoot me a

skeptical look over the top of his shades. "Week-old sandwiches from a bus station vending machine wasn't what I had in mind."

"I'm surprised you want to eat at all, considering you felt too hungover to drive." I bit my lip and backed Jason's SUV into a space as he located a small bottle and popped two white tablets. "I just have to do something. You can wait here. I'll crack a window."

"Right. Because I'm a child or a puppy." He followed me out of the car and downstairs.

The inside of the bus terminal seemed unnaturally dark and dingy in contrast to the bright morning outside. A tired-looking woman hauled a screaming toddler toward the restrooms while a junkie rocked back and forth on a bench. A few security guards wandered through the crowd, their yellow shirts the only spots of color.

"Middle America at its finest," muttered Jason. The corners of his mouth twisted down as he watched a cleaning lady mop up a puddle of vomit. "Want to explain why we're here?"

I pushed back the coins on the bracelet I wore—Amy's bracelet—to peer at my watch. I hadn't factored in traffic and we were a few minutes late.

"You can't seriously think Kyle's been hiding out in a hole like this." Jason made it sound like we were standing on skid row. To someone as rich as he was, maybe the distinction didn't seem that big.

I fingered the edge of a coin and swallowed. I had rehearsed what I would say all morning, but now that we

KATHLEEN PEACOCK

HILL

 KATHERINE TEGEN BOOKS
An *Imprint* of HarperCollins*Publishers*

Katherine Tegen Books is an imprint of HarperCollins Publishers.

Thornhill

www.epicreads.com

Library of Congress Cataloging-in-Publication Data
Peacock, Kathleen.
   Thornhill / Kathleen Peacock. — First edition.
        pages   cm
   Sequel to: Hemlock.
   Summary: "Mackenzie, who recently solved the mystery of her
best friend's murder by a werewolf, goes in search of her boyfriend and
uncovers secrets of a werewolf rehabilitation camp from the inside"—
Provided by publisher.
   ISBN 978-0-06-204868-4 (hardcover bdg.)
   [1. Werewolves—Fiction.   2. Juvenile detention homes—Fiction.
   3. Rehabilitation—Fiction.   4. Mystery and detective stories.]
I. Title.
PZ7.P31172Tho 2013   2012051734
[Fic]—dc23   CIP
                                                                  AC

Typography by Torborg Davern
13 14 15 16 17   LP/RRDH   10 9 8 7 6 5 4 3 2 1

First Edition

were here, all my practiced words deserted me.

Before I could recapture them, the crowd shifted and someone squealed my name. I caught a split-second glimpse of dark skin and bright fabric before I was tackled by five feet and one inch of enthusiasm.

"Human ribs," I gasped. "Can't. Breathe. Se—re—na."

A flicker of embarrassment crossed Serena Carson's face as she released me. "Sorry. I forgot." She raked a hand through her shoulder-length curls and scanned the crowd to see if anyone had noticed her minuscule slip. Serena was usually very good at hiding her condition. She had to be. Like Kyle, and thousands of other werewolves living underground, she'd be sent to a government rehabilitation camp if anyone found out she had lupine syndrome.

She turned back to me and frowned as she catalogued the bags under my eyes and my rumpled clothes. "Don't take this the wrong way, but you look like hell. And I'm saying that as someone who spent the night on a Greyhound listening to the life story of a guy called Murray the Rat." She slipped a backpack from her shoulder and tossed it at Jason.

He caught it effortlessly, his eyes impossible to read behind the sunglasses. "Carson. Fancy seeing you here."

I shot Jason a nervous glance, then flashed Serena a small smile. "Not all of us dress like every day is a casting call for *America's Next Top Model*."

She glanced down at her outfit—a turquoise bomber-style jacket over a belted pink shirt and gray capris—and grinned. "The shoes don't really work," she said, gesturing to the blue Chuck Taylors on her feet, "but I figured flats would be better for pounding pavement."

"They look good. Tess has a pair just like them." Guilt flooded me at the thought of my cousin. "Is she okay?"

Serena nodded. "Upset and worried, but okay. At least you're providing the mother of all distractions from Ben. No sign of him," she added, before the question could leave my lips.

I exhaled. I still wasn't sure how—or if—I should tell Tess that Ben was the white werewolf who had terrorized Hemlock and killed Amy. As far as she knew, he had dumped her and skipped town to hook up with his ex. I wanted it to stay that way until I figured out what to do.

Serena glanced at Jason and arched an eyebrow. "Speaking of distractions, I told everyone at school that you went to Vegas on a bender. Mac and Kyle are supposedly tracking you down before you marry a hooker and sign away the family fortune."

Without a word, Jason turned and headed for the parking garage, striding through the crowd like he expected them to clear a path for him. Most of them did.

Serena shot me a bewildered glance. "Okay, since when does Jason Sheffield care about his reputation?"

I sighed. "It's not that. I sort of didn't tell him you were coming."

The look on her face slid from bewilderment to reproach. "So he doesn't know why I'm actually here? Oh, this is going to be fun."

"I just couldn't figure out how to tell him."

"Well, you'd better think fast," she said, falling into step next to me as I started after Jason.

"Did you really tell everyone we were in Vegas?"

She nodded. "Figured it was either that or say you had a pregnancy scare and ran away because you didn't know which of them was the baby daddy."

"Soap opera much?"

Serena shrugged. "We do live in Hemlock."

Truer words had never been spoken. I shook my head. "Thanks for coming."

"Are you kidding?" She grinned. "Denver is like the ultimate werewolf hot spot. I've been dying to check it out for years."

We reached the stairs to the upper parking level. Jason was almost at the top. The set of his shoulders was stiff and he dangled Serena's backpack by one strap, gripping the fabric so tightly that his hand shook.

"Jason?"

He kept walking.

I jogged up the stairs. Serena didn't follow, trying to give us the illusion of privacy even though she'd hear every word. Werewolf hearing.

"Jason? Would you stop for a second?" I grabbed the other strap of the bag.

He turned and slipped off his shades with his other hand. His expression was carefully blank as he slid the glasses into his jacket pocket, but his eyes glinted like pieces of broken glass. The backpack dangled between us, each of us holding a strap like it was the prize in a tug-of-war. "You want to tell me why Serena's here?"

I swallowed. "I thought she could help."

"So you called her without telling me?"

"You like Serena," I reminded him. "At least you used to." The *before you found out she was infected* hung heavy and unspoken.

"Sure. For a—" He caught himself. "—for what she is, she's great." He ran a hand over the light stubble on his face. "That's not the point. If you think Serena can help, fine, but you can't get pissed about me meeting the Trackers without telling you and then call her behind my back."

"It's not the same thing."

"It's exactly the same. You never trust anyone."

The idea of being lectured about trust by Jason was so ridiculous that only the look on his face stopped me from laughing. "I trust people who deserve to be trusted." I wasn't sure what else to say.

"Like Kyle? Leaving you a Dear John letter and slipping out before you woke up is really deserving of trust." Almost at once, Jason realized he'd gone too far. His eyes widened and the expression on his face softened. He released his grip on the bag and it thudded against my legs. "Mac . . . I didn't . . ."

I set the bag down and crossed my arms, using them like a shield even though the words had already hit. What Kyle had done, he had done to try and keep us all safe. That had to make it better, didn't it? "It doesn't matter," I said, even though it did.

I glanced over my shoulder. Serena was at the top of the stairs. I sucked in a deep breath and turned back to Jason. "Serena's here to help us find Kyle, but if we don't have any luck by morning, the two of you are going home. I'll stay here and keep looking, but you're going back to Hemlock."

"You've got to be joking." Jason stared at me, incredulous. "I do one thing you don't like and you want me gone?"

I was pretty sure meeting the Trackers and falling off the wagon counted as two things, but I didn't point that out. "I can't look for Kyle and worry about you at the same time."

"You can't force me to leave." Jason's voice came out with the edge of a growl, almost as though he were infected.

"You're right." Serena was suddenly beside me. She flexed her hand and muscles shifted under her skin. "Mac can't force you, but I can." She didn't look happy when she said it, but she flashed him a wolf's grin, showing teeth that were a little too long and a little too pointed.

Jason swore under his breath and walked away. When he realized we weren't following, he turned. "Are you coming?"

I hesitated and he pushed a hand roughly through his hair. "Look. I want to find Kyle. You want to find Kyle. We can argue about everything else"—his gaze darted to Serena and a thunderstorm played out across his face—"later. The Trackers said Montbello was fleabag friendly. It's one of the few parts of Denver we haven't checked."

"You're still going to help?" Serena asked the question before I could.

"It's not like I have a choice."

I followed him to the SUV. "Jason, you've always had a choice."

"Kyle's my best friend and you . . . you won't come back to Hemlock without him." He pulled open the driver's-side door and slid behind the wheel. "Choice doesn't factor into things."

.

3

A SMALL WOODEN SIGN JUTTED OUT OVER THE NARROW brick building. The words *Jumping Joe*—barely visible in the fading light—were carved in block letters and painted the color of coffee beans.

Serena stared up at the sign. "I wonder if they have smoothies. I'm dying of thirst."

Jason tugged on his turtleneck, making sure his tattoo was still hidden. "Yeah, all that flirting you did back there must have left you parched." A set of bells jangled as he pulled open the door.

"Don't hate on my investigative methods," Serena chided as we followed him inside.

Jason made a noncommittal noise and headed for a table. We'd spent the day combing Montbello and the immediate surrounding area with no luck. A guy working at the last place we tried—a 7-Eleven on the edge of the neighborhood—had given us the name of the coffee shop in exchange for Serena's number.

The mingled scent of coffee grounds and baked goods

made my stomach rumble as Serena and I joined the line in front of the counter. Framed posters of old art deco travel ads covered espresso-colored walls and most of the illumination came from sleek, cylindrical lamps hanging above small round tables.

Serena's phone buzzed. She pulled it from her pocket, glanced at the display, then slipped it back without answering. "Trey," she said in response to my questioning look.

I cringed at the thought of all of the things her brother would say to me—most of them justified—when I got home. "I can't believe he let you come on your own."

She snorted. "I didn't call and tell him until I was halfway here. Even then, I didn't say where I was going."

Trey wasn't going to just yell at me. He was going to outright kill me.

"Don't worry," Serena said, catching the look of panic on my face. "I wanted to come and he needs to be less obsessively overprotective. This will be good for him."

Somehow, I doubted Trey would see things the same way.

I pulled my own phone out and scrolled through the photos until Kyle's face smiled up at me. Warm brown eyes, sharp features, and chestnut hair that always needed a cut.

An ache spread through my chest. Without him, Hemlock wasn't home.

I glanced around the shop and my eyes locked on Jason. He was sitting at a table near the window, legs sprawled out and hands clasped behind his head as he stared up at the ceiling. Who would watch over him if I made him go back without me? Not his parents; they treated him like a prob-lem they could just throw money at.

Serena started bouncing on her toes, providing a blessed distraction from my thoughts. "How are you not exhausted?"

"It's one of the perks."

Right. Superstrength. Superspeed. Less need for sleep. If you could bottle the benefits of LS without the whole turning-furry thing, people would line up to get infected.

We reached the front of the line. Serena got a mocha latte and I ordered two large coffees, knowing there was no way Jason would turn down caffeine after a night like the one he'd had. I handed the girl a ten and waved off the change, earning a small smile. She was about our age. Her shoulder-length hair was black with an indigo streak and when she brushed it away from her face, I caught sight of a Claddagh ring on her right hand.

I glanced over my shoulder. There was no one behind us.

"I was wondering if you've seen this guy." I held out my phone, screen up. "He would have come in over the last cou-ple of days."

The girl took my cell and frowned down at Kyle's picture. "Maybe," she said slowly. She chewed on her lower lip for a moment. "It's dead in here right now, but it's usually pretty busy." She glanced over her shoulder. "Eve?" Silence. "Eve!"

Another girl ducked out of a back room and approached the counter. She was short—maybe as short as Serena—and compensating with a pair of combat boots that looked regu-lation until you realized the soles were at least five inches thick and the laces were blue ribbon. Her apron, jeans, and

19

T-shirt were all black and her scarlet hair was pulled back into a high ponytail.

She tilted her head to the side. "Yeah?" she asked, the word a smoky rasp.

The girl with the ring handed her my phone. "They want to know if we've seen this guy."

Eve glanced at Kyle's picture. Her eyes widened a fraction of an inch as her gaze darted from Serena to me. "Boyfriend?"

If I said yes, she'd probably think we were stalking him.

"Friend," Serena said, picking up on my hesitation.

A shroud of indifference fell over the redhead's face as she set the phone on the counter. "Sorry. Hasn't been in."

"Are you sure?" asked Serena. "You barely looked."

"I looked. Never seen him." Underneath her low tones, there was a defensive edge the question hadn't warranted. Her fingers strayed to a large leather cuff around her wrist, twisting it as though letting off the tiniest bit of restless energy.

She was hiding something; I was sure of it.

But it wasn't like I could lunge across the counter and throttle her for answers. If the Trackers were right and Montbello was popular with wolves, the girl could be infected. It was hard to force anything out of a werewolf—especially when you were a reg.

I hauled a pen from my jacket pocket and scribbled my cell number on a napkin. "Can you call me if he does come in?"

She shrugged. "Sure."

I tried to smile. "Thanks." I slipped the pen and my phone back into my pocket, picked up my drinks, and headed for a small cart that was stocked with coffee fixings and plastic lids. Serena followed. She sipped her latte and kept an eye on the counter as I added cream to my coffee and sugar to Jason's.

"She just tossed your number in the garbage," whispered Serena as the grinder started clanking.

"Think she was lying about not seeing Kyle?"

"Definitely."

As I fitted the coffee cups with lids, I glanced up at a community bulletin board. There were a few flyers advertising open mic nights and people looking for roommates. I wondered if Kyle had found a place to crash. He had the Honda so it wasn't like he'd end up sleeping on a park bench, but I hated the thought of him spending his nights in the backseat of the car.

He's a werewolf, Mackenzie, I chided myself. *Don't you think he can take care of himself?* No. If I really did think that, I wouldn't be here. With a small sigh, I turned away and trailed Serena to the wobbly table Jason had claimed.

Out of the corner of my eye, I saw the redhead watching us from the counter.

"They haven't seen Kyle," I said as I set the cups down. I plucked a discarded newspaper from the chair opposite Jason and sat. Let the girl think we believed her. For now.

Jason didn't comment, but he did take the coffee. I hoped that meant his anger at me was starting to fade.

I sipped my own drink as I scanned the front page of the

paper. A smiling brunette with a streak of white at her temple stared up at me from under the caption: *Winifred Sinclair Claims Thornhill on Schedule to Open in Six Months.* My stomach twisted. Thornhill was the first of five new facilities the LSRB—the Lupine Syndrome Registration Bureau—was constructing to deal with overcrowding at the existing camps. It was the kind of place Kyle and Serena would be sent if they were ever turned in.

Below the Thornhill piece was an article about a speech Amy's grandfather—Senator John Walsh—had given urging jail time for regs who failed to report infections.

I wondered if he'd still be so vocal if he knew why Amy had really died.

The bell above the shop's door jangled as a trio of gazelle-like girls in yoga-chic wandered in. I tossed the paper onto an empty chair as they walked by, hoping Serena and Jason hadn't noticed the articles. From the tightness at the corners of Serena's eyes and mouth, I hadn't been fast enough.

I glanced at the counter. Eve was ringing in three bottles of overpriced water. She didn't look our way, but I had the distinct feeling she was still keeping an eye on us. "We should get going."

Jason raised an eyebrow. "We just got here."

I shrugged. "They haven't seen Kyle. There's no point in staying." I shot him what I hoped was a meaningful glance before heading outside.

"You realize you're the world's worst actress," he said, once we were out on the street. "Didn't you learn anything from Amy?" I turned in time to see him cringe. "Sorry."

"Why?" The air felt static-charged and heavy, the way it gets before a thunderstorm, and dusk had deepened to full dark while we had been inside. "It's not like she didn't keep things from you, too." The bracelet on my wrist felt like a hundred-pound weight as I walked to the SUV.

Behind me, Serena filled Jason in on the barista. "She obviously recognized Kyle's picture. And she's infected."

I leaned against the hood of Jason's car. "I thought wolves couldn't detect other wolves when they're in human form."

Serena shrugged. "We can't. That leather cuff on her wrist is hiding scars. It rode back when she reached for the phone."

Jason let out a low, skeptical noise. "Scars on her wrist? You've just described half the girls at school who've seen *Girl, Interrupted* and own copies of *The Bell Jar*."

"The scars were on top of her wrist, moron," said Serena. "And they were rough. Scratches, not cuts."

Jason sighed and cracked his neck. "Okay. So we come back tomorrow and stake out the coffee shop in case Kyle shows."

I shook my head. "I'll come back in the morning. After you and Serena leave for home."

Jason opened his mouth to argue, but Serena waved us silent and pulled us around the back of the SUV. She yanked Jason so hard that only her grip on his arm kept him from falling. She pressed a finger to her lips and nodded toward the shop.

Eve stepped out onto the street, a jacket held loosely in

one hand. She stretched her arms back and rocked up on the toes of her gigantic boots. For a second, it looked like she hovered on the edge of taking flight, but then her heels touched pavement. She pulled on her jacket as she headed for a Thunderbird parked halfway up the block. Just before climbing behind the wheel, she slipped a phone out of her pocket and sent a text.

I turned to tell Jason we should follow her, but he was already reaching for his keys.

"Are you sure you've never tailed anyone before?" asked Serena as she leaned between the front seats.

The ghost of a grin crossed Jason's face. "Is that a compliment?" He pulled over and killed the engine before reaching across me for the pain pills in the glove compartment.

"Still hungover?" I asked.

"Just a headache." He tossed back two pills. "Plus the whole getting-cut-up-with-a-bottle thing."

"Don't worry," said Serena, patting his upper arm and smirking when he winced, "lots of women like men with mileage on them. Not me, personally, but lots of women."

"If it keeps me off your list, I'll add a scar or two."

A block ahead, Eve slipped out of the Thunderbird and crossed the street. The neighborhood was filled with overgrown lots and ramshackle warehouses and had a serious postapocalyptic vibe, but she walked as though she were untouchable—all swagger and confidence and big boots.

She disappeared around a corner.

Jason stopped me as I reached for my door handle. "Give

her a sec. You don't want to spook her."

Serena let out an exasperated sigh. "She's a werewolf, not a horse." Before Jason could object, she slid out of the car and started down the block, leaving us to follow.

Eve had parked across from a four-story brick building. It looked like an old factory, but there were no signs to identify it. The windows were all either boarded up or busted, and the whole thing was surrounded by an enormous chain-link fence.

I walked the length of the fence and turned the corner. It was completely unbroken. There were no openings or gates.

"I think she went over," said Serena. "I can hear music coming from inside. . . ." She peered up at the fence. "It's high, but I could definitely make it."

Jason stared at her. "It's at least fifteen feet."

She shrugged. "So?"

He shook his head. "Just . . . wondering what it would actually take to keep one of you out." He ran his fingers over the fence. "Too thick for wire cutters. Why would anyone build a fence without a gate?"

Rough hands suddenly spun me around and thrust me against the fence. "Because we don't need gates." Eve's eyes—a gray green the color of mist on a pond—flashed. She pressed her arm across my neck: hard enough to make breathing difficult but not so hard as to actually crush my windpipe. She was smaller than I was, but size didn't matter when you were up against a werewolf.

Without looking at them, she addressed Jason and Serena. "I can pulverize the reg's neck before you get to me.

You might want to back up a step. Or three."

To me, she said, "Why are you following me?"

I tried to answer and ended up coughing until she relaxed her hold a fraction of an inch.

"We're looking for our friend," said Serena quickly. "The one we asked you about."

The colors in Eve's eyes seemed to darken and swirl. "I told you: I've never seen him." She was great at lying with her face and voice, but her eyes were as changeable as the weather. They gave her away.

"Don't believe you," I rasped.

"This friend of yours? He's a werewolf?" She waited for me to give a small nod. "No offense, but most wolves who come to Denver don't want to be found. At least not by regs."

"What makes you think she's a reg?" Jason sounded closer, as though he had eased forward despite the warning.

"If she were infected, would you have listened to me when I told you to stay back?" Eve released me unexpectedly and I had to grab the fence to keep from landing on my butt. "Do yourselves a favor and go. This isn't a mixed neighborhood."

I swallowed and lifted a hand to massage my throat. Kyle was in Denver and Eve had seen him. If I hadn't been sure before, I was now. Relief flooded my chest. "Please, if he's inside, just tell him I'm out here. If he doesn't want to see me, I'll go." Out of the corner of my eye, I saw Jason raise an eyebrow. "Please. My name is Mac. Mackenzie Dobson. Just tell him I'm here."

Confusion flashed across Eve's face. It was replaced, a second later, by anger. "Lying about your name doesn't make me want to help you."

I stared at her, baffled. "Why would I lie?"

"You tell me." With inhuman speed, she reached around me and plucked my wallet from my back pocket.

"Hey!"

She fished out my driver's license, tilted her head to the side, and went completely still. Emotions flickered through her eyes but none of them made any sense. Surprise, resignation, and something that looked almost like fear. "Mackenzie Dobson from Hemlock."

"I don't know you." I was very sure of that, despite the too-familiar way she was staring at me.

Eve shrugged. "We know someone in common."

Hadn't we already established that I was looking for Kyle?

Serena was apparently thinking the same thing. "Kyle Harper," she said. "Mac showed you his photo in the coffee shop. The person we've been talking about for the past five minutes."

Eve's mouth twisted into a small smile, one that looked more pained than amused. "Right. Of course. You might as well follow me."

I exchanged worried glances with Serena and Jason as we trailed Eve around the corner. None of this was adding up.

Eve tugged on a section of the fence. It lifted on hidden

hinges, creating an opening just large enough to crawl through.

"Maybe you guys should stay here," I whispered, forgetting, momentarily, how futile whispers were.

Jason shot me a scathing look that clearly said we were not going to have this conversation.

Eve glanced back. "All three of you are coming. I'm not risking any of you running off to tell someone what you've seen."

"All we've seen is a fence and an abandoned building," muttered Jason.

She shrugged. "If the night patrol were doing their job, you wouldn't have gotten within half a block of this place."

Eve gestured at the opening. With a frown, Serena dropped to her knees and wormed her way through the small gap. Jason went next, barely managing to squeeze his broad shoulders through. I went last, followed by Eve.

I climbed to my feet on the other side and dusted clumps of dead grass from my palms and jeans. The lot surrounding the building was a knee-high tangle of weeds and shrubs. Without hesitation, Eve waded into the brush, moving as silently as a ghost and leaving just as much of a trace.

The path she took us on curved around the building and eventually led to three stone steps and a steel door. Eve climbed the steps slowly, almost reluctantly. She wrapped her hand around the door handle and paused. The fear that she was second-guessing her decision to let us in thundered through my chest as she turned and shot me a piercing glance that was almost a glare. I had never met her before today, so why did I get the feeling she hated me?

She gave her head a small shake, then pulled the door open and disappeared inside.

I climbed the steps. Just before I crossed the threshold, Jason's fingers skimmed my hand. "Are you sure about this?"

"No."

4

A WAVE OF LIGHT AND SOUND CRASHED OVER US. THE entire first floor of the building was one gigantic, open space broken only by support beams. Trance music picked up the frantic beating of my heart while a kaleidoscope of colors—purple, orange, red, and blue—swept a dance floor and illuminated several dozen dancers.

Although I wasn't sure if what they were doing could accurately be called *dancing*.

Dancing implied normal, human movement. This was motion supercharged by the strength and grace that came with LS. It was bodies leaping high in the air, twisting in ways that should have been painful and that would have broken a reg body to pieces.

It was beautiful. And disconcerting. As were the low shadows that stalked the edge of the crowd, wolves whose fur looked ultraglossy under the multicolored glow.

A bar hugged one side of the room and people were lined up three-deep for drinks.

It was a club. A werewolf club.

Gooseflesh swept down my arms. Having LS didn't make you a monster—I knew that—but being surrounded by so many people who could rip me to shreds left me feeling claustrophobic and off balance. Especially so soon after Ben.

I glanced at Serena. Purple and red light bounced off her dark complexion and an expression that looked almost like longing flashed across her face. She mumbled something that might have been "wicked," but it was hard to hear over the music.

Jason, on the other hand, looked like he was ready to crawl out of his skin. A muscle jumped in his jaw, and I wasn't sure if it was the mere presence of so many werewolves that left him looking slightly ill or the thought of what they might do if they found the symbol hiding under his collar.

Eve scanned the crowd and called over a giant who looked capable of picking up Jason and tossing him across the room.

Most of what they said was lost under the music, but I caught the tail end of their exchange during a gap between songs.

"Shit, Eve. I only came in for a minute." He tugged on a silver hoop—one of many—in his ear.

"Think he'll care? Just keep them out of trouble until I get back, okay?" Before the man could argue, she disappeared into the crowd.

I started after her as the music swelled up again.

A heavy hand on my arm pulled me back. "Stay put,"

growled the giant, his voice rising over the music.

Eve had lied about not recognizing Kyle's picture back at the coffee shop. There was no way I was just going to stand here and trust her to bring him to us.

I glanced at Jason. From the look on his face, he was thinking the same thing, but he shrugged and nodded meaningfully at the dance floor. If we drew attention to ourselves, it wouldn't be three against one: it would be three against every wolf in the room.

Serena rolled her eyes at us and stepped between me and the wolf. Just before she turned her head, I glimpsed a smile that could have made armies crumble. One male werewolf didn't stand a chance.

She rose up on tiptoe and said something near the man's ear before moving around to his other side.

His gaze followed her like a compass finding north, and Jason and I slipped away.

We skirted the crowd, weaving around small groups of conversation and wolves who danced like it was their last night on earth. I scanned each face we passed. None of them was Kyle's.

I headed for a staircase in the corner of the room, giving a wide berth to a couple making out in the shadows. The music faded to bearable levels as we climbed to the second floor.

A trio of wolves with midnight-black fur bolted past us as we reached the landing, and I couldn't quite suppress a shiver before glancing around.

Here, it was less dance club and more pool hall. It was

the kind of place I would find my father in on Sunday afternoons when I was a kid. Lamps hung like spotlights over scarred pool tables where money was put down, lost or won as angles were worked and tempers flared.

A blond man, his back half to us, leaned over a table as he lined up a shot. My heart tried to leap in different directions before momentarily stopping completely. *Ben.*

I wanted to move, but I was paralyzed.

The man straightened and turned. The air escaped my lungs in a rush as my heart kicked back into gear. *Not Ben.* I pressed a hand to my chest.

Jason was staring at me, brow creased. "Are you all right?"

I opened my mouth to lie, to tell him I was fine, but the words died in my throat. Standing thirty feet away, staring out one of the few windows that wasn't boarded up, was Kyle.

He didn't notice me. Not at first. He leaned against the window frame and pressed the knuckles of his right hand to the wood, a soft punch that might have been frustration or boredom. Then, with a deep breath, he straightened and turned.

Even at a distance, dark hollows were visible under his eyes, and it looked like a toss-up between what he had done last: slept or shaved. It had only been a few days, but he seemed somehow thinner and taller, like he had been stretched out.

I started to step forward and then hesitated. Relief. Hurt. Worry. A small flash of anger. I'd left everything behind to find him, but now that he was in front of me, I wasn't sure what to do or feel.

Kyle's eyes found mine.

I wanted to run; I forced myself to walk.

Twenty questions chased shock across his face as I came to an uncertain stop in front of him. I desperately wanted to cross those last two feet, but I couldn't. I stood before him—gutted with every emotion exposed—and waited for him to say something. Anything.

After a long moment, he reached out and cupped my cheek with his palm. *"Mac?"*

A tremble radiated out from my chest and stole my breath. Caught between wanting to laugh with relief or cry, I settled for closing my eyes and turning my face into the touch.

Kyle's hand fell away and I opened my eyes. "Hi," I whispered, the tiny word hesitant and inadequate.

"What—" Kyle's voice was a shock-choked rasp. He had to swallow and start again. "What are you doing here?" Something sparked in his eyes, and before I could answer, his lips were suddenly on mine, crushing and hungry and maybe a little desperate.

We were standing in the middle of a werewolf bar in a strange city, but it all faded as I wrapped my arms around Kyle's neck and kissed him as though we were the only two people in the world.

After a moment, he let out a rough sigh and eased back slightly. I pressed my cheek to the cotton of his shirt—the gray Arcade Fire shirt he'd been wearing the day he left—and listened to the rapid thud-thump of his heart. Even for a werewolf, it seemed to beat too fast.

Kyle pressed his lips to the top of my head. "Idiot," he breathed. "I can't believe you came after me." The words were chiding, but the tone was gentle. Almost relieved.

I pulled back just far enough to stare into his eyes. "What did you expect us to do?"

"Us?" Kyle scanned the room. His gaze focused on a spot just over my shoulder and his eyes darkened.

I turned.

Jason.

"He wanted to help." I wasn't sure why I felt the need to explain. Despite everything, they were best friends. Of course Jason had come to Denver.

"You shouldn't be here. Either of you." Kyle put a hand on my back and steered me toward the stairs.

I sidestepped him. Hating the way my voice trembled, I said, "You're coming with us, right?"

"I . . ." Kyle shook his head. "The reasons I left haven't changed."

Jason was close enough to hear. "Come to the motel. We'll talk. If you still want to stay, we'll go, but you at least owe Mac that."

I caught a flash of brightly colored fabric near the stairwell. The giant who was supposed to be watching us had one hand wrapped firmly around Serena's arm and was searching the room. We were out of time.

"Please, Kyle." I didn't want to beg—shouldn't have to beg—but I would. "Just come with us for a little while." If we could just talk to him away from this place, he'd see that he belonged back home.

The Adam's apple in his throat bobbed as he swallowed. "I can't. It'll just make things too hard. Trust me." His hand was suddenly on my back again, steering me forward. I twisted away as Jason grabbed his arm.

"What about how hard this is on Mac? Have you thought about that?"

Kyle pulled free of Jason's grip. "Stay out of it, Jason."

"I can't. I've spent the past four days watching her get her hopes crushed and listening to her cry when she thought I couldn't hear."

I froze. Our second night in Denver, I had given in to the tears I'd been holding back since leaving Hemlock. I'd tried to be quiet—locking myself in the bathroom and burying my face in a towel—and I had thought Jason was asleep, but he had heard.

He had heard and hadn't said a word.

Jason didn't look at me; he was totally focused on Kyle. "The guy I know would care about that."

"You think I don't care?" Kyle's laugh was so bitter it sent shivers down my spine. "Everything I'm doing is because I care."

He turned away.

He turned away and everything happened too fast.

Jason grabbed Kyle's shoulder and Kyle shoved him. Hard. Harder than he meant to, judging from the shock that flashed across his face.

Jason stumbled six or seven feet, collided with one of

the pool tables, and slid to the floor. A group of werewolves looked up from their game.

I stared at Kyle, angry and bewildered and beyond hurt. This wasn't how things were supposed to happen. "That's your best friend." My voice cracked. "He came to Denver to help find you and *that's* your response?"

I went to Jason's side and reached down to help him up. "You okay?" He hesitated, then took my hand and staggered to his feet.

"Sure," he muttered. "My week's not complete until someone hits me." He shook his head as though trying to clear it, and the fabric at his neck gaped open. I stared, horrified, as his tattoo was fully displayed.

I quickly pulled his collar closed, but I was too late. One man was already setting down his pool cue. He swore under his breath as he drew closer.

A single word was tossed from wolf to wolf: Tracker.

Games and drinks were abandoned as a semicircle of wolves closed around us. Kyle and Serena yelled our names, but I couldn't see them through the crowd.

Jason's fingers tightened around mine, and my hip bumped the pool table as I stepped back.

"He's a spy. They sent a spy." I couldn't see the speaker, but it didn't matter: the accusation was picked up and passed along until every face reflected a dangerous combination of fear and anger.

Kyle managed to break through the throng. He put himself between us and the nearest wolves. "He's not a Tracker."

A heavyset man with a lion's mane of gray hair stalked

forward. The muscles in his arms moved under his skin. "He has the tattoo."

Kyle repositioned himself so that he was partially blocking Jason from their view. His voice was steady but with an unmistakable undercurrent of desperation. "He didn't go through the initiation. The tattoo's not complete. He's not one of them."

"You expect us to believe you? After everyone saw you talking to him? What did you do, give him the address?"

"No one gave us the address," I said breathlessly. I caught a glimpse of Serena as she tried to make her way to the front of the crowd. "We came with Eve. She knows we're here."

"Bullshit," replied the wolf. "Eve would never let a Tracker in." The wolves pressed forward, a noose tightening around our necks.

The back of Kyle's shirt was damp with sweat and I thought I could see muscles twitch under the fabric. "I swear: he's just an ordinary reg. Harmless."

"And her?" rose a voice in the crowd.

Kyle glanced at me and hesitated. Which version of the truth would get us out of this unscathed?

The wolves didn't wait for him to decide.

In a blur of motion, a woman—partially transformed with inhuman hands and teeth—broke through the throng and tore me away from Kyle and Jason. My knees collided painfully with the floor as she forced me down. Serena shouted my name a second before the woman shredded the collar of my shirt and jacket with her claw-tipped fingers. Cold air hit my neck as she pushed my head to the side, looking for the Tracker's brand.

Kyle was on her in an instant. His face was a mask of fury, and for the first time, I looked at him and saw a man who had killed to keep me safe. He pulled the woman off of me but lost his grip when she started to shift completely.

Bones cracked, muscles tore, and clothing fell away until a wolf with fur the color of honey had taken the woman's place.

I tried to stand, but someone grabbed me from behind and shoved me back to my knees.

"ENOUGH!" A roar split the air, and the silence that followed was deafening.

A man strode through the crowd, two gigantic rust-colored wolves padding at his side. I strained to glimpse his face, but a hand on the back of my skull forced my gaze to the floor.

The man placed himself between me and the bulk of the wolves. "Let her go."

That voice. I *knew* that voice.

The pressure on my skull fell away. I looked up just as the man turned his back on me. He was tall and lean and he held himself like someone who was used to violence. His hair, black with hints of gray, just grazed the collar of a flannel shirt.

The set of his shoulders and the way he tilted his head to the side were horribly familiar, but I couldn't see his face.

"They're Trackers, Curtis." The wolf with the gray hair stepped forward. "He has the brand."

Relief washed over me. The voice hadn't really been

familiar. *Curtis*. I knew how disposable names could be, but I seized it like a lifeline as I pushed myself to my feet.

"And you were what? Going to send him back in pieces? Start a war?" Each syllable was a threat.

The other wolf backed down and withdrew into the crowd.

Slowly, the wolves drifted away, returning to the pool tables and their drinks. My rescuer watched them go and then turned.

Legs threatening to buckle, I stared into my father's eyes.

5

"HANK?" MY STOMACH DROPPED AS I TRIED TO WRAP MY mind around the man in front of me.

He grabbed my arm, and even though I had just watched him toss a werewolf across the room, I tried to twist away.

"That name died three years ago," he said as his gaze locked on my friends.

Jason and Kyle were both on their feet. A trickle of blood ran from Jason's mouth and he leaned against Kyle as though he couldn't fully support his own weight. Kyle didn't look much better. He ducked out from under Jason's arm and Serena took his place.

Kyle stepped toward me, but at a shake of Hank's head, three men blocked his path. "Keep an eye on them. Make sure they don't get into any more trouble." Hank raised his voice so that it reached every corner. "No one touches them. For now."

He crossed the room, pulling me in his wake. I tried to dig in my heels, but I couldn't so much as slow him down. "I'm not leaving my friends!"

"I'm not giving you a choice."

I thought I heard Kyle—or maybe Jason—yell something, but then Hank hauled me through an entrance and a door slammed shut behind us. He forced me down a drab gray hallway and then pushed me through another door.

I stumbled forward and barely caught my balance on a leather chair.

My father glanced at his hand. "I'm used to dealing with wolves."

I rubbed my arm. The words almost sounded like an apology, but Hank never apologized. "You're infected."

He nodded. "Three and a half years. Almost four."

That meant he had been infected while I was still living with him. That meant that one more aspect of my small, crappy life had been a lie.

I studied the room because I couldn't look at him. Not for a few seconds, at least. The space didn't match the rest of the club or the man I remembered. It was all leather upholstery and polished wood and—I looked down—Oriental rugs. The man I had known would never have set foot in a place like this unless he was pulling some sort of con.

Hank sat on the corner of a massive wooden desk, and I finally forced myself to look at him. His clothes didn't suit the surroundings, but he filled the room like he had every right to be here.

There was a heavy silver ring on his right hand that I didn't recognize. It caught and reflected the light as he gestured to the chair. "Sit." I didn't want to do anything he said—not even something so small—but my legs were still shaking from the fight and the aftereffects of an adrenaline rush.

I sank into the leather and fought the urge to put my head between my knees. "Assume crash positions," I whispered.

A muscle in Hank's jaw twitched. Anger or amusement? I couldn't tell.

"You want to explain what you're doing in a werewolf bar in Denver? With a Tracker?" Anger, definitely anger.

My father's voice had always been intimidating. Add the edge of a werewolf growl and it was downright scary.

"He's not a Tracker," I said, trying not to flinch.

I pressed a fingernail into the padded arm of the chair. This one piece of furniture was probably more expensive than anything Tess and I owned. Added together, the cost of everything in this room might be more than my cousin made in a year. "Instead of me telling you why I'm here, why don't you explain what you're doing in a room like this?"

Hank leaned forward. His hair was longer than he used to wear it and going gray at the temples, but his eyes were the same. Flat and blue like a winter sky and just as empty. "I am not playing games, Mackenzie. Why are you in Denver?"

"Why do you care?"

"You're my daughter." He shrugged like it should be obvious.

The muscles in my chest contracted. He didn't have the right to those words. He'd lost it years before he finally left. I shook my head. "Why did that wolf call you 'Curtis'? Why

43

did the wolves listen to you?"

"Goddamn it, Mackenzie. Do you have any idea how many wolves the Trackers have rounded up or killed in this city? If the pack had really challenged me . . ." He took a deep breath and cracked his knuckles. They still bore spiderwebs of scars, souvenirs from fights that were too old for LS to erase.

I had poured peroxide over some of those cuts when they were fresh. A wave of déjà vu rolled over me and an insistent throbbing started just above my eye socket, like someone was trying to drill through the bone.

"I want to know what you were doing with that boy."

After a long moment, when it became clear I wasn't going to answer, Hank said, "He called me Curtis because that's how they know me. Hank Dobson had too long a rap sheet to be useful."

So he had cut the name loose. Just like he had cut me loose. "And you came to Denver."

"We lived here for a few months when you were a kid. Even then, it had more werewolves than anywhere else in the country."

"Strength in numbers," I muttered. It was part of the reason Jason and I had assumed Kyle had come here. I couldn't remember ever having lived in the city—nothing over the past few days had seemed familiar—but when you never stayed in the same place for more than a couple of months, everything became a blur.

"When did it happen? Exactly?" I don't know why it made a difference, but I suddenly needed to know.

"The day I wouldn't let you go back for your bag."

Sometime around age eight, I'd started keeping a backpack of anything that really mattered. A teddy bear. A picture of some woman Hank claimed was my mom. A plastic figure of a knight on a white horse and a handful of small bills pilfered from Hank's wallet. As I got older, the cash increased and the contents of the bag changed, but it was always packed and ready. No matter what Hank was running from, there was always time to at least grab the backpack.

Until one day there wasn't.

That had been at least six months before he ditched me in Hemlock. Six months when he had hidden the fact that he was infected. "You always were good at lying," I said softly.

The office door creaked open and Eve walked in without knocking. She didn't hover on the threshold, she just crossed the room, her heavy boots muffled by the thick rugs on the floor. Like Hank, she didn't match the surroundings but looked completely at home.

"I told you to wait in the bar."

The glare Hank leveled at her would have made hardened criminals crumble, but she just shrugged. "Figured you'd want to know they put the Tracker and the two wolves in the storeroom." A strand of scarlet hair fell over her face and she absently pushed it aside. "Heath was worried some of the wolves might challenge your orders."

"Orders I wouldn't have had to give if you hadn't let them inside."

A blush darkened Eve's cheeks. "Sorry. I thought you'd

want to see her." But she didn't sound sorry, and the look Hank shot her made it clear he thought she should be.

Sorry. Sorry for letting us inside. Sorry for making me his problem.

My eyes burned. I wasn't his problem. I wasn't anyone's problem. All I needed was for Hank to hand over my friends and show us the door. After that, he'd never have to see me again.

"Do something useful and take her back to the house. The wolves can stay with the Tracker until I figure out what to do with them."

I was on my feet in an instant. "You're not doing anything with them. Jason and Serena were with me. All we wanted was to find Kyle and get out."

"You expect me to believe a Tracker is friends with two werewolves?"

"I told you: he's not a Tracker. He left them before going through with the initiation."

Eve's gaze ping-ponged between the two of us as she twisted the leather band over the scars on her wrist. She stood close to Hank—closer than he let most people get—and I realized she knew his history. She knew who he really was. "That's why you let us in," I said, staring at her. "You recognized my name."

She shrugged. "Wouldn't have if I'd realized you were with a Tracker."

"He's not—"

Before I could repeat myself, a shrill ring tone cut through the air. Hank hauled a phone from his pocket and glanced at the display before answering. "What?"

He listened for a moment, then, "I'll meet you down-stairs."

He hung up and stood. To Eve, he said, "A group of Trackers caught a wolf out near Elitch Gardens. The wolf's alive. Barely."

Eve swallowed. "One of ours?"

Hank walked around the desk. "They're having trouble identifying him, but they think so."

He took my arm and steered me to the door. Eve trailed us out of the office and down the corridor. "I'm coming with you," she said.

"No. If it's a hunting party, they might still be in the area." Hank paused and turned to pull open a steel door that I hadn't noticed earlier. He pushed me over the threshold and I caught a glimpse of Kyle, Jason, and Serena before I whirled back to face him.

Hank's eyes flickered to Jason, then locked on mine. They were cold and impossible to read. "I'll be back soon."

Eve suddenly reached around him and went for my pocket. Before I could jerk away, my phone was in her palm. "Can't let the Tracker call anyone," she said as she handed it to Hank.

The door slammed shut.

I tried the knob. We were locked in.

I don't know how long I stared at the closed door. Long enough for Kyle to stand. Long enough for him to cross the room and put a hand on my shoulder.

"Mac?"

I barely heard him over the roaring in my head.

I'd had so many fantasies about confronting my father. But in not one of them had Hank saved me from a pack of werewolves only to dump me in a locked room while he took care of things that were more important.

I squeezed my eyes shut and sucked in a deep breath.

An apology. That's what he had wanted from that girl. "For having to deal with me," I whispered.

"Mac? Are you okay? Did they hurt you?" Kyle's voice became increasingly insistent as the touch on my shoulder fell away.

I wanted to answer him, but my throat was clogged with all of the things I should have said back in the office. A cold black wave rose up as my hand curled into a fist. I lashed out, aiming for the door even though my eyes were closed.

The impact came too soon and was too soft.

My eyes sprang open. Jason stood in front of me, his palm a barrier between my hand and the metal. His lip was split and swollen, but other than that and the torn shirt, he looked all right. Better than seemed probable.

"If you're going to hit something, hit something a little softer." He closed his hand around mine, cradling my clenched fist. "Trust me. I've had plenty of practice."

He glanced at Kyle and then quickly dropped my hand and put some distance between us.

Kyle shot Jason a look I couldn't decipher, before focusing on me. Gently, he tugged the shredded fabric of my shirt and jacket aside and ran his fingers over my neck and shoulder.

Relief flashed across his face. "Back in the pool room . . . I couldn't tell if you had been scratched."

"Don't worry," I said, voice stretched thin as I rubbed my sleeve over my eyes. "Plenty of wounds. None physical."

"The guy who dragged you out of there," said Serena, "Curtis? You called him 'Hank.'"

I turned. She was sitting on a cot in the corner, surrounded by boxes and busted bar stools. A ripped futon mattress hugged the opposite wall. The only source of illumination was a bare bulb screwed over a stained sink, and the room's one window was boarded up tight.

It was a junk room, filled with things—and now people—that weren't important.

I shoved my hands in my pockets, reasoning that would stop me from lashing out again. "His real name is Hank, not Curtis. Hank Dobson. He's my father." I tried to keep my voice level, but it shook on every word. "I didn't know he had LS. He hid it."

Jason turned to Kyle. "Did you know?"

"Of course not," snapped Kyle, surprise warring with anger in his voice. "It's not like Mac keeps pictures of her dad around."

He reached out to touch my arm and I moved away. "It's not you," I said quickly as hurt flashed behind his eyes. "If you hug me or touch me right now, I'll cry."

And I really didn't want to cry.

Kyle nodded, then walked to the cot and sat a few feet from Serena. "He goes by Curtis Hanson. Eve introduced me to him when she brought me here a few nights ago. He's the leader of the Eumon pack."

"Pack leader?" I echoed just as Jason said, "Eve was the one who brought you here?"

Hank had always hated responsibility. The idea of him leading a club full of werewolves didn't make sense.

"I met Eve my first night in Denver," explained Kyle. "She tried to tear a chunk out of me before realizing I wasn't local."

Serena frowned. "Why? Everything I've ever heard makes Denver sound like the be-all and end-all for wolves. What difference would it make whether or not you were local?"

He shrugged. "Turns out there are three separate packs in Denver and they all have territories. I wandered into Eumon turf and she thought I was from another pack. She's small, but strong."

There was a strange note of respect in Kyle's voice that made my stomach do a small flip. I told myself that I had nothing to be jealous of, but why had Eve lied about knowing him? What could she possibly have had to gain?

"Anyway," continued Kyle, "she felt guilty so she brought me here. Introduced me around. Found couches for me to surf on. Eumon is the only pack in the city that takes rogues—people not infected by someone already in the group. It was come here or try to go it on my own."

"You could have come home." I shook my head and corrected myself. "You *can* come home."

"It's not that simple. I can't just—" Kyle checked himself

and flexed his hands. "You guys are safer without me around."

Serena snorted. "Richie Rich joined a right-wing hate group and Mac's legal guardian was dating a mass murderer. Compared with that, you're about as dangerous as a carton of two-day-expired milk."

I walked to the cot and crouched in front of Kyle. A knot formed in my chest as I rested my hands on his knees, and when I spoke, my voice came out high and a little unsteady. "Don't you want to come home?"

Kyle's gaze darkened, but he didn't answer. Maybe he just couldn't believe I had asked something so stupid.

With a sigh, I pushed myself to my feet and walked to the window. One board looked like it might be a little loose. I pulled at it, then tried ramming my shoulder against it.

Jason cleared his throat. "What are you doing?"

"Looking for a way out." I glanced at my friends. "You don't seriously want to stay in here all night, do you?" I hit the board again. "We." *Hit.* "Are." *Thud.* "Getting out of here." With each hit, I visualized Hank's face.

I stopped to catch my breath, and Jason was suddenly at my side, reaching past me to try and pull the board free. It groaned but didn't give.

"Regs," Serena muttered affectionately as she stood and nudged Jason aside. She bit her lip and lashed out with her fist. The bottom of the board moved just enough for her to slide her fingers under the edge. After that, she was able to pull all of the boards off in seconds.

She examined her nails. "And the manicure is still intact."

Fresh air filled the room. I sucked it down until my lungs were close to bursting.

And then I took a closer look at the window. It was small. Too small for any of us—even Serena—to squeeze through.

I picked up one of the boards and hurled it at the wall as my eyes filled with tears. We were close enough to the outside that I could feel the fresh air on my face and hear the distant sounds of traffic, but we were still trapped.

I walked to the ripped futon mattress and sank down. Hank and his wolves had put us in a box and we weren't getting out unless they let us. I pulled my legs to my chest and pressed my forehead to my knees.

After a minute, Kyle came and sat next to me. This time, when he tried to put an arm around me, I let him.

"Tess?" I pushed open the door to my cousin's room. The mattress had been stripped and the closet stood open and empty. A lone wire hanger dangled on the rod.

"She's not here." Amy walked across the room and flopped onto the bed.

I swallowed. "You're going to leave a stain." As soon as the words slipped from my mouth, a pool of red appeared on Amy's white cotton T-shirt.

She sighed and sat up. "You are such a buzzkill. Besides, it's not like Tess is coming back here."

A tasseled pillow had been abandoned on the floor. I picked it up and hugged it to my chest. "She'll come back. She wouldn't leave me."

Amy shot me a small, sympathetic smile. "Everyone leaves you. Haven't you figured that out yet?" I flinched and she frowned. "Sorry. You know everything gets twisted in here. I end up being the me you think you deserve."

I didn't argue.

I wondered, suddenly, if Jason and Kyle had their own versions of Amy, if their guilt, like mine, warped her like a fun-house mirror.

Amy reached back and touched a small indent in the mattress. "He laid his head here, you know."

A shiver swept down my spine. I didn't have to ask who she was talking about.

She stood and stretched, then frowned thoughtfully. "Doesn't it bother you that Ben and Kyle have the same disease?"

"No." I didn't even have to think about it. "Kyle's not Ben and a disease doesn't change who someone is."

"Ben thought it did." She walked to the window and drummed her fingers on the sill, fast and furious like the beat of a werewolf's heart. "Can you really date one of them? I know I was with Trey, but he never told me what he was. And you do have options. Jason wants you so badly, it's a miracle he doesn't spontaneously combust."

I flushed. "I'm not talking relationships with you."

"Why not? They're fascinating." Amy turned to stare at me, her expression so earnest that I almost believed it was really her. "It always breaks down to relationships. My relationship with Jason. Ben's relationship with his father.

My family tree and the fact that my grandfather is a senator. Everything happens because of a connection. Cause and effect. Kyle knows it. That's why he ran away from you. He's scared he'll be the cause of you getting hurt or infected or dead."

She sighed. "He hasn't figured out that no matter what you do, some people just end up broken."

As she spoke, the shadows in the room thickened and lengthened. Smokelike tendrils stretched out from the darkness. One wrapped itself around my wrist and my skin blistered and peeled.

Amy gazed at me sadly. "You can't outsmart fate."

I started awake. Kyle's arm tightened reflexively around me, but his breathing stayed deep and steady. Even in sleep, he tried to keep me safe. It took me a second to remember where we were, to remember falling asleep with Kyle on the futon mattress.

A few feet away, Jason and Serena were passed out on the cot. Jason slept sitting with his back against the wall and Serena—weirdly enough—had fallen asleep with her head on his shoulder. They weren't far away, but it was hard to see them clearly.

I blinked. A cough clawed at the back of my throat as my eyes teared.

Smoke.

The room was filling with it.

6

"KYLE!" I SHOOK HIS SHOULDER AND CHOKED OUT HIS name.

He jerked awake in a sputtering, coughing start as I staggered to my feet and stumbled to the door.

I touched the metal with my fingertips. It wasn't hot—yet—but the smoke at this end of the room was growing thick.

Kyle roused Serena and Jason. The next second he was by my side, moving me out of the way so he could throw himself at the door.

It didn't budge.

Serena joined him in the assault—both of them yelling for someone to let us out. Through the haze, I caught glimpses of dark smears on Kyle's hands: blood. He and Serena were tearing themselves apart against the door, but it wasn't doing any good.

I glanced back at Jason. He hauled off his jacket and grabbed Serena's from the cot. He doused them in the sink, then, coughing, squeezed past Kyle and shoved the fabric along the bottom of the door. The flow of smoke slowed but didn't abate.

Screams and crashes drifted up from somewhere below us.

Serena backed away from the door and pressed her hands to the sides of her head.

"Serena?" I coughed her name and reached for her shoulder. She knocked my hand away so hard that I winced and cradled my wrist against my chest.

"Oh, God. Oh, God. Oh, God." Her eyes were wild and the words were a repeated gasp.

The fire at her house, I realized, *she's remembering the fire.*

The smoke tore at my lungs. I stumbled back toward the window. The air here was easier to breathe, but not by much. Light-headed, I slumped to the floor. That's what you were supposed to do in a fire, wasn't it? Crawl underneath the smoke?

A few feet away, Jason had the same idea. None of us would hold out against the smoke for long, but he and I had the added disadvantage of reg lungs.

The ceiling pressed down and the walls closed in, mirroring the constriction in my chest.

I don't want to die here.

Jason groped for my hand and I wasn't sure if I had thought the words or if I had managed to choke them out.

Kyle was suddenly there. He crouched next to me and pressed something cold and damp over my mouth and nose: his shirt. He had shredded it and soaked the rags in the

56

sink. He waited until I held the cloth in place on my own before turning to Jason and pressing a second piece of fabric over his face.

I couldn't see Serena through the smoke, but I could hear the thuds as she continued to throw herself at the door.

It was hopeless. It had to be if Kyle was here and not helping her.

The pounding stopped.

Serena had given up.

An image of Tess filled my head as I struggled to my feet. We couldn't give up. I wasn't giving up.

I made it across the room and began running my fingers along the edge of the door. There had to be a hinge or a gap. *Anything.* Kyle and Serena had tried brute force, but there had to be some other way out. Tears streamed down my face. I could barely breathe, but after a minute, my fingers found part of a hinge and the notch in a screw.

"Screwdriver," I choked out. "What could we use as a screwdriver?"

Before anyone could answer, there was a screech of metal and then smoke-filtered light poured into the room from the hall. A voice that was almost-familiar-but-not rasped, "Come on."

I wiped a hand across my eyes and squinted into the haze. Eve. Her long red hair was a mass of knots and her jacket was ripped at the shoulder. Smudges of dirt and ash dotted her face.

"What's going on? What happened?" My throat was raw and it took me two tries to get the words out as I stepped into the hall, the others behind me.

"A raid. Trackers." Eve threw a glare back at Jason before heading down the corridor, trusting us to follow. "There are dozens of them downstairs."

The smoke thinned and my lungs and head cleared. "Where's Hank?"

Eve pulled open another door, revealing a barely lit stairwell. "He went to check on that wolf and hasn't come back." Her voice was thick and constricted.

Shouts echoed at the other end of the hall. Eve grabbed my arm and flung me at the stairs. I barely avoided dashing my brains out against the wall. "Go! Don't stop until you reach the top floor!"

"Up?" I spun and stared at her. "The building's on fire and you expect us to go *up*?"

"There's an escape route on the top floor. A ladder." She grabbed my shoulder and half shoved, half turned me back to the stairs.

"I trust her," said Kyle. "Go!"

Figuring we had no choice, I ran, taking the steps as fast as I could, glancing back once to make sure everyone was behind me.

My sneakers slapped the third-floor landing just as a door below flew open.

"We've got a group on the back stairs," yelled a rough voice.

Trackers.

Now we really had no choice but to keep going up.

There was a noise like a tin can fired out of a cannon, and

it was followed by a burst of light so bright that I instinctively looked over my shoulder.

Kyle pushed past Jason and Serena and grabbed my hand. "Tear gas." His grip was slick in mine as he urged me to move faster. There was a second rattle and flash—so much closer—and then a caustic smell that stripped my throat and nose when I inhaled. I tried desperately to hold my breath as we ran the last few steps to the fourth floor.

We stumbled into a cavernous space that was filled with dozens of large, industrial machines. Moonlight streamed through a wall of broken windows, and when I glanced up, I saw gaping holes in the roof.

Serena and Jason came crashing out of the stairwell.

Serena's eyes were red-rimmed and she was supporting Jason with one arm. Face shining with tears and sweat, he leaned away from her and vomited. Eve tumbled after them a moment later, retching as she hauled off her powder-caked jacket and dropped it to the floor.

Eyes and nose streaming, Eve staggered past us and headed for the far side of the room. She thrust aside a plastic tarp revealing a wall so covered in graffiti that it looked like a living organism.

She ran her hand over a patch of blue paint as we approached. Her fingers closed on a metal loop that had been all but invisible, and arms shaking, she hauled out a section of wall.

I peered over her shoulder and into a passageway that was little more than a crawl space.

"It leads to a fire escape." Eve stepped away from the

entrance and turned. "It'll let you out on the south side of the building."

The space was less than a foot and a half wide. It was so narrow that you'd have to walk sideways and anyone taller than me would have to stoop. Complete blackness fell a few paces from the opening. Once the wall was closed, you'd be blind. I stared into the darkness and imagined being roasted alive as fire consumed the building.

"I'll try my luck with the Trackers," said Serena, voice shaky.

"We don't have time for this," snapped Eve. "The fire is on the other side of the building. The three of you have time to get out if you go now."

She glared and the look on her face reminded me of my father.

"I'm going to regret this," muttered Serena as she eased into the passage.

I hesitated as Eve's words sank in. "Three?"

"Curtis isn't here, and I don't know how many people the Trackers have nabbed." In a blur, she grabbed Jason's arm. Her eyes locked on mine. "I got you out for Curtis, but the Tracker stays."

"Eve, he didn't have anything to do with this." Kyle's torso shone with sweat and the muscles in his shoulders and arms were so tense it looked as though he had iron under his skin. "Even if he had wanted to tell the Trackers about the club, there wasn't any way to reach them without our phones."

Eve's gray-green eyes flashed. "Maybe. Maybe not. Either

way, he's leverage." She stared at Kyle like she was willing him to understand. "All of my friends are down there. Everyone I know."

"If you think we're letting you take him, you're crazy." I took a step toward her, but Jason shook his head.

"I'll be all right, Mac." With his free hand, he reached up and yanked on his torn shirt, ripping it even farther so that there was no way the black brand on his neck could be missed. "Enough Trackers saw me last night that someone will recognize me."

"Jason . . . No. Absolutely not."

He turned to Kyle. "Make sure she gets out." His gaze flickered to Serena, just visible in the opening to the passage. "Both of them."

Kyle nodded and grabbed my arm. I struggled but couldn't break his grip. "Kyle! No!"

With his werewolf strength, it was entirely too easy for him to shove me into the passage behind Serena. "We can't just leave Jason!"

He squeezed his eyes shut for a quarter heartbeat. "I'm not," he said before slamming the door.

The darkness was absolute.

The walls pressed against me. For a second, I couldn't breathe, and then I threw myself against the door. It didn't budge. There was no release from this side. "Kyle! Kyle, open the door!"

Serena's hand clamped over my mouth. Her skin smelled like smoke and a sharper, stomach-churning scent that was probably the tear gas.

There was a crash followed by shouting on the other side of the door.

A thud shook the wall and someone screamed. It sounded horribly like Jason.

Serena pressed her mouth to my ear. "If we can find the exit, maybe we can loop back and help them."

As quickly as we could—which wasn't quickly at all since we could only move sideways and I couldn't see—we made our way down the passage.

There was a sudden grinding sound behind us and I glanced back as a triangle of light pierced the darkness.

"Go! I'll be right behind you!" I pushed Serena. She was faster than I was. She could get away even if I were caught.

In response, she grabbed my hand. Holding it in a death grip, she hauled me through the rest of the passage.

Fresh air hit my face as the walls unexpectedly fell away. I stumbled forward and only Serena's grip kept me from hurtling off the narrow metal platform at the top of the fire escape.

I glanced down: the ancient contraption of ladders and platforms looked like a rusted death trap.

"Come on." Serena started down, moving at a dizzying speed before remembering I was a reg and slowing her pace.

Four stories down should have been easy, but my hands and feet kept slipping on the rungs. The metal let out a non-stop chorus of squeals and groans underneath my weight, competing with the shouts and screams coming from inside the building.

Just as we passed the second floor, a heavy, masculine

voice crashed over us. "Come down slowly."

Serena froze.

Heart in throat, I peered around her to the ground below.

Three Trackers had gathered around the bottom of the fire escape. For a second, I considered going back up, but then I realized that one of the men held a rifle. As I watched, he trained it on Serena.

There wasn't any choice. We slowly made our way to the ground. Serena stepped off the ladder, and then held her hands in the air as she moved aside. I followed right on her heels.

Two men with Kevlar vests and Tracker tattoos pulled my arms behind my back and snapped a pair of heavy cuffs around my wrists. A second later, Serena suffered the same fate. One of the men grabbed her a little too roughly and she elbowed him in the ribs.

Gasping, the man reached for the butt of a holstered gun and started to pull it free.

"Kill her and it's one less head we get paid for," snapped one of the others before radioing in that they had found two more wolves.

Ash and burning shingles drifted to the ground around us as we were marched to the front of the building. The chain-link fence—which, just a few hours ago, had surrounded the property and made it a fortress—lay flattened on the ground. My sneakers caught on the links as we were herded to a group of wolves—two dozen, maybe more—who waited curbside in cuffs. Black shapes patrolled the edge of the small crowd: Trackers with guns drawn.

From this vantage point, it looked like the building was beyond saving. The fire had spread to the upper two floors and the roof was quickly becoming engulfed in flames.

I whirled as a familiar, smoke-raw voice asked if I was okay. Kyle. There was a burn on his arm and a gash across his chest, but that was nothing to a werewolf; his body would heal the damage in no time. He was all right.

I leaned into him and he pressed his chin to the top of my head. A shudder wracked my body as I pulled in what felt like the first real breath I had taken since he had shoved me into the passage.

After a moment, I pulled away. "Where's Jason?"

A shadow crossed Kyle's face. "I don't know. They saw his tattoo and separated us as soon as we were out of the building."

My stomach lurched. Under normal circumstances, the tattoo on Jason's neck would keep him safe from the Trackers, but he had been found in the middle of a were-wolf club. If he could convince them that he had gone in for some sort of nefarious purpose, he'd be okay. But if they suspected—even for an instant—that he had any werewolf sympathies . . .

A large truck rumbled down the street and came to a jerky stop in front of us. Two Trackers pulled open the doors to the cargo hold and threw down a ramp. It hit the pave-ment with a clang that seemed to reverberate in my chest.

The crowd shifted as people were herded aboard. I spot-ted Eve's red hair a second before she disappeared inside.

Serena was shoved forward, then Kyle, then me.

I tried to stop, to turn and search the milling Trackers for Jason, but another push sent me stumbling up the ramp. As I reached the top, I heard one of the men say a candle had started the blaze.

I slipped on a small pool of blood and fell to my knees just over the threshold. With my hands bound, there was no way for me to break my fall. I bit back a pained gasp. Werewolves didn't cry over scraped knees, and if the Trackers realized I was a reg, I'd lose my only chance to find out where Kyle and Serena were being taken.

I shimmied away from the edge of the truck and found a space along the wall. There were no benches or seats: it was a truck built for freight, not people.

I looked up.

Jason.

He was trying to push past a Tracker who looked capable of breaking him in two. He was shouting, but the scene was too chaotic and he was too far away for me to catch a single sentence.

His face and clothes were streaked with ash and he looked crazed—as crazed as any wolf with bloodlust—but he was okay. He wasn't in cuffs and the Trackers hadn't beaten him to a pulp. He was all right. He would be all right.

His gaze locked on mine. Fierce. Desperate. Determined.

"It's okay," I whispered, even though he wouldn't have believed the words even if he could have heard them. "I promise, it'll be okay."

Jason's eyes were the last thing I saw before the doors slammed shut.

7

WE HUDDLED IN THE DARK FOR WHAT FELT LIKE HOURS.
The combined scent of sweat, fear, and smoke was nauseating. Some people cried and others prayed. Most were too scared to make a sound.

A few wolves managed to get cell phones and iPods out of one another's pockets. No one could get a signal, but they used the devices as flashlights. The dim electronic glows pierced the dark and somehow made things slightly more bearable.

Very slightly.

"We're going to die." The voice was young and male and it cracked around the edges.

"We are, aren't we?" No one answered and the silence seemed to push him over some invisible line. *"Aren't we?"*

He climbed shakily to his feet and began to pace. Back and forth. In and out of thin bars of light.

His steps carried him a little too close, and I could feel Kyle and Serena tense on either side of me.

There wasn't enough light to see clearly, but I could hear

the cracking and popping of bones and muscle as fear frayed the boy's control. The cuffs were heavy, but I wasn't sure if they would hold during a shift.

My heart tried to break free of my rib cage as I strained against my cuffs to reach Kyle's hand.

Another figure stood. It took me a moment to recognize Eve in the semidark. "Bastian . . ."

The boy ignored her.

Swaying with the motion of the truck, she moved forward and blocked his path. "Bastian, listen to me." Her voice was firm. Commanding. "We are not going to die."

He started to object and she cut him off. "*Listen to me*: If they wanted us dead, they'd have sealed off the exits when the fire started or shot us on the street. They won't kill anyone unless we give them a reason. Shift and you give them a reason."

I held my breath. After a small eternity, the boy shuffled over to the wall and slid to the ground.

Next to me, Serena exhaled in a soft rush.

"We'll be okay." Eve turned in a slow circle as she addressed the wolves. "Curtis will think of something. The pack will come after us. We just have to stay calm until then."

Only exhaustion and fear kept me from laughing.

No one was coming after us. Least of all my father.

I stared at Eve and wondered, again, who she was and how she was connected to Hank.

The truck hit a patch of rough road and Serena choked back a sob. Her eyes glinted and I realized she was crying.

The only other time I'd seen Serena cry had been the night a group of Trackers had gone after her and her brother.

"I'm so sorry." The whispered words weren't enough. I had asked Serena to come to Denver. I was the reason she was here.

She didn't respond and each moment of silence increased the pressure in my chest. Finally, she said, "You couldn't have known this would happen." Then she closed her eyes and edged slightly away—a rebuttal to further conversation.

Kyle squeezed my hand and pressed a gentle kiss to my temple. "It's not your fault," he whispered.

"Yes it is."

I rested my cheek on his shoulder. His bare skin was warm and smelled faintly of smoke. "So I guess my attempt to save you from the life of a teenage runaway was a colossal failure." My throat constricted and my voice came out thick. "If I hadn't gotten you locked up, you might have gotten out."

A tear leaked from the corner of my eye and Kyle stiffened as it landed on his chest. He let out a deep breath, almost a rough sigh. "I love you. You know that, right?"

"Me too." It occurred to me that the only times either of us had managed to say those words had been either during or just after mortal peril.

The truck shuddered to a stop.

Fear flooded my chest and sweat soaked the back of my shirt.

Next to me, Serena let out a small, strangled noise.

I had to find a way to get her out of this. To get both her and Kyle out of this.

The doors were thrown open. People struggled to their feet and moved back, hugging the shadows as two Trackers lowered the ramp and two more covered us with guns. As impossible as it seemed, they made the Trackers I'd come across in Hemlock seem tame.

Like cattle, we were forced off the truck and counted before guards in blue uniforms took over and herded us across an expanse of pavement. They carried guns that looked every bit as dangerous as the ones the Trackers were toting and made sure no one made a run for it.

Not that there was any place to run to.

We were in a courtyard behind a massive gate. A thirty-foot-tall fence topped with loops of razor wire stretched out from either side of the entrance and disappeared into the dark. It was easy to imagine that it went on forever.

Serena tilted her head to the side. "It's electric," she murmured.

"She's right." The girl from the coffee shop—the one with the indigo streak—was standing with Eve. "I can hear the voltage." She took a step back and bumped into the wolf behind her. She shook her head sharply, the gesture almost violent. "I can't be here. I can't be in a camp."

"It's okay, Mel. We'll be okay." Eve's tone was reassuring, but her eyes darted nervously to the guards and Trackers.

"It's not me I'm worried about." The look Mel shot Eve was pure misery. "What about my nan? Without someone there to look after her and make sure she takes her meds . . ." She swallowed. "What happens to her when I don't come home?"

Eve didn't answer.

I turned away.

Across the courtyard, a three-story building stood sentinel against the night. Ivy crawled up its redbrick walls and its roof rose up in a peak sharp enough to puncture the sky. It looked old and out of place compared to the collection of one-story buildings that ranged out behind it.

There was nothing to indicate which camp—and Mel was right, it had to be a camp—we were in.

A man with a clipboard strode forward. "I need you to form two lines. If you're eighteen or younger, line up on the left. Over eighteen, line up on the right."

I stood between Kyle and Serena. Only three wolves moved to the right. The man walked down our line, unlocking our cuffs. The weight around my wrists fell away, and I tried to massage some of the feeling back into my skin.

No one uncuffed the wolves in the other line as guards ushered our group past a row of identical white jeeps and to a brick building—also white—near the gate. A small sign on the building's door read Admissions.

Inside, we were left in a windowless room with white tile walls. Fluorescent lights were embedded in the ceiling. One bulb was on the fritz: it flickered and hummed like those lanterns people hung outside to zap bugs. The room was completely devoid of furniture except for three booths— identical black tables enclosed by floor-to-ceiling glass on all sides—along the far wall. They looked vaguely familiar. When I realized why, I shivered: the glass walls reminded me of Houdini's Chinese water torture cell.

No one went near the booths. Instinct or mob mentality kept us pressed tightly together, as far away from that side of the room as we could get without actually stepping on one another's feet.

After a few minutes, two guards with holsters around their waists—Tasers on one side, guns on the other—led a man into the room. The man was young with dark skin and wide-set eyes. He was dressed in white and pushed a large steel cart in front of him.

He cleared his throat. "I need you to form three lines, one in front of each booth."

No one moved.

The guards began dividing us up, threatening to use the Tasers when people didn't obey quickly enough.

I ended up being the sixth person in the middle line. Serena was directly in front of me. Kyle was the first person in the line on the far left.

"Walk into the booth opposite you when directed," said the man in white, "and just follow the instructions. First group in!"

My heart twisted and I had to fight the urge to run forward as Kyle crossed to a booth, pulled open the door, and stepped inside.

After a second's hesitation, the other two wolves entered their own booths, letting the doors swing shut behind them. There was an audible click once all three were inside—as though a deadbolt had been thrown.

The wolf in the middle cell—a girl with waist-length dreadlocks and an Emily the Strange T-shirt—tried to open her door. Her mouth stretched in a silent shout when she realized she was locked in. She raised her fists and pounded on the glass as Kyle and the boy on her right looked on.

The man in white walked to an intercom to the left of the booths. He pressed a button and leaned toward a small speaker. "The glass is shatter resistant and soundproof. Just calm down and follow the instructions. It will all be over in a minute." He returned to the steel cart.

Shoulders shaking and fists clenched, the girl turned to the table in her booth. Kyle's gaze locked on mine for an instant before he followed suit.

My stomach somersaulted as I stared at Kyle's back. I was convinced that something horrible would happen, but after a few moments, he turned around, something clenched in his fist.

"Next group in," said the man in white as the locks disengaged. The three wolves exited the booths and walked toward him. They each handed over what looked like a small plastic square and were told to wait at the back of the room.

Three groups later, it was Serena's turn. She flinched as the door closed behind her but came out unscathed.

"Next!"

I could practically feel Kyle's eyes on me as I walked forward and stepped into the booth. *It's okay*, I told myself.

If it wasn't, Kyle would be flipping out. Nevertheless, I had to push back a wave of claustrophobia and panic when the door locked behind me. A strong smell—like bleach—filled my nostrils and burned my throat.

I glanced to either side. Mel—the girl from the coffee shop—was in the booth on my right while an unfamiliar boy was in the booth on the left. Unlike the glass door, the walls between the booths were frosted up to chest-level.

An automated voice rang out of a hidden speaker. "Take a slide from the dispenser in the middle of the counter."

Sure enough, there was a stack of glass slides on the tabletop. I pulled one out and held it between my thumb and forefinger.

"Place the slide on the counter and then press your index finger to the red *x*."

A few inches from the dispenser was a white circle with a red *x* in its center. I hesitated, but did as the voice said.

"Ouch!" I hissed through my teeth as something pierced my finger.

"Press your finger to the slide until a sample of your blood is clearly visible, then take a second slide from the dispenser and set it on top of the first. If you heal before you can accomplish this, simply place your finger back on the red *x* and repeat the process."

Being a reg, healing too fast wasn't an issue.

"Once you have successfully acquired a sample of blood," continued the voice, "take an envelope from the dispenser on the side of the table and place your slide inside."

Following the instructions, I slipped my sample into an opaque plastic envelope.

My mind whirled. Nine months ago, CutterBrown Pharmaceutical—a company run, in part, by Amy's father—had announced they were working on a test to detect LS. Almost a year later, they still hadn't had any major breakthroughs—at least none they had publicized.

Was it possible they had successfully developed the test and were using it in the camps?

I glanced at Mel through the glass. She was obviously having trouble getting a sample. Tears ran down her face, but she didn't seem to notice.

Something slammed into the wall on my left and I spun. The boy in that booth was having some sort of panic attack. He shouted words that only he could hear as the muscles in his arms jumped and twitched. With horror, I realized he was on the verge of shifting.

The man in white headed for the intercom again. "The girl in the middle and the girl on the right, please exit and give me your samples."

There was a click as our doors unlocked.

Mel stepped out, envelope held loosely in hand, shoulders hunched. I remembered what she had said about her grandmother back in the courtyard.

She had every reason to need out and I had two very important reasons to stay in.

Three more guards rushed into the room and headed for the booths. Mel paused to watch. Everyone in the room was watching. In that second, my decision was made.

As the guards flung open the door to the last booth and tased the boy inside, I backed up quickly—as though frightened—and collided with Mel as hard as I could.

Startled, she dropped her blood sample. Mine hit the ground a nanosecond later as a bolt of pain shot through my shoulder.

"Sorry!" I gasped. I crouched and scooped up the plastic envelopes before she had a chance. Trying for an apologetic smile, I handed her my sample.

Mel frowned as she took the envelope, then focused her attention back on the guards as they hauled the boy—now unconscious—out of the room. "He has trouble around blood," she said, her voice a faint croak.

There's an understatement, I thought.

I turned and headed for the cart.

Kyle was staring at my hand. He started forward, but one of the guards stepped toward him, Taser out, and ordered him to stay with the others. Kyle did as he was told, but didn't take his eyes off me.

My stolen envelope suddenly felt like it weighed a ton. It was a relief to hand it—along with my first name—to the man in white.

I rejoined Kyle and Serena. Kyle opened his mouth, but then snapped it shut. We were surrounded. He couldn't say or ask anything without being heard.

Before the last samples were collected, two more wolves had freak-outs—one because of the blood and another because she was claustrophobic. The claustrophobic wolf was given a second chance. The other was tased and dragged from the room.

Once it was over, the man in white left and the remaining guards followed.

We waited. After a while, a few people were brave enough to pull out their cell phones, but just like in the truck, no one could get a signal. No one spoke. It was like we were all scared the guards would return at the first whispered word.

Eventually, wolves began getting called out of the room in groups of twos and threes as the results of the blood tests came back.

All but Mel. She was taken back the way we had come. As long as she didn't argue when they called her a reg, she'd get a ticket out of here.

At least I had managed to help someone.

Kyle and I ended up the last two.

He glanced at the door, then turned and gripped my arms. "Tell me you didn't do something with the samples. Tell me you didn't do anything stupid." He stared at me as if he knew the answer but was praying he was wrong.

I swallowed. "I swapped."

Kyle uttered a string of profanity that would have left Jason impressed, then stopped abruptly and sucked in a deep breath. I could actually see the effort he exerted to bring himself under control. "You have to tell them the truth. They'll retest you. They'll have to."

I shook my head. "I'm not leaving you. Or Serena. It's my fault you guys are here."

"Mac, it's a camp. You'll get torn apart." He ran a hand over his face. "If you don't tell them it was a mistake, I will."

"If you do, that other girl—Mel—will just get yanked back. You heard her in the courtyard. This'll give her the chance to go home. Do you really want to take that from her?"

"You don't belong here." The words were a low growl.

"Neither do you or Serena," I tossed back. "We don't even know what camp this is. If I stay for a few days, maybe I can learn something. Something that could help get you out. Something the RfW could use, maybe." The RfW—Regs for Werewolves—was one of the few groups who lobbied for werewolf rights. "You know they'd kill to find out what's going on in the camps."

Kyle stared at me as though I had completely lost my mind.

"There's Hank!" I said, desperately grasping at straws even I didn't have faith in. "You heard Eve: She thinks he's going to come for us. And there's Jason." I grabbed Kyle's arm in a death grip. "I'll keep my head down and watch what's going on—at least find out where we are—and in a few days, I'll tell them I'm a reg. That way I can at least let Trey know where Serena is. Please, Kyle, just a few days."

Emotions cycled across his face. Worry. Frustration. Guilt. And then resignation. He reached out and brushed the hair back from my forehead.

The door to the waiting room opened. Finally, he nodded.

We were led to a room that was small, sterile, and white. It reminded me of those interrogation rooms you saw in movies, a feeling not helped by the mirror that ran the length of one wall or the two guards—a man and a woman—who watched us with detached boredom.

The man was tall and lanky with a shock of red hair and pale skin. The woman had a gray crew cut and a body as square as a brick. Both looked like they'd rather be in bed.

They weren't the only ones.

A woman with tortoiseshell glasses and a black blazer covered a yawn before telling us to hold out our left arms. I was so panicked at the thought of another blood test that I was almost relieved when the male guard stepped forward and snapped a three-inch-wide metal cuff around my wrist. A four-digit number was stamped on the front.

"These ID bracelets are designed to expand and contract when your body shifts," explained the woman in a voice as dry and uninterested as a desert wind. "Any attempt to remove them will trigger an automatic alert to the warden and security staff."

I ran my hand over the cuff. It was thick and there were seams halfway around, like someone had sliced it in two. The seams weren't welded together, and when I tugged on the top half of the bracelet, I caught a glimpse of another circle of metal nestled inside.

The glare the woman shot me was so sharp that I flinched. "I was just looking," I said, quickly letting go. "I wasn't trying to take it off."

She pursed her lips and handed Kyle and me each a clipboard. "Fill out these admission forms in the waiting room."

The guards ushered us through the door, down a hall,

and into a long, narrow space that looked more like a holding pen than a waiting room. There were three doors—the one we had just come through and two at the far end—and the ceiling was so low that I could have touched it had I reached up and stretched.

Every surface was painted a dull gray; the only color came from the teens who were sitting on the floor, their backs resting against the walls as they filled out admission forms.

I breathed a sigh of relief when I saw Serena, but she looked less than thrilled to see me. "Tell me she didn't do what I think she did," she said as the wolves next to her slid down to make room for Kyle and me.

"Don't get him started," I said, eyeing the guards as they took up positions across the room. I lowered myself to the ground and dropped my gaze to the admission form. *Seriously?* I thought as I reached for a pen that had been tied to the clipboard. *They kidnapped us and they're worried we're going to steal office supplies?*

I shook my head and focused on the questions.

Full Name? Mackenzie . . . I racked my brain for a fake last name and somehow found myself writing down *Walsh.* Amy's last name.

Age? Seventeen.

How old were you when you became infected? Did you have any health conditions prior to infection? Do you often feel weak and dizzy outside of shifts? How many times a month, on average, do you involuntarily shift?

For most of the questions, I snuck glances at Kyle's and Serena's answers and just put down something in the middle.

Just as I reached the last question, the woman with the glasses reappeared with the man who had collected our blood samples. They began taking clipboards, pausing a moment to scan each set of answers before moving to the next wolf.

The woman's brow creased in a frown as she glanced over Serena's form.

Apprehension fluttered in my stomach as she pulled one of the two guards—the man with the red hair—out into the hall.

A moment later, they were back.

The woman cleared her throat. "Serena, I need you to come with me."

Serena reached for my hand and squeezed so hard it was all I could do not to flinch. "Mac . . ." Her voice was a strained whisper.

When she didn't move right away, the guards started forward.

Kyle pushed himself to his feet and stepped in front of us. "What do you want with her?"

"We just need to ask her a few more questions," said the woman with the glasses.

I peered around Kyle's legs. The woman's tone had been reassuring, but her eyes were dead. Hank always said there was a world of difference between lying well and being able to lie with your eyes.

Kyle caught it, too. "Why can't she answer them here?"

In response, the guards drew their Tasers. The wolves to either side of us parted like the Red Sea, and my pulse pounded so loudly that the blowback rang in my ears.

All Kyle had done was ask a question.

I waited for them to order him to sit or move, but there were no commands and no warnings. In the space between heartbeats, the female guard squeezed the trigger.

I screamed Kyle's name as he fell to the ground. I tried to reach for him but Serena held me back as he was hit by another Taser.

Kyle's spine bowed and I thought I heard something crack before he fell horribly still. Other than the rise and fall of his chest, he looked dead.

Without giving either Serena or me a chance to fully absorb what had just happened, the male guard started toward us.

Serena panicked. Her hand shattered around mine, and I pulled free of her grip just in time to avoid being scratched. I scurried back on my butt as her body tore itself apart. Fur flowed over skin and then a coal-black wolf rose shakily to its feet.

My gaze darted to Kyle. He had recovered enough to push himself to his hands and knees. He was trying to force himself back up, to reach us.

Suddenly, he collapsed.

He and every other wolf in the room.

They slumped to the floor with their hands clasped to their heads. The bones and muscle in Serena's body snapped and tore as she shifted back. The only people unaffected were the woman in the blazer, the man in white, and the two guards.

And me.

Unsure what was going on, I huddled on the floor like the other teens and watched the room from under my lashes.

"We had it under control," muttered the female guard, holstering her Taser.

"Of course," said the woman in the glasses as she slipped something into her pants pocket. "This was simply . . . neater."

The door behind her opened and two men dressed like hospital orderlies stepped into the room.

The redheaded guard walked around us. I heard a sharp exhalation of breath and a small grunt as he lifted Serena. Every instinct I had screamed at me to do something, *anything*, as he carried Serena across the room, but if I moved, they would know I wasn't like the others. They'd know I was a reg; I'd get kicked out and wouldn't be any help to anyone.

There was nothing I could do but watch.

In a gesture that surprised me, the woman in the glasses shrugged off her jacket and draped it over Serena, partially covering her nudity as the guard eased her into the arms of the orderlies. Serena was too out of it to notice. She looked small and helpless and broken.

They carried her through the door. The sound of the latch catching slammed through me like a bullet.

Around me, the wolves began to stir.

Eve met my gaze from halfway across the room. A

thoughtful expression crossed her face as she pressed the heel of one hand to her temple, but I didn't have the energy or the interest to puzzle out what the look meant.

I crawled to Kyle as he sat up. His skin was ashen and his face was covered in sweat. "Are you okay?" I whispered.

"Think so. It felt like someone was driving an ice pick into my brain." His voice was raw and his chest heaved as he pulled in a deep breath. "Serena?"

"They took her."

"Where?"

I shook my head as I helped him to his feet. "I don't know." Saying the words made it hard to breathe.

"It'll be all right," said Kyle as he wrapped his arms around me. "You heard what they said. It's just some questions. She'll be okay." The words were reassuring, but unease colored each syllable.

The voice of the male guard rang across the room. "Girls through the door on the left. Boys through the right."

It wasn't supposed to be like this. We weren't supposed to be separated. I had conned my way into staying with Kyle and Serena and they were both being taken from me.

I pulled back. "Kyle, I . . ." I wanted to tell him that I loved him, but the words felt too much like good-bye.

He pressed his forehead to mine and let out a deep breath. "Me too," he said, echoing the response I had given in the truck.

His hands ran over my shoulders and slipped down my back and then, suddenly, his lips were on mine, delivering a crushing kiss that tasted like honey and copper. My lips parted under his as he pulled me so close that I wasn't sure where my body left off and his began.

I'd been scared to say the words aloud, but he had to know they were there: they were in every second of the kiss.

My eyes flew open as rough hands locked around my arm and pulled us apart.

More guards had shown up. Two pulled Kyle across the room. He wrenched free but went stone still as one of the guards pulled out a Taser and pressed it to his side.

A dark, animalistic look crossed Kyle's face. For a horrible second, I thought he would fight back, but then the guard holding me drew her own Taser.

Kyle's eyes locked on mine. Any hint of resistance drained out of him, and I suddenly knew they didn't need Tasers or physical force to make him do what they wanted: all they had to do was threaten me.

He shot me one last, desperate look before letting them shove him through the door on the right.

The guard holding my arm pulled me to the door on the left.

I knew it wasn't too late: I could tell her that I wasn't really infected. It was what Kyle—even Serena—wanted. I could walk out the gates and call Jason. He'd pick me up and enfold me in a hug and never once say I had done the wrong thing. I would spend the rest of my life blaming myself, but no one else would blame me at all.

I didn't have to go through the door.

I didn't have to be here.

Choice doesn't factor into things. I remembered Jason's

words in the parking garage and imagined the look of horror that would cross his face if he knew I was using them to justify walking into a camp.

But just because he had never intended for the words to apply to a situation like this didn't make them any less true.

With a deep breath, I walked through the door.

8

WHITE TILE WALLS. BENCHES. LICKS OF STEAM CURLING out of an archway. Of all the things that could have been lurking behind the door, a locker room hadn't been high on my list.

A folding chair sat in the middle of the floor and just behind it was a row of blue plastic bins—the kind Tess had for recyclables but forgot to use unless I nagged.

If we don't get out of here, it'll kill her.

And Jason.

The twin thoughts sent a stab of pain through my chest. Before I could dwell on them, however, a female guard and two women—one short and round, the other an escapee from a bodybuilding magazine—strode into the room.

The muscle-bound woman walked to the first bin and turned. Her tan polo shirt strained over biceps the size of cantaloupes and her skin had an orange tinge, like a faded self-tan. Her hair hung down her back in a braided whip. "One volunteer in the seat. Everyone else: line up."

No one moved.

The other woman yawned and glanced at her watch. "Langley, just pick one. I'm exhausted."

The woman with the orange skin scowled and gestured to Eve. "You."

Eve walked forward with her shoulders squared and her head high, but when she turned to sit, she wiped her palms on her faded black jeans.

Langley withdrew a pair of electric shears from the first bin. They clicked and hummed as strands of Eve's scarlet hair piled up around the chair. When it was over, Eve pushed herself to her feet and ran a hand through her now chin-length locks. A frown was her only concession to emotion.

Hank would approve, I thought, and then pressed my nails into my palm. This whole thing was his fault.

The other woman led Eve past the row of bins and raised her voice so we would all hear her instructions. One container for cell phones and electronics. Another for jewelry. The last for clothes. Nothing from outside was allowed into the camp.

I looked away as Eve shucked her T-shirt, and my gaze fell on Amy's bracelet. It was one of the only things I had of hers; I couldn't lose it. Besides, Amy had always claimed it was lucky. Right now, I needed all the luck I could get.

Using the girl in front of me for cover, I fumbled with the leather tie holding the bracelet in place, then switched the coins to my other wrist—the one with the metal cuff. A bead of sweat ran down the back of my neck as the guard walked by. Once she was past, I pushed and pulled on the band. It dug painfully into my skin, but I was able to stretch it out just enough to slip Amy's bracelet underneath.

A sliver of copper peeked out from under the cuff, but I didn't think anyone would notice—not unless they were looking for something out of the ordinary.

The line advanced and then, suddenly, it was my turn in the chair.

I stepped forward and sat. The woman with the shears, Langley, seemed to delight in yanking sections of my hair, and I struggled not to grimace as chunks of blond fell to the floor.

"Done."

I reached up as I stood. My stomach gave a strange flip-flop as my fingers grazed the ends of my hair. For the first time I could remember, it was above my shoulders.

The other woman led me down the row of bins. I walked right past the one for jewelry, but any triumph I felt at keeping Amy's bracelet was crushed under a wave of humiliation as I was ordered to strip.

I angled my body and kept my arm pressed to my side as I slipped out of my clothes. I still bore souvenirs from my final encounter with Branson Derby: bright pink scar tissue and a row of stitches on my forearm. The fact that the gash was still healing would instantly mark me as either a reg or as someone who hadn't gone through the thirty-day LS incubation period.

Either way, they'd probably retest my blood. Just to make sure I was infected.

Keeping the cut pressed to my side, I walked into the

showers and headed for the spot farthest from the door and the other girls.

Needles of ice water hit my skin as the guard patrolled up and down the room. It felt like a prison scene in some horrible movie, and I was hit with an urge to cry so strong that the muscles in my chest ached. I reminded myself that there was another locker room on the other side of the wall; I couldn't see him, but Kyle was going through the same thing a few feet away.

I sucked in a deep breath and grazed the wet tile with my knuckles. It wasn't so bad. No one had actually hurt me. I just had to keep thinking about Kyle and Serena.

A voice bellowed, "Everyone out," and we trudged, shivering, back into the locker room where we were each handed a stack of clothing and a pair of white canvas sneakers.

"You swapped, didn't you?" hissed Eve as she took a place next to me. Another girl shot us a curious glance, but the words were vague enough that it wasn't obvious just what Eve was talking about.

I quickly pulled on underwear and a pair of gray cargo pants. "Yeah."

"Idiot. If Curtis knew, he'd be furious."

A soft, bitter laugh escaped my lips. "He wouldn't care. In case you haven't noticed, he's the reason all of this happened."

Eve's newly shorn hair swished around her face as she shook her head. "He didn't know we'd be raided."

Maybe not, but if Hank had just let us take Kyle and go—if he had listened when I told him Jason wasn't really a

Tracker—we'd have been on our way back to Hemlock hours before the raid.

Eve gave me a long, evaluating look. "Why Mel?"

I shrugged. "She seemed to need it." I pulled on a heavy sweatshirt—gray like the pants—and tugged the sleeves over my wrists so that they hid my arm. A black logo on the front of the shirt drew my gaze. A circle of twisted vines surrounded a single word: *Thornhill*.

I frowned and bit my lip. How could we be in a camp that wasn't supposed to open for another six months?

Before I could give it any real thought, we were rushed through dressing, and then herded back through the admission building.

Outside, Langley and her partner took the lead while the guard took the rear. There was no sign of Serena as they marched us across the pavement and past the old three-story building at the other end of the courtyard. Nor was there any sign of Kyle or the rest of the boys from the raid.

We reached a path and made our way through the camp, passing what had to be at least two dozen one-story structures, a few of them still under construction. All of the buildings had signs painted on the outside indicating their purpose. Dorms. Classrooms. A dining hall.

I'd been expecting overcrowding and riots and death—all the rumors I'd grown up hearing—but this place looked more military school than concentration camp.

"Orientation is in three hours," said Langley's partner as we stopped between two dormitories. "I suggest you all get some sleep." She pointed at Eve and me. "You two are in dorm seven. Head straight through the common room to the sleeping quarters. Just claim an empty bunk for tonight."

Orientation? I wanted to ask, but one glance at the impatience on Langley's face and I mutely followed Eve into the building on our right.

We wove through a moonlit room crowded with armchairs and sofas, and then stepped into a long, narrow space filled with two rows of metal bed frames. Jane Eyre would have felt right at home. A few girls stirred as we passed, but no one spoke.

I counted the beds as I walked. Thirty, if you included the two empty ones at the far end of the room.

It was easy to see why no one else had claimed them. They were practically right on top of the bathroom and neither had sheets or blankets.

With a sigh, I chose the first bed and stretched out on my side. The mattress was almost as comfortable as a blanket laid over cracked asphalt; it made the beds back at the motel look luxurious.

I squeezed my eyes shut and thought of Jason.

I remembered the way his eyes had locked onto mine just before the truck door slammed shut. Stomach knotting, I pictured him going back to our room. I imagined him flicking on the light and staring at the empty beds as he tried to figure out what to do.

It was probably too much to hope he had gone back to Hemlock. *He'll be okay as long as he doesn't do anything crazy,* I thought, and then wondered who the hell I was kidding. Jason was recklessness personified.

Eve's low voice pierced my thoughts. "Back in that room . . . when we all hit the floor . . ."

I opened my eyes and watched as she stretched out on the other bed and searched for a way to ask if I'd been affected without any of the wolves in the room picking up on it. "No," I said.

She nodded as though I was just confirming what she already suspected. "That could be useful."

"Maybe." I shrugged halfheartedly. She might be right, but I sure as hell hadn't been very useful earlier.

"Curtis will think of something," she said suddenly. "The Trackers and the LSRB have never snatched more than four Eumon at a time. Last night, they nabbed thirty-one of us and burned down Curtis's club. He'll retaliate. He'll find a way to get us out."

It was the same conviction she'd shown in the truck.

"What's the deal with you two?" Hank would never chase a teenage girl—one of the few standards he did have—and I couldn't figure out their connection. For some reason, not knowing bothered me.

Eve hesitated. "A year and a half ago, Curtis found me on the streets and took me in. I was . . ." She bit her lip. Discomfort and uncertainty crossed her face and she looked suddenly young in the semidark. "I was in a bad spot. He got me out. Curtis let me stay with him and brought me into the pack. He looked out for me when I didn't have anyone."

I shook my head. "Hank doesn't help people. Not unless he's getting something out of it."

All trace of emotion and vulnerability left Eve's face.

"He told me what he was like before. He's different now. He lost you when he became infected. Losing a kid—it changes people."

Abandoned, I wanted to say, *not lost*. But it was like a shard of glass had lodged itself in my throat. Why? Why would Hank ditch me and then take care of some other girl? I felt a pinprick at the corner of my eyes but forced it back. It had been a long time since I had cried over my father and I wasn't going to start now.

Finally, I managed to speak. "If Hank had really told you what he was like before, we wouldn't be having this conversation. You'd know that anyone who counts on him always gets hurt." I turned over onto my other side before she could respond. I didn't need to be told who my father was or fed some fairy tale about how losing me had been the low point that made him turn his life around.

I'd spent my childhood watching Hank lie, cheat, and steal. He could be anything to anyone—as long as it suited him.

The man Eve thought she knew was as fake as the name he was using.

We were on our own.

"Remember that ghost story? The one Grandpa John told us the week we spent at the cabin?"

My eyes sprang open as Amy leaned over me and whispered in my ear. Her breath left a thin layer of frost on my cheek and I cringed away.

Hurt flashed across her face. She pulled back and I tried

not to feel guilty. In life, I had never been scared of Amy. In death, I didn't want her touching me.

I sat up and swung my legs over the side of my bunk. It was daylight and we were in the dorm room. Each of the other twenty-nine beds had been neatly made, but there was no one in sight. The faint smell of smoke hung in the air.

"He told us dozens," I said, wondering where this was going.

Amy's family owned a cabin about five hours from Hemlock. The summer Amy turned fifteen—the last summer she was still more tomboy than heiress—she, her brother, Stephen, and I had spent a week hiking and fishing with her grandfather. In the evenings, John—because "Sir" and "Mr." made him feel old—played chess against Amy while telling us ghost stories. The trip had been her father's idea, but we barely saw him; he'd spent most of the time glued to a satellite phone.

"The story with the dolls?" A red splatter appeared on Amy's white T-shirt, but she brushed her hand over the fabric and the stain faded to nothing.

I shook my head and a sad smile pulled at the corner of her mouth. For a second, she looked small and disappointed and desperately unhappy—the real Amy she'd kept hidden behind too-bright grins and her Stepford life. "Isn't it funny? I used to love ghost stories. Couldn't get enough of them—even though they scared me." She twisted a strand of hair around her finger. "I never thought I'd be one."

"You're not a ghost." I was sure of that. Wherever the dreams came from, they weren't really her.

"Of course I am." Amy shook her head. "That's all memories are. Ghosts and demons kicking around upstairs."

Sharp pain erupted at the base of my skull and radiated down my neck. For a brief, dizzy second, another room was superimposed over this one. The same size, only the paint on the walls had blistered and turned gray with ash. The same number of beds, only they weren't empty. Twenty-nine charred bodies fused to blackened mattress springs with crows picking at the bones.

I retched and scrambled off my bed.

"Easy, Toto," whispered Amy. "You're not in Kansas anymore."

9

A SHRILL WHISTLE DROVE INTO MY EARDRUMS LIKE A spike. My eyes flew open as I half scrambled, half fell out of bed.

A low rumble of complaints and curses swept the room as twenty-nine werewolves were jolted from sleep.

Eve was already on her feet, eyes narrowed as she stared at the door.

I turned and followed her gaze.

The female guard from last night—the one with the crew cut and square build—stood in the archway to the common room. One hand held a clipboard, the other a silver whistle. She fought back a yawn.

I swallowed. "Where's my friend?"

She ignored the question. "You were the only two assigned here last night, correct?" Without waiting for a reply, she said, "I'm supposed to take you to orientation," and then turned and disappeared through the arch.

A few girls cast bleary gazes in our direction as Eve and I walked past. One—a brunette with a sharp, foxlike face and features that looked vaguely Native American—glared as she raised herself on one elbow. "Great. More Eumon trash."

Eve stopped and turned. A predatory grin split her face as she took a step toward the girl.

"Guard outside," I hissed—more out of self-preservation than concern for her well-being.

"I wasn't actually going to start anything," she muttered unconvincingly, before spinning on her heel and heading through the common room. "Seriously, though, someone needs to teach that girl a lesson. She can't insult everyone just because her mom is the head of the Carteron pack. Like that's so special. It didn't keep her from winding up in here."

I followed Eve out of the dorm, half wishing for a jacket as I crossed my arms against the chill morning air. The guard told us to turn right at the end of the path and then walked behind us, giving directions as we made our way through the camp.

She could tase either of us in the back and we wouldn't realize it until the electricity hit. The thought made me shudder.

Daylight didn't diminish Thornhill's military school vibe. The buildings and lawns were neat and precise— even the ones that were still under construction—and the sky above the camp was an endless gunmetal gray. As we walked, I occasionally caught glimpses of a silver ribbon in the distance: the fence.

We reached a fork in the path at the same time as a group of boys. Each sported a crew cut and an olive version of the gray uniforms Eve and I wore. Kyle wasn't with them, but the guard herding the group was the redhead from last night.

"Tanner," said our guard, "I thought you were supposed to be off with the nightshift at six thirty."

"Donaldson quit." The redhead shrugged. "I got stuck with his shift."

They herded us toward a redbrick building with Auditorium painted on an arch above a set of heavy wooden doors. Though the structure was a simple rectangle with a flat roof, it seemed to match the large building near the courtyard: it looked decades older than the dorms and had the same ivy-covered walls.

We filtered into a space that had clearly once been a gymnasium. The lines of the basketball court were still visible and an ancient scoreboard—the kind where someone actually had to flip the numbers—hung at one end of the former court.

No way could anyone play a game in here now, though. The room was filled with three sections of benches, all facing what would have been the sideline.

Only the first two rows of each section were occupied. I quickly scanned the handful of wolves who were already seated; a small spark of fear raced down my spine as I realized Kyle and Serena weren't among them.

"You two," said our guard, "section on the right. First row."

My eyes were drawn to three huge banners on the wall as Eve and I claimed seats on the mostly empty bench.

CONTROL OVER ANGER.

CONSTRAINT IS FREEDOM.

YOUR DISEASE IS NOT A WEAPON.

My skin crawled.

The banners were white text on black fabric and they reminded me of that book we'd read in English last year: *1984*. Amy had hated it.

Below the banners, a black podium had been placed in the middle of a row of ten folding chairs. The podium had the Thornhill crest stenciled in white on the front and had been carefully positioned so that the center of the crest appeared directly underneath the word *freedom*.

"Subtle," I muttered.

I tore my gaze away and glanced over my shoulder. One section over and one row back, four boys were finding their seats. My heart gave a small lurch as I realized one of the boys was Kyle.

The guards at the back of the room were talking among themselves. They dealt with wolves as they came in, but only occasionally glanced our way. I darted across the aisle to Kyle's section.

Relief flashed across his face when he spotted me, and he swept me in a hug as soon as I reached him.

"Longest three hours of my life," he said, voice rough as he held me tightly.

I buried my face against his neck and breathed in the scent of his skin. "No kidding."

After a moment, I eased back and studied him. It was

hard to believe it had only been a few hours since we had been pulled apart. Kyle looked years older. The olive uniform deepened the color of his skin, making him look almost tanned, and his newly shorn hair highlighted the strong planes and angles of his face. The stripped-down appearance made his eyes impossible to ignore; they held shadows of everything he'd seen and done over the past few weeks, things no seventeen-year-old should have to carry.

Things he carried because of me.

Turning away before he could catch the flash of guilt on my face, I scanned the auditorium. It only took a second. As far as I could tell, only the wolves caught in last night's raid were here.

Kyle didn't have to ask who I was looking for. "I don't think Serena's here." Almost as an afterthought, he added, "The two guys who were tased during the blood test are, though."

I couldn't remember what the boys looked like—especially with everyone dressed the same—but I took Kyle's word for it. I bit my lip and allowed him to pull me down to the bench. Why would they be here when Serena wasn't?

A wolf in the next section turned his head to talk to someone behind him. For a split second, I thought he had a tattoo on the side of his neck, but then I realized it was just a thick mound of scar tissue. I swallowed. "Do you think Jason's all right?"

"Probably," said Kyle slowly. "Getting caught in a building full of werewolves doesn't look great, but Jason could teach a class in bullshitting. He'll have talked his way out of it."

Before either of us could say anything else, the auditorium doors closed with a bang that made several wolves jump.

The gunshot slap of heels rang out as a woman strode toward the front of the gathering. She looked oddly familiar, but it took me a moment to place her: Winifred Sinclair. The woman whose photo I had seen in the paper.

The picture hadn't done her justice. Her hair—a rich, chestnut brown except for the single streak of white—was set in curls so precise they looked sculpted, while her pinstripe suit emphasized her height and slender frame.

Two women and three men—all dressed in white—followed in her wake and claimed the folding chairs on the right as she took her place behind the podium.

Every whisper fell silent as Sinclair's gaze swept the room. When her eyes passed over me, it felt like someone had slipped an ice cube down my back.

"My name is Warden Sinclair and I'd like to welcome you all to Thornhill. Though the camp isn't fully operational yet, we've been able to open our doors to a select number of wolves to ease overcrowding at other facilities." She swept a hand over the top of the podium as though clearing away dust. "I want to stress how lucky you are to be here."

Lucky? There was a collective intake of breath. How could anyone—even someone who ran a camp—call being rounded up at gunpoint "lucky"?

Something about the raid—some snatch of memory that

didn't quite make sense—hovered at the edge of my mind, but Sinclair pulled my attention back to the here and now.

"Van Horne is the nearest rehabilitation camp. Last month, there were eighteen deaths, food shortages, and riots. Similar conditions are found at almost every camp in the country."

She paused, letting her words sink in.

"Thornhill is different. We are developing a pilot program that truly focuses on rehabilitation. You were sent here, instead of Van Horne, because you are young enough to make the most of this opportunity."

Young enough? I guess that explained why they had separated everyone over eighteen.

The boy in front of me raised his hand and the warden nodded.

"I don't understand how you can rehabilitate us." His voice cracked and I realized it was the boy from the truck, the one who had almost lost control. "I mean, there's no cure, is there?"

There was an oddly hopeful note in his voice. Next to me, Kyle inhaled sharply and leaned forward. The Adam's apple in his throat bobbed as he swallowed.

"Not yet."

I was watching Kyle, not the warden. Disappointment and pain flashed across his face. His hands rested on his knees and he stared down at them, studying them. When he glanced up and realized I was watching, he looked embarrassed, then a little angry, like I had spied on something private.

Sinclair was still speaking. "The best medical minds in the country are looking for a cure. There may someday be a breakthrough. If that happens, wolves at places like Van Horne won't be released. The camps will have robbed them of any humanity LS left behind, and they will not be able to reintegrate into society. Thornhill will help prepare you for life in the event a cure is found. For rejoining the outside world and adjusting to a single physical form. The *right* physical form."

I thought of Ben and shuddered. He'd gone into the camps a normal teenager. After getting out, he had willingly signed on for a killing spree.

Sinclair curled her fingers around the edge of the podium, clutching it so tightly that her knuckles stood out like sharp points. "You've been given this opportunity over hundreds of other werewolves, but be warned: If you do not treat Thornhill like the privilege it is—if you cause trouble or fall behind in your classes—the program coordinators behind me will hear about it. If they decide that you are not a suitable candidate for our program, you will be transferred—either to Van Horne or to work on one of the other camps currently under construction, all of which are being built using wolf labor. Neither option will improve the quality of your life."

She flashed a small, empty smile. "I hope we're all on the same page."

10

AFTER AN HOUR OF SPEECHES AND LISTS OF DOS AND don'ts, we were ordered to stay in our seats while the warden and program coordinators left. Once the last white uniform disappeared through the doors, timetables were handed out and guards were assigned to each row of werewolves.

Group by group, we were led outside.

"Line up in twos and follow me," snapped our escort, a grizzly of a man with acne-scarred cheeks. "And pay attention. After today, you'll be responsible for finding your own way around this place. Guards and counselors have enough to do without walking you to and from every class and work detail."

"Right," muttered a female voice from somewhere behind Kyle and me, "because it would really be possible to get lost in this place."

She had a point. Sooner or later you'd just hit the fence.

I glanced at Kyle's timetable and compared it to my own. Every day of the week was scheduled, though evenings were considered "free time" until curfew. We had the same morning classes, but our afternoon work details—physical labor assignments to help us build character and the camp save money—were all different.

"Self-control," said Kyle, reading off this morning's class. "Sounds . . . cheery."

I looked up, a reply on my lips, and caught a glimpse of white on the path ahead.

One of the male program coordinators had stopped to talk to a counselor. According to the orientation speeches, the tan-clad counselors oversaw classes and work details while the program coordinators designed the curriculum and made bigger decisions—like who got to stay and who ended up being transferred.

We weren't supposed to talk to the program coordinators directly, but if anyone could tell me where Serena was, it would probably be one of them. I tugged on Kyle's sleeve and glanced meaningfully in the man's direction. Kyle nodded and we slowed our pace, falling back to the end of the line and then falling out completely.

"Excuse me?" I said as we approached the pair. The coordinator turned. I had a second to register his sandy-blond hair and a birthmark like a thumbprint on his cheek before my gaze slid to the woman at his side. A lead weight settled in my stomach as I recognized the counselor from last night: Langley.

She stared at us and her mouth pressed into a line that was ruler straight. I had never seen her before arriving at Thornhill, but I had the distinct impression she hated me— hated anyone interned here—on principle.

I swallowed and focused on the coordinator. He held a computer tablet under one arm and he seemed very young— maybe as young as his midtwenties—for his position. Somehow, I hoped youth would make him more sympathetic. Determined to get my question out before the guard leading our group noticed Kyle and I were missing, I spoke in a rush. "One of my friends was held back last night and she wasn't at orientation this morning. I was wondering where she was?"

"A few wolves were over eighteen. They were transferred this morning." He turned back to Langley, clearly dismissing us.

"She was seventeen," interjected Kyle. "They didn't hold her back until after we were through admissions."

Langley's eyes narrowed. "I suggest you spend less time worrying about others and rejoin your group."

"But . . ." I started to object, and Kyle placed a warning hand on my arm. Our guard had brought the others to a halt and was making his way back down the path toward us.

I knew we should walk away—quickly—but I still hesitated.

A flicker of annoyance crossed the coordinator's face. He lifted the tablet. "What are your names?"

A chill swept through me. He hadn't said or done anything threatening, but he had the power to move either of us to another camp if he decided we were troublemakers— the warden had said as much herself. I shook my head and backed away. "Never mind. Sorry to have bothered you." The words were cardboard and paste in my mouth as I turned and followed Kyle back to the line.

The guard scowled and rested his hand on the top of his holster as we rejoined the group. Thankfully, his ire seemed only to last until Langley and the program coordinator looked away, then he muttered something about not being paid enough and headed back to the front of the line.

I slipped my hand into Kyle's as we passed a dorm and a few classroom buildings. "Do you think she's all right?"

"Serena's tough," he replied.

It wasn't an answer.

We reached a large white building with the personality and charm of a shoebox. I dimly remembered walking past it last night.

The guard's voice rang out. "Dining hall. You've still got twenty minutes for breakfast—assuming the other wolves left you any."

Waves of conversation and the smell of burned eggs crashed over me as Kyle and I followed the others into a cavernous cafeteria. The whole room seemed to be shades of brown and beige: brown tile floors, brown painted walls, long beige tables. The rest of the camp had risen while we were in orientation and there had to be close to three hundred wolves inside.

The last thing I felt like doing was eating, but Kyle headed for a stack of trays—brown, of course—and pushed one into my hands. I tried to object, but he just said, "You won't be any help to Serena if you pass out from hunger."

I tried to remember the last time I had eaten. The only thing that came to mind was the coffee I'd had yesterday afternoon.

Yesterday.

I followed Kyle down the line, mindlessly accepting helpings of food without realizing—or caring—what any of it was. How was it possible that so much had changed in less than twenty-four hours?

"I asked her to come to Denver." The words carved a hollow in my chest. "I'm responsible. If anything happens to her, it's my fault."

"I know the feeling."

We reached the end of the line. I lifted my tray and glanced up at him. "You didn't ask me to come after you."

Kyle held my gaze for a handful of heartbeats and then shrugged. "But you're still here."

Before I could respond, he headed for an empty table at the far end of the room.

My sneakers squeaked against the linoleum floor and I could feel curious eyes on me as I crossed the cafeteria. Eve sat at a table with a bunch of kids I dimly recognized from last night. At orientation, we'd been told that packs were banned in the camp—like Thornhill was a big, happy family or one of those colleges that outlawed sororities—but it looked like the Eumon wolves were intending to stick together.

I slid into a seat across from Kyle and halfheartedly pushed my food around with my fork. "The program coordinator didn't seem big on answering questions," I said, stating the obvious.

"None of the staff are." A boy with a blond crew cut was suddenly towering over my right shoulder. "Cool if I sit?" Without waiting for a reply, he set his tray—and himself—next to me.

Kyle made introductions. "Mac, this is Dex. He's in my dorm."

The boy turned his head and I bit back a gasp.

He had the kind of rugged jaw you saw in shaving commercials and wide-set brown eyes that a girl could lose herself in, but his right cheek was covered in a network of intricate white scars. It looked like someone had carved symbols into his flesh with a scalpel.

"Freakish, isn't it?"

"Umm . . ." I had seen some horrible scars before—Kyle's back, Ben's chest—but never anything like this. They had the pull of a car wreck on the side of the highway: I didn't want to stare, but I couldn't look away. "Are those . . . *letters?*"

"I think so." Dex rubbed his cheek with a hand big enough to palm a basketball. "But don't ask me what language it is or what it says. A werewolf decided to use my face as a Post-it after I broke into his car."

"What . . ." I swallowed. "What happened to the wolf who did it?" There were other questions I wanted to ask—things like *Were you conscious?*—but I figured I was better off not knowing the answers.

"Curtis dealt with it." Eve slid into the seat next to Kyle and snagged a piece of toast from his plate. I had been so focused on Dex's scars that I hadn't noticed her arrival until she sat. "The wolf wasn't one of ours, but the Denver packs have an agreement not to draw attention to ourselves."

"And my face is pretty high profile." Eve started to object, but Dex swept her words aside. "It's not like I haven't seen a mirror, Evelyn."

She shook her head and a smile flashed across her face. "Damn, it's good to see you. I think I even missed you calling me that."

Dex pressed a hand to his chest. "Don't tell me you were actually worried about me."

"Kinda. But tell anyone and I'll deny it."

"I'd expect nothing less." He sobered. "I heard the club got raided."

"Raided and torched." Eve dropped the toast back onto Kyle's plate, her appetite apparently lost. "Where's your girlfriend?" she asked as though trying to distract herself from the memory of last night.

A pained look crossed Dex's face, twisting the shape of his scars. "Don't know."

Eve stared. "What do you mean you don't know? Everyone said you got picked up during the same raid."

"We did. Six weeks ago, Corry and I arrived together. After we were here a few days, two guards showed up and took her out of class. They said they had some questions for her."

A prickly feeling crept down my neck. It was what the

woman had said last night before they had taken Serena—that they had questions for her. Kyle reached under the table and skimmed my knee with his fingertips, a quick, comforting touch.

A guard walked by. Dex waited for him to move out of earshot before continuing. "Corry didn't come back. When she didn't show up at dinner, I went to her dorm. Her bunk was completely stripped. I kept asking where she was—asked so much I got tased. Finally, they told me she had gotten violent and was transferred."

Eve frowned. "Corry's never struck me as someone who has a lot of self-control issues."

"She doesn't. She has more control than any wolf I've met." Dex's words were fierce and sharp. They cut through the air, and I realized the noise around us had died down. I glanced at the next table. All conversation had ceased. The wolves were staring at their trays, but they were obviously hanging on every word.

"There are things you don't ask about here," continued Dex as he ran a hand over the numbers on his wrist cuff. "Classes. Work details. Disappearances. *Especially* disappearances."

"Next, he'll be telling them about Willowgrove," muttered a voice at the other table, just loud enough to carry.

The words were accompanied by a scattered chorus of nervous laughter.

A faint blush darkened Dex's cheeks, but when he spoke, his voice was low and angry rather than embarrassed. "They think I'm crazy. They'd rather pretend this place actually cares about rehabilitating us than admit something strange is going on."

"Why?" I asked. "What's Willowgrove?"

"A Thornhill urban legend. The bogeyman for werewolf boys and girls." Dex shrugged. "People say it's a secret camp—one so bad they don't tell anyone about it. If you disappear from Thornhill, that's where you get sent."

I frowned. "That doesn't make sense." Werewolves didn't have rights and the camps already had horrible reputations. It was hard to imagine one so bad the LSRB would keep it secret.

"No," agreed Dex, staring at me levelly, "it doesn't."

Kyle leaned forward. "So what do you think it is?"

"A fictional camp to balance the books or a lie to tell the wolves they nab so they'll go more quietly." Dex's eyes darkened. "Do you know why prisons let inmates out early for good behavior?"

"As an incentive," said Kyle with a shrug.

"To save money and free up beds," I corrected softly. I shot a quick glance at him, wondering what it would have been like to grow up in a house where conversations didn't regularly start with some variation of "If-slash-when I go to prison."

"Every wolf they pick up is a lifer," said Dex. "You and I? We represent sixty years of taxpayer dollars going down the drain, and I'm guessing budgets at the camps are already stretched thin. Sooner or later, they're going to need a way to keep the population in check. Sinclair is just doing it sooner."

Eve cleared her throat. When she spoke, her tone had a razor edge. "What, exactly, are you saying?"

"I'm saying Willowgrove is the ultimate solution. Kill a few wolves here and there and no one gets suspicious. Do it often enough, and eventually the whole overcrowding thing sorts itself out."

The silence at the other table had spread. Every wolf in the dining hall seemed to be listening, and guards were starting to notice the change in atmosphere—notice and pinpoint our table as the epicenter.

Dex pushed himself to his feet. His gaze locked on me. "Kyle said they took your friend during admissions?"

Throat dry, I nodded.

"If she's still alive, she's probably in the sanatorium."

The words *still alive* hit me like a slap. I struggled to find my voice. "Sanatorium?"

"The big building near the courtyard. It used to be a hospital for tuberculosis patients. It's off-limits to wolves unless you're dying or sent to the detention block."

Two guards headed our way, and the look Dex shot them was enough that one of the men unsnapped his holster and placed his hand on the butt of his Taser.

Eyes on the guards but still speaking to me, Dex said, "In the whole camp—unless you count the gate and the fence—that's one of only two places they really don't want you to go."

"What's the other?"

But he was already walking away, guards trailing him until he left the building.

I rose from my seat, intent on following and getting an answer, but before I could, an amplified voice boomed through the air with a crackle of static. "All new wolves scheduled for self-control class proceed to the lawn in front of the dining hall."

11

Sixteen of us, including Eve, followed Langley down paths and across lawns. We left the buildings behind and passed a fenced-off area that was completely empty and almost the size of a football field. A sign posted near the path read Authorized Shifting Zone.

During orientation, we'd been given rules about shifting. It was only allowed in two areas: the shifting zone and the self-control class. Thornhill had a zero-tolerance policy for wolves who transformed anywhere else.

"Glorified dog park," muttered Eve, earning her a small smile from Kyle.

I felt a tiny flash of jealousy. I hadn't seen that smile very many times since he had become infected.

"Why let anyone shift at all?" I wondered softly, glancing over my shoulder for one last look at the field.

A few wolves shot curious glances my way, but Kyle quickly covered for me. "You haven't been infected long. Even wolves with really strong control have to shift sometimes. Otherwise, they risk losing their temper and blowing up."

"And taking a swipe at whoever happens to be in the way," added Eve. Something dark passed over her face and I wondered, suddenly, how she had become infected.

We skirted the edge of a wooded area until we reached another field.

It should have been beautiful. The grass was a green so bright it was practically Technicolor and wildflowers dotted it like exclamation marks. It was the kind of spot you saw in perfume ads or Disney movies—except for the cage.

It sat in the middle of the field like a fly trapped in honey, and the sight of it sent goose bumps racing down my arms. It was almost the size of my apartment back home and fully enclosed. The only way in or out was through a small door made of thick wire.

Langley unlatched the door and turned to face us. "Part of self-control is learning to resist external stimuli and suppress your wolf. Those of you who can demonstrate restraint this morning may receive special privileges. Those of you who can't . . ." She let the words trail off ominously as she reached into her pocket and withdrew a small red object. A pocketknife.

She slid open the blade as her gaze swept the wolves. Her eyes lingered on me. "You were full of questions this morning. Roll up your sleeve."

I felt, more than saw, Kyle go completely rigid. My gaze darted from Langley to the knife in her hand. She couldn't be serious.

"Your sleeve. Unless you'd like to explain to the coordinators why you refused to participate in class."

Heart thudding, I reached for my sleeve.

Kyle caught my hand.

Langley's eyes narrowed. "Is there a problem?"

"Of course there is. Everyone's frightened and exhausted and you just pulled a knife."

I turned.

Eve rocked back on her heels. Everyone else looked alert and on edge, but her face was a mask of boredom. Only her eyes—sharp and calculating—hinted that she was just as tense as the rest of us. She cracked each knuckle in her right hand and then yawned.

"Congratulations," snapped Langley, "you just volunteered to take her place. Arm out."

Eve stepped forward without hesitation.

I stared, stunned. She had provoked the counselor so I wouldn't be hurt.

Why? I thought, confused, as Eve rolled up her sleeve and held out her arm. We weren't friends. She didn't owe me anything. I couldn't understand her motivation, and that made the idea of her taking my place even more unsettling.

Langley singled out eight wolves, including Kyle, and ordered them into the cage. Once they were inside, she turned to me and held out the knife.

She had to be joking.

"Take it."

I shook my head. No way.

Langley's gaze shifted to the cage and hovered meaningfully over Kyle. Sweat beaded on my forehead. She could try to have him sent to another camp—or worse—just to punish me for defying her. And she would. The expression on her face didn't leave room for doubt.

Kyle gave a small, barely perceptible shake of his head. He slipped his fingers through the links of the cage, gripping the wires so tightly that I worried he'd slice his skin.

"Do it," said Eve.

I glanced at her and her eyes locked on mine, almost like a challenge.

I licked my lips nervously and reached out to take the knife. It was heavier than it should have been and the handle was oddly cold in my hand.

I wondered how Langley could be crazy enough to give a prisoner a weapon, then realized how stupid the thought was: wolves carried knives under their skin 24-7. Just because they weren't supposed to shift outside of this class and the zone didn't mean they wouldn't.

"Make an incision and then follow her into the cage."

Eve's eyes widened, and something that looked like worry crossed her face. She hadn't counted on this, I realized. She hadn't expected me to follow her in.

She shook her head. "This isn't a fair test. Everyone is running on empty. You put a bleeding wolf in there and most of us will shift just because our minds and bodies are overloaded."

Langley's lips pressed into a thin, hard line as she regarded Eve. "If you'd rather not participate, I'm sure a spot can be found for you at Van Horne."

Still, Eve hesitated. She lowered her arm.

I couldn't let her get herself into that much trouble. Not

to protect me. Stomach plummeting and heart rate skyrocketing, I slashed out with the blade.

It slid through Eve's pale skin as though she were made of paper.

But paper didn't bleed.

Blood welled to the surface of her arm and an answering wave of acid rushed up my throat. The pocketknife slipped from my hand and fell to the ground. It made a muffled thump as it hit the grass.

Eve walked quickly to the cage, swearing under her breath and holding her arm away from herself. Kyle tried to block the entrance, but she shoved him. I had just enough time to slip inside while she hissed at Kyle that it was my choice.

Langley slammed and locked the door.

Eyes a firestorm, Kyle stepped around Eve and reached for me. He tried to keep his body between me and the other wolves as we backed toward the far end of the cage.

Langley addressed the other half of the class, the wolves outside the cage. "People don't like to admit it, but many werewolves—not just those with bloodlust—find it difficult not to shift in the presence of blood. And, of course, the temptation to shift when wounded or when another wolf loses control is incredibly strong."

Blood ran down Eve's skin and dripped onto the grass. I watched, horrified and fascinated, as she sucked in deep, ragged breaths and folded to her knees. Her spine bowed with a sound like river ice snapping during a thaw and then her body tore itself to pieces. When it was over, a silver wolf climbed to its feet.

Three, then five, then six of the wolves lost control and shifted. One had white fur, and the reminder of Ben sent my heart hammering against my breast bone and stole the air from my lungs.

My shoulder blades hit the wall of the cage and I flinched.

One wolf took a swipe at another and the result was like a match thrown onto a pile of gas-soaked rags.

Teeth gnashed and blood flowed as other wolves got pulled into the fray. It was hard to believe the creatures in front of me had been human just moments before. They were like true animals—animals who had more in common with Ben than with Kyle or Serena.

No. No. No. No. The single word echoed in my head and only when it drew the attention of the white wolf did I realize I was mumbling it aloud.

Kyle stayed in front of me. His presence should have been reassuring, but his sleeves were rolled up and I could see the muscles twitch and writhe under his skin. The white wolf padded toward us and Kyle let out a low, dangerous growl— the kind of growl a human throat shouldn't be capable of.

The wolf continued its advance, and Kyle kicked out so hard that I heard a sickening crack as his foot connected with the wolf's skull.

Only one other person in the cage, a boy who looked younger than everyone else, hadn't shifted. "I'm. Not. Going. To. Change . . . ," he panted, curling his hands into fists as the bones tried to snap.

Suddenly, he clamped his hands to his head and fell to

the ground. In front of me, Kyle did the same. All of the wolves—inside the cage and out—collapsed. The ones who had retained human shape covered their ears and the ones who had lost control shifted back.

It was just like what had happened when they took Serena.

I covered my own ears and crouched next to Kyle. I tried to look helpless and in pain—not much of a stretch given how scared I was—as I watched Langley from beneath my lashes. She held a small black device in her hand that was about the size and shape of a remote car starter. After a minute, she slipped it into her pocket and the wolves began to come to.

Langley's voice swelled over the class. "Guards have Tasers and guns. Counselors have HFDs: high-frequency devices. Fall out of line and a counselor will use an HFD. Get too close to the fence or a restricted zone and an HFD will automatically be triggered."

There was a hint of excitement in her voice, and I had the sickening suspicion that she had enjoyed hurting us, that we were little more than animals to her.

Kyle shakily lifted himself to a sitting position as around us, people grabbed the shredded remains of clothing, desperately trying to cover their nudity.

"Are you okay?" I whispered.

"Yeah. I think so." His voice was raw as he stood and reached down to help me up. "You?"

I hesitated, then nodded. I couldn't tell him that seeing that many wolves shift had scared me almost as badly as the

LSRB and the Trackers said I should be.

Trying not to think about the way Kyle's muscles had moved under his skin, I reached up and took his hand. *Still Kyle*, I reminded myself, *he'll always be Kyle.*

I glanced skyward as I gained my feet. As I did, I noticed something I had missed when entering the cage: High on each corner were four cameras, all pointing inward.

Langley's voice pulled my gaze away. "First group out, second group in."

The other group had their turn in the cage. Not one of them was able to hold back from shifting. Afterward, the wolves grabbed fresh uniforms from a row of plastic bins. Once everyone was decent, we sat on the grass and listened for two hours as Langley told disturbing—and graphic—tales of wolves who had lost control and killed.

By the time the buzzer signaled lunch, every person in the class was emotionally battered and physically drained.

Every person except Langley, of course. There seemed to be a spring in the counselor's step as she led us back through the camp. I could just imagine the meetings she must have had with her high school guidance counselor as she explored career options that would let her both torture *and* humiliate.

I watched Kyle out of the corner of my eye as he walked beside me. He had barely said a word since stepping out of the cage, and his eyes, his expression, even his posture, were all hard and closed down.

"Are you okay?" I whispered, skimming his hand with

my fingers as the side of the dining hall came into sight.

"I should be asking you that." His brow furrowed as we passed a small stand of trees. "C'mon." He shot Langley a quick glance before twining his fingers around mine and stepping out of line.

"You have forty minutes and then a fifteen-minute warning bell will . . ." Langley's voice faded as I followed Kyle to the circle of trees. He dropped my hand as soon as we were under the branches.

The spot wasn't completely private—someone walking past would be able to see us if they were close enough and paying attention—but from what I knew of the camp's layout, most people would probably be approaching the dining hall from the other side of the building.

An ornately carved stone bench—a holdover from the days when this place had been a hospital—stood in the middle of the trees. I sat on the edge and traced an epitaph with my fingertip. *In Memory of Miriam.*

I expected Kyle to sit next to me, but he leaned against a tree and crossed his arms.

The six feet between us felt like six thousand.

"What's wrong?" I realized the absurdity of the statement and shook my head. "I mean, other than the fact that we're in a rehabilitation camp and Serena is missing and my hair looks like it was cut by a blind man using a rusty hacksaw blade."

The scowl on Kyle's face was so deep it was in danger of becoming permanent. "That last bit was a joke," I said, somewhat unnecessarily.

A muscle in his jaw twitched. I had the distinct feeling he was holding himself back from saying a dozen things—none of which I would want to hear. Finally, voice tight, he said, "Do you have any idea what could have happened in that cage? Did you listen to the stories Langley told us? Forget getting scratched—one of them could have torn your throat out or crushed your skull. They don't know you can't heal."

"I know." I pulled in a deep breath and let it out slowly. "But I'm okay. Nothing happened."

"If Langley had waited any longer to set off that HFD, it would have."

"Maybe," I admitted, because I could neither deny nor admit how scared I had been. I didn't want Kyle to know that a small part of me had been afraid of him, too, that it still frightened me when I saw muscles twist and tear beneath his skin.

I slipped a finger under my wrist cuff and touched the edge of Amy's bracelet. "What happened?" I didn't want to ask, but somehow, I couldn't stop myself. "Why did they turn on each other?"

"Blood plus exhaustion plus a confined space? Even regs would have had a hard time not taking swipes at one another." He uncrossed his arms and ran a hand over his jaw. His eyes darkened, and I knew he was thinking about how close he had come to losing control with the others.

"Why didn't you shift?" I asked softly.

He swallowed and gazed out at the camp. For a moment, I thought he wasn't going to answer. "You," he admitted finally. "I was scared of what would happen if you were the only one who didn't shift. And I didn't want you to see me like that."

"Kyle . . ." I stood and closed the space between us, then slipped my hand into his. He didn't pull away, but he didn't return my grip and he didn't meet my eyes. For a moment, it was like he was somewhere else, locked someplace inside his head where I couldn't follow. "I've seen you shift before."

"Five times," he said. "I didn't want to make it six." He finally looked at me. With his free hand, he reached out and brushed a strand of hair back from my face, letting his fingers linger on my cheek for a moment. "I wish I could be human for you."

I shook as a slow ache spread through my chest. "Kyle, you *are* human."

"No. I'm really not." His gaze became resolute. "You need to tell them what you are. You need to tell them you're a reg."

"You know I can't." I stared at him, willing him to understand. "There's no way I can leave without knowing Serena's okay—especially after that stuff Dex said at breakfast."

Kyle stared right back, but didn't speak. It was like a contest: whichever one of us blinked first lost.

"I'll be careful. I'll be safe. We don't have self-control for another week, and that's the only place wolves are allowed to shift outside the zone." I laced my fingers with his. I didn't need his permission to stay—it wasn't a contest or vote—but I couldn't afford to spend every free moment arguing. "I need to know that Serena's okay and I need you to help me." I squeezed his hand so tightly that my arm shook. "Please, Kyle."

"You're insane, you know that, right? You're like a member of PETA with a death wish." The words were mocking, but the look in his eyes was lost and a little sad. Voice rough, he said, "Regs aren't supposed to care this much about werewolves."

"All werewolves start off as regs," I countered.

In response, he kissed me.

It started off gently—just the brush of his lips against mine—but I reached up and clasped my hands behind his neck, drawing him closer. My lips parted under his and the kiss deepened to something that was a almost fierce in its intensity.

Everything inside of me twisted and shattered.

Without breaking the kiss, Kyle switched our positions so that my back was against the tree. His hands stroked my hair and my shoulders and grazed my sides when my shirt rucked up a few inches. His fingers left trails of fire on my skin, the sensation only occasionally dampened by the touch of the metal cuff around his wrist.

No wrist cuffs, I thought, *no Thornhill. Just us.*

Moments later, when I was in danger of completely forgetting where we were, Kyle made a low, frustrated noise deep in his throat and gently pulled away.

He turned his head and scanned the area beyond the trees. Following his gaze, I saw a female guard headed our way. Squinting, I could just make out a pack of cigarettes in her hand as she shook out a smoke.

"There's probably still time to get some lunch," I said as Kyle and I stepped out from the trees.

He shot me a small, slightly rueful smile. "Sure. If you're going to insist on throwing yourself into dangerous situations, we should probably make sure you keep your strength up."

"Speaking of which . . ." The roof of the sanatorium was just visible over the dining hall. "Dex seemed sure that was where Serena would be."

"It makes sense. If she were in the main part of the camp, we'd have seen her at breakfast or orientation."

"So all we have to do is figure out a way to get into the only place we're not allowed to go. Well, one of," I amended, thinking of Dex's cryptic statement about there being two. "Should be easy." I meant the words to sound joking, but they hung heavy in the air, filled with doubt and trepidation.

"We'll figure something out," promised Kyle, and I knew part of the determination in his voice was the belief—or hope—that I'd leave once we knew Serena was safe.

But even if we found her, how could anyone ever be safe in a place with counselors like Langley and where—according to Dex—people disappeared?

I took one last glance at the sanatorium roof before it slipped from view.

No: finding Serena was just step one. There was no way I was leaving Thornhill until I figured out how to take both her and Kyle with me.

12

MY ARMS THROBBED AS I TRANSFERRED ANOTHER LOAD of wet sheets to a dryer that was big enough to sleep in. The humidity in the air plastered my shirt to my skin and made my lungs ache. Before this afternoon, I wouldn't have said laundry was actual torture, but before this afternoon, I had never tried to do laundry for a few hundred people.

"You! Over here!" The counselor—a chubby woman with a nose ring and olive skin—raised her voice above the din of the machines.

Twelve pairs of eyes turned toward her as we each tried to figure out which one of us she was talking to. At the machine next to me, Eve dropped the armful of Thornhill shirts she was holding and pushed back her sweat-damp hair.

The counselor's gaze locked on me. "Over here," she repeated.

I followed her across the long, narrow room to where two-dozen wheeled bins awaited an ever-rotating supply of uniforms, sheets, and towels. She gestured at two smaller bins set off to the side. Unlike the others, they had lids but no wheels. One was labeled *Gloves*, the other *Smocks*.

"These need to go to the garden sheds by the produce fields. Can you manage?"

A sinking feeling filled my stomach as I tried to figure out how much each bin might weigh.

When I didn't immediately answer, the counselor frowned. "Are you going to pick one up?"

Good question, I thought.

There was no choice but to try. Hoping gloves would be lighter than smocks, I lifted the nearest bin—

And almost dropped it. Not because it was too heavy— though I could feel the strain in my arms and shoulders—but because I could barely reach around it; no wonder the counselor had asked if I could manage.

"You'll need help." She turned to the room and asked for a volunteer.

I tried to keep the surprise from my face when Eve raised her hand.

The counselor waved her forward and gave us directions as Eve gracefully lifted the bin full of smocks. "They go in shed fifteen. Head past the auditorium and take a left at the next path. Don't worry about making it back for the end of the detail. We only have ten minutes left and it'll probably take you that long to get there."

We made our way out of the building. For a few moments, I luxuriated in the sensation of the afternoon breeze cooling the sweat on my face and the chance to breathe air that wasn't as heavy as a wet gym sock. But the mental break lasted only until the laundry building was out of sight.

"What do you want, Eve?"

"Who said I wanted anything?"

I glanced at her out of the corner of my eye. Her expression was too guarded for someone who wasn't working some sort of angle. "Come on. First you bailed me out in self-control—thanks for that, by the way—and then you volunteered to lug this stuff across the camp."

"Beats staying in the laundry room," she said with a shrug.

Up ahead, a pair of men rounded a bend in the path. Both wore jogging shorts and blue T-shirts—outfits that were completely at odds with the holsters bouncing on their hips. Even at rest, the guards were armed.

We stepped off the path to make room. Once they were out of sight, Eve set down her bin, readjusted her hold, and then picked it back up. I was tempted to do the same, but given the way my arms were starting to shake, I wasn't sure I'd be able to lift it a second time.

"We need to get out of Thornhill," she said. "We can't just sit around, doing nothing."

I raised an eyebrow. "What happened to all that stuff you said about Hank getting us out?"

She considered her answer as we passed the auditorium and took the left the counselor had told us about. Here, close-crowded trees bordered the path, and I realized we were on the other side of the woods we had passed on our way to self-control earlier in the day.

"Curtis *is* going to try and get us out," Eve said slowly,

ignoring the short, skeptical noise I made, "but if he can't, then we have to figure out something on our own. This whole place was built to control wolves like me, not regs like you. You can go places I can't. We can use that."

She blew a strand of hair off her face. "I am *not* spending the rest of my life in here."

We neared the edge of the produce fields and Eve fell silent: enough wolves were working that private conversation was impossible.

The fields were located on the farthest outskirts of the camp and were nothing more than glorified vegetable patches—straggly ones at that. An old water tower rose near the edge of one. Covered with rust and balancing shakily on four spindly legs, it looked like it had been here long before the camp—maybe even before the sanatorium.

Shed fifteen was just past it. Beyond that was the fence.

Large signs warned wolves not to get within eight feet of the wires, and someone had enhanced one of these by adding a stick figure with lightning bolts shooting out of his fingertips and the top of his head.

"Funny," muttered Eve as she headed for the shed.

She pulled open the door and stepped inside, but I stopped when I was still several feet away. On the other side of the fence was some sort of steel grid. I stared at it, puzzled, but then my stomach lurched as I realized I was looking at the early stages of a reinforced concrete wall.

All of the camps had them. They kept regs from getting near the electrified fences and wolves from talking to anyone on the outside. Some regs left memorials along the walls or spray-painted tributes to infected loved ones inside the camps. There were websites where you could see photos of the graffiti.

This wall was barely under construction—there couldn't have been more than sixty yards of steel set up and only a few feet of solid concrete in place—but once completed, it would rise forty feet and completely encircle the camp. You wouldn't be able to see out unless you looked up.

I was suddenly hit by a wave of loneliness that left me feeling like one of those paper snowflakes kids made: all stretched out and full of holes. If I couldn't find a way to get Kyle and Serena out of here, they would spend the rest of their lives cut off from everyone and everything—including me if I ended up on the outside of the wall.

And if I didn't end up on the outside—if I stayed in here with them—I would never see Tess or Jason again.

The thought of never hearing another one of Tess's sugar-fueled rants about men, or never seeing Jason's green eyes or that look he got on his face when I was driving him crazy, made my chest ache.

I pushed the feeling away. I couldn't afford to think like that. I couldn't afford to get bogged down in what-ifs and maybes.

I headed into the shed and deposited my bin. The muscles in my arms spasmed, and my spine twinged as I was able to stand up straight for the first time since leaving the laundry building.

Eve watched me stretch, a strange look on her face that made me uncomfortable in a way I couldn't quite define. It looked a little like longing, but more . . . wistful.

When she realized I had caught her in the act of star-ing, she blushed. "Sorry," she said with a shrug that seemed uncharacteristically self-conscious. "I was just trying to remember what it was like."

"It?"

"Those small aches and pains you get when you're a reg." Before I could say anything else, she pushed past me and walked out of the shed.

The buzzer signaling the end of the work details sounded as I stepped outside after her. She glanced at me and her face was as blank as an unlined page in a notebook. Whatever had prompted the brief moment of sharing was clearly over.

The wolves from the fields were already heading back toward the main part of camp. We trailed after them slowly, by unspoken agreement giving them enough time to get out of earshot.

"So . . ." I kicked at a stone on the path. "You want my help coming up with a plan in case Hank doesn't come through." No need to tell her the odds of that were about 150 percent.

"I think you can find information that might help me come up with a plan in case he can't help us, yes." She stopped walking and tilted her head to the side as she gave me a long, considering look. I had the feeling Eve didn't ask people for help very often.

"You can get past the HFDs and you can watch what happens after one goes off. The pain in my head when they use those things is so bad that a marching band playing death metal could walk past and I'd be oblivious."

I considered it.

Kyle would hate the idea. He would more than hate it. Just a few hours ago, I had promised him that I would be careful and be safe; agreeing to help Eve spy and plan a breakout was pretty much the opposite of that.

But if it led to a way to get him and Serena out . . .

"Okay," I said slowly. "But I have a condition."

Eve raised an eyebrow.

"You want to find a way out. I want to find out what's happening to Serena."

Eve nodded. "Fair enough. You help me, then I'll help you."

"Serena first. You need me more than I need you." I held my breath. Until moments ago, it wouldn't have occurred to me to ask Eve for her help, but I suddenly wanted it. Badly.

She hesitated, then nodded grudgingly. "Fine."

I exhaled. She was the only other wolf in Thornhill who knew I was a reg, and unlike Kyle, she wouldn't try to protect me at the expense of getting out of here. And as much as I disliked the loyalty she had for my father, anyone who had been living with Hank—anyone who'd been raised by him for a year and a half—had probably picked up the kind of skills that would come in handy when breaking out of a government facility.

"Do we spit on our palms and shake on it?" I asked.

Eve rolled her eyes and started walking again. "You know," she said after a minute, "even before the stuff Dex said, this place wasn't adding up. Did anything seem strange about Sinclair's overcrowding explanation to you?"

I thought about the raid, about the memory that didn't quite fit. *Kill her and it's one less head we get paid for.* "If the camps are so overcrowded," I said slowly, "why are they paying Trackers to go on raids?"

"Exactly." Eve started to say more but her voice trailed off as a guard came into view. Even at a distance, I recognized the lanky figure and red hair of the man who had helped them take Serena, the man the female guard had called "Tanner."

He left the path and headed for the trees, his stride quick and purposeful. One hand gripped the handle of a black case the size of a toolbox.

"A guard heading into the woods with a big black box," said Eve. "Because that's not suspicious."

"Follow?"

"Follow."

We shared a glance and a split second of camaraderie, which left me feeling awkward and confused as we trailed the man into the woods. I wasn't sure I wanted to like anyone crazy enough—or blind enough—to trust my father.

The guard followed a wide path, but Eve and I glided through the underbrush. Well, she glided. I stumbled awkwardly behind, trying to make as little noise as possible.

The trees began to thin around us and I caught glimpses of a chain-link fence through the foliage. What on earth could they possibly need to fence off way out here?

The guard stopped in front of a metal pole. He set the toolbox on the ground, crouched down, and hauled out what looked like an iPhone. He pointed it at the top of the pole, waited, then sighed and tossed the device back into the box.

He stood and slipped a radio from his belt. "Number thirty-five is working fine. Were you guys just messing with me?"

The reply was lost under a burst of static. "Funny," muttered the guard. "Real funny." He picked up the toolbox and headed back the way he had come.

We waited until we were sure he was out of visual range and then crept forward. I tugged on the fence. It wasn't as impressive as the one surrounding the camp and it wasn't electrified, but it was solid and secure.

I approached the pole the guard had examined. It was about twenty feet tall with spikes on the sides that formed a sort of ladder. On top was a box that looked like a small speaker.

I turned back to Eve.

She was on her knees, her hands clamped to the sides of her head. I hadn't heard her go down.

I glanced from her to the box and then quickly ran to her side.

"Sorry," I muttered, crouching next to her.

"I'm okay," she groaned as she pushed me away. "I'm all right." But she retched until it sounded like she was on the verge of bringing up internal organs.

Wiping her mouth with the edge of her sleeve, she climbed unsteadily to her feet.

"There's an HFD on top of the pole," I said, standing. "They must be motion activated."

Eve frowned. "Then why didn't it go off when the guard was near it?" She glanced down at her wrist and ran a hand over the metal cuff. She held out her arm and slowly walked forward. When she was about five feet from the pole, she flinched and yanked her arm back. After a moment, she held out her other hand. This time, she seemed perfectly fine.

"It's the cuffs." She twisted the metal around her wrist. "They must have some kind of sensor in them that sets off the HFD when you get too close."

I glanced from Eve to the pole and then back. Careful to stay out range, I walked to the fence and peered through the links.

There was a path. It ended about thirty feet away with a waist-high gate. It was the kind of barrier that would be easy to slip over. With the HFD covering the path, they probably didn't worry about wolves just hopping the gate.

But I wasn't a wolf.

"What was it Dex said at breakfast? That there were two places in the camp they didn't want wolves to go?"

"You think this is number two?"

"I think a fence and an HFD is going to a lot of trouble if it's not." I turned back to Eve. "I can get over the gate. If I waited five minutes, do you think that would be enough time for you to get out of range?"

Eve shook her head. "I'm staying."

She couldn't be serious. "The second I get within five feet of the pole, it'll go off."

"Not for long. Unless you're planning on strolling at a leisurely pace, it should only hit me for a minute."

I opened my mouth but then shrugged. Who was I to argue if Eve wanted to sign up for another dose of pain?

Still, just because I wasn't going to argue with her didn't mean I wanted to hurt her any more than necessary. I made a run for the opening of the path, not slowing or glancing back as I raced past the HFD. She'd be all right once I was out of range; I just had to get there as quickly as possible.

I rounded the edge of the fence and almost did a face plant as I clambered over the gate. I caught a glimpse of Eve's red hair out of the corner of my eye as I hurtled down the path, but I didn't stop until I had gone another fifteen feet.

Eve was already standing by the time I looked back. She nodded at me, once, and I did the same before continuing on.

The chain-link fence rose at least ten feet into the air on either side of the path and left just enough space in the middle for a jeep to squeeze through. It was creepy and claustrophobic and I couldn't shake the feeling that the whole thing was going to snap down on me. The breeze—which had been gentle and welcome when we left the laundry building—picked up strength and pushed at my back.

After a few minutes, the path curved to the right and then ended in a small, overgrown clearing. The fence branched out on either side, looping around an area that was too perfectly square to be anything other than man-made. When I glanced around the edges of the clearing, I noticed HFDs along each side of the fence.

The space was completely empty. I bit my lip. Why go to all this trouble to keep people out of an empty field?

I waded into the straggly grass and tripped as my sneaker caught on the edge of something hard.

I pitched forward and barely caught my balance. Letting out a low curse, I glanced down. A small rectangle had been set into the ground. I crouched and brushed thick weeds away from a granite slab. It was a grave marker, the name and dates worn smooth by time and weather.

I stood and walked down two rows of identical stones. There were fourteen in total, and only one had retained a legible date: 1933.

If the main building had been a hospital for tuberculosis patients, it made sense that there would be a graveyard, but why hide it? Who would care?

The markers in the next row looked different. Curious, I walked forward. The grass was slightly less overgrown, here, and the markers were metal, not stone. They weren't decades old—the oldest was dated just five months ago—and each had a four-digit number where a name should be.

My blood turned to ice as I glanced at my wrist: four digits.

What if Dex was right?

Pulse thudding, I walked forward, counting as I went. There were six rows of seven markers and each row was progressively less overgrown. When I reached the last row, the graves were covered with plain dirt that looked like it could have been turned yesterday.

All of the dates were within the last four weeks.

I reached the last marker.

I couldn't look down.

I had to look down.

My knees threatened to give out in relief as I stared at the slab of metal and read the date. Six days. The date was six days past. Whoever was buried here, it wasn't . . . it wasn't Serena.

A gust of wind whipped my hair around my face as a low rumble of thunder sounded in the distance. A flutter of yellow a few feet away caught my attention and all the relief died in my chest.

A wooden stake—the kind they used on construction sites to show where things should be placed—had been driven into the ground right where the next marker would be.

A roaring sound filled my head, louder than the distant thunder.

There were only two reasons why a stake would be there: either a body had been buried and the marker hadn't been placed yet or . . .

I stumbled back, struggling to keep my balance as the first drops of rain hit my face.

. . . or they were marking where the next body would go.

13

"POP QUIZ, MACKENZIE DOBSON . . ."

"I'm not playing."

"Spoilsport." Amy laced her fingers through the links of the fence and stared at the cemetery. Her pale-blue sundress seemed to glow slightly in the dark and her bare feet and legs were splattered with bits of mud and grass.

She stared at the markers—small, dark shapes barely visibly in the mist. "Why do you think they took their names? They took their names and left them with numbers no one would remember them by. It's sort of sad."

Blood dripped off her hands and landed on the grass. For a moment, I thought she had cut herself, but then the moon slipped out from behind the clouds. The entire fence was coated in blood. Thick red beads ran down the links and fell to the dirt below. The earth soaked it up like a sponge, and when Amy shifted her weight, the ground beneath her gave a soft, wet sigh.

"If I could see them," continued Amy as though nothing

were wrong, "if I could talk to the Thornhill ghosts, do you think they'd talk back?"

"Amy . . ." I swallowed, fighting the urge to run, "whose blood is that?" A better question would have been *Why is it on the fence?* but I could only handle one thing at a time.

"It's everyone's." Amy shrugged and nodded toward my arm.

I followed her gaze. Blood soaked the sleeve of my shirt and coated my hand like a glove.

"Everything runs red here."

A gasp lodged itself in my throat as I woke in a tangle of sweat-damp sheets. The room was filled with blue-black shadows, but early morning light slipped past the curtains. I had overslept.

I dressed quickly, making sure to pull my sleeve down to hide my arm—the same arm that had been bleeding in my dream. I wasn't sure how my dorm mates would feel if they discovered I was a reg, and I didn't want to find out. Hank always said people hated being lied to almost as much as being stolen from. He oughta know: he was an expert at both.

Eve raised herself up on her elbow.

From liar and deserter to pack leader and caregiver. How was it possible for two people to have such different opinions and expectations of the same man?

"Sure you're up for this?" she whispered. Her gray-green eyes reflected the light from the bathroom doorway.

I nodded. After what I had found in the woods, Eve and I had regrouped with Kyle. There was no way I could wait another day before trying to get into the sanatorium—not with the implications of the grave markers and that yellow stake.

Since injury and detention were the only excuses a wolf had for being in the building, Kyle would injure himself. I'd play the part of the hysterical girlfriend and insist on going with him. Once inside, I'd try to slip away and find some sign of Serena. Eve had volunteered for the job, but given that we didn't know if there were HFDs inside, I was the logical choice.

Plus, there was no way in hell I was letting Kyle go in there without me.

As far as plans went, it was about as sturdy as a house of cards in Tornado Alley. We just didn't have much choice.

"Good luck," said Eve. Then, just in case I was in danger of thinking we were on our way to becoming BFFs, she added, "Don't screw it up."

Tossing her a glare, I bent down and grabbed my shoes. Then, sneakers in hand, I walked past the sleeping girls and out of the dorm.

Puddle water soaked my socks as I stepped outside.

It had stopped raining sometime during the night, but the paths and grass still shimmered wetly as the sky lightened to mauve.

A shadow broke away from the side of the building: Kyle.

Warmth flooded his eyes, and for a brief, heady second, I actually believed I could be the center of someone's world. A small voice in the back of my head reminded me that he had left me and run away to Denver, but I pushed it aside.

"Tired?"

"Exhausted," I admitted as I pulled on my sneakers. I curled my toes inside my damp socks. "I spent most of the night trying to figure out if there was a way to get inside the building that *wouldn't* involve you hurting yourself while trying *not* to think about the graveyard *and* trying to convince myself that Serena is all right."

Kyle wrapped an arm around my shoulders as we started walking. "She's okay," he said. "We'll find her and figure out what's going on."

I wanted to believe him, but I knew he was just telling me what he thought I needed to hear.

We walked in silence until the sanatorium came into sight. If possible, the building was even more imposing in the early morning light. It threw a shadow over the entire courtyard and loomed over the admission building and the small cluster of white vehicles near the gate. It was a photographer's dream—all harsh angles and creeping ivy. In its own way, it was oddly beautiful, but I couldn't quite shake the feeling that its dozens of dark windows were somehow watching us.

Kyle let his arm fall from my shoulders as we stepped off the path and headed for the side of the sanatorium where an extension was being built. We reached the edge of the construction site, and he gracefully hopped up into the partially completed wing.

I hoisted myself up after him—much less gracefully—then brushed wood shavings from my clothes as I stood and looked around.

There wasn't much to see. Piles of lumber and discarded tools littered the floor while skeletal walls supported wires and plumbing. The wing was larger than it had looked from the outside. Almost cavernous.

I turned to Kyle. There was a familiar, unsettling expression on his face: it was the one he always got right before telling me something he knew I'd hate.

He ran a hand over the back of his neck. "I've been thinking. Me slicing my arm might not be enough."

I tried to ignore the twinge of alarm in my chest. "What do you mean it might not be enough? What do you want to do instead?"

"We're not supposed to shift outside the zone and class. I have to be hurt badly enough that the injury won't heal without shifting but not so badly that I lose control." Kyle hauled his shirt over his head and let it fall to the floor. "It's going to take more than my arm."

I swallowed. "How much more?"

In response, Kyle walked a few feet away and picked up a long copper pipe. It was at least two inches in diameter and the edges were jagged, like it had teeth. He came back and held it out to me. "I figure it'll look like I fell and accidentally impaled myself."

"Kyle, no. . . ." I took a step back as bile rushed up my throat. "This isn't what we agreed on." This was crazy. Insane.

Kyle let out an exasperated sigh. "I'm a werewolf, Mac. I'll heal."

"Like you healed after the fire at Serena's? You were in a

coma for an entire night! They weren't even sure you would wake up." The memory of sitting at his bedside—scared and bargaining with God—sent a shiver rocketing up my spine.

Kyle shifted his grip on the pipe. "This is different. I know how much damage my body can take."

"Bullshit." I meant the word to sound fierce; instead, my voice broke over the second syllable. "You've only been a full-fledged werewolf for a couple of weeks. How do you know?"

"Think about Serena," he shot back. "This is our best chance of finding out if she's okay."

My vision blurred. "We'll find another way." Without giving Kyle a chance to respond, I turned and headed for the edge of the construction site.

There was a sudden clang—metal on wood—followed by a heavy thump.

I spun.

Kyle was on his knees, fumbling for his shirt. He balled it up and pressed it to his stomach. Blood soaked the fabric in the three seconds it took me to reach his side.

He pushed himself to his feet and swayed. I caught his weight and just barely managed to keep him from hitting the floor.

I pressed one hand over his, trying to help him hold the bloodstained shirt against his stomach. "Shift." I swallowed. "Please, just shift." He was hurt badly—a reg would be in real trouble—but if he shifted, he would be okay.

Probably.

Panic threatened to pull me under.

"I'm fine." Kyle's voice was pinched and far away. "Were-wolf, remember?" A shudder wracked his body, and his face shone with sweat. "I'll be okay. I can hold on."

The muscles in his back writhed under my arm, jumping and crawling like things lived under the skin. It took every-thing I had not to cringe back.

The only way this would work would be if Kyle had the self-control not to shift. When the plan had been for him to cut his arm, I hadn't been worried. But this . . .

He started walking and I supported as much of his weight as I could. "Just need to get inside," he said through gritted teeth. He repeated the words like a mantra.

By the time we reached the glass doors at the front of the building, his voice had faded to barely audible, nonsensical mumbles. At one point, he called me Amy and the mistake cut like a blade.

The guard at the door took one look at Kyle and told us to take a left followed by a right.

We finally staggered into the infirmary, and a doctor with hair as white as his lab coat looked up from his coffee and donut.

"What happened?" Keeping just out of Kyle's reach, he ushered us through a door and into a tiny room with metal walls. It was like a vault.

I hesitated on the threshold, holding Kyle back as I bit my lip and took in the heavy bars and locks on the door.

"It's all right," said the doctor. "The room is just rein-forced in case a wolf needs to shift."

The explanation didn't make me feel any better, but Kyle

pulled free of my grip and walked forward, bearing his own weight until he sank onto an examination table in the middle of the small space.

He closed his eyes. For a horrible second I thought he had passed out, but then he shifted his weight and arranged himself more comfortably. A ripple swept through his torso as his muscles tried to tear themselves apart. Kyle clenched his fists and the movement stopped.

I brushed a strand of hair from my face and caught sight of my bloodstained fingers. My stomach did a slow flip. You couldn't catch LS through blood—you had to be bitten or scratched by a fully or partially transformed werewolf—but it was Kyle's blood and the idea of it on my skin left me feeling shaken and sick.

The doctor was speaking to me—had clearly been speaking to me for at least a minute or two. I forced myself to focus on his repeated question. *What happened?*

"He spotted something up in the rafters at one of the construction sites. He climbed up to take a look, but the boards were slick and he slipped. . . ." My voice cracked.

"Why didn't he shift?"

Kyle's face twisted in pain, but he opened his eyes and stared at the ceiling. That had to be good, right? Eyes open had to be better than eyes closed. *Focus.*

"He was scared he'd get in trouble. I would have taken him to the zone, but the infirmary was closer."

The doctor's gaze fell on my hands, and a sympathetic look flashed across his face. "There's a sink in the outer room," he said as he turned his attention fully to Kyle.

He asked Kyle a series of inane questions, and something inside my chest unknotted when Kyle choked out his favorite color and the name of the president.

Legs shaking, I walked to the sink. The water ran pink and I couldn't get all of the blood out from under my cuticles, but I could at least stand the sight of my hands.

I headed back to the small room—the vault—and hovered in the doorway.

The doctor was still asking questions.

Kyle's eyes locked on mine and he gave me a small nod.

Telling myself that wasting this chance would mean he had hurt himself for nothing, I slipped out of the infirmary.

The wing housing the infirmary was made up of locked doors and identical gray hallways that were all empty save for the occasional—improbably healthy-looking and utterly ginormous—potted plant. I passed three of the things before realizing they were fake.

How long had I been gone? Five minutes? Ten? Long enough for the doctor to send someone after me, probably.

I had to find Serena, but so far all I'd managed to do was run around like a rat in a maze.

I rounded a corner and froze. A white-clad program coordinator and a guard were standing at the end of the passage. Their backs were to me as they spoke in hushed tones.

Move, I ordered my legs. *Move!*

I rocketed back around the corner.

Someone had wedged one of the plastic plants into a small nook. I squeezed in behind it and crouched down. My knee hit the base, and my heart went into cardiac arrest as the plant tilted and almost fell.

Please don't look this way. Please don't look this way. I mouthed the words like a prayer as footsteps approached.

"It's just a few more tests. You want help, don't you? You don't want to be sick, do you?"

"No," said a frail female voice, the syllable uncertain and unspecific.

Hope leaped in my chest. The voice was so weak that it was barely audible, but it was Serena. It had to be.

I peered around the plant as the voices reached the intersection of the two hallways. The program coordinator half turned in my direction just as I got a clear look at the girl. It wasn't Serena. It wasn't anyone I had seen before.

Disappointment threatened to crush me, but was quickly shoved aside by the girl's appearance.

Her skin looked like tracing paper and the shadows under her eyes were so dark they could have passed for smudges of ink. Her lank brown hair grazed the collar of a shapeless white tunic. She was wearing the same sort of wrist cuff we'd all been fitted with, but her arms were so thin, I wasn't sure how it didn't slip off.

She really did look sick—desperately sick.

The guard wheeled an IV stand. The plastic bag was filled with liquid that was the same light blue as the windshield wiper fluid Tess kept in the trunk of the car. It dripped down a tube that wound around the girl's arm and into her skin.

I bit my lip. Werewolves weren't supposed to get

sick—except for bloodlust. And whatever was wrong with the girl, it couldn't be that. Less than 2 percent of people with LS developed bloodlust. It left you wild and frantic, and she didn't look like she had any strength at all. She looked like she was being drained from the inside out.

"I think . . . if I can go back to my room . . . I'd feel . . . if I could rest . . ." She twisted the hem of her shirt between her fingers.

The program coordinator ignored her words and started ushering her down my hallway.

Fear constricted my lungs. I tried to make myself smaller behind my plastic plant, but there was no way they could walk by and not see me.

Suddenly, the girl collapsed. The guard just managed to keep her from falling while the program coordinator lunged to catch the IV stand.

"What's wrong with her?" The guard supported the girl with his left arm, keeping his right hand—his shooting hand—near his holster.

"Exhaustion and stress, probably." The program coordinator kept one hand wrapped around the IV stand. With his other arm, he helped take some of the girl's weight. "She hasn't slept in days. We'd better take her to the infirmary, though. Just to be certain."

They headed straight down the hall, bypassing my corridor completely. Either I had gotten turned around, or they knew a faster way back to where I had left Kyle.

Relief surged through my muscles as their voices faded.

I crept out of my hiding place and approached the spot

where the hallways intersected. The coast was clear.

Nerves buzzing, I turned left. That was the direction they had come from. With any luck, it would be where I'd find Serena. The fact that I didn't have a plan beyond "make sure she's okay and don't get caught" suddenly seemed more than a little problematic, but I forged ahead.

This corridor was different from the others. It had white tile instead of gray carpet, and most of the doors had key-pads next to them. After a short distance and another turn, the hall ended in a heavy steel door. I had a feeling I had just found the detention block.

"What are you doing here?"

I whirled. A guard stood ten feet away.

His uniform strained over the kind of bulk that had more to do with Dunkin' Donuts than muscle. Thick black brows pulled together as he took in my hair and clothes. He stared at me like I was a bomb on the verge of exploding. "How did you get in here?"

I struggled to string words together, but my throat wouldn't cooperate.

He reached toward his holster.

He's going to tase me. The thought ripped through my brain as he hauled his weapon free.

I threw all my weight forward, aiming myself at his shoulder like a cannonball. I didn't have the strength of a werewolf, but I knew how to hit someone and leave them off balance.

The Taser went skidding across the floor and the guard stumbled.

I didn't make a grab for the weapon or wait to see if he went down; I just ran.

Within moments, I was lost. Every corridor looked the same. I pressed a hand to my side as my muscles pulled in a stitch. Somewhere behind me, I heard a stream of obscenities and thunderous footsteps. How was it possible for one person's footsteps to be so loud?

Because it wasn't just one person. The realization slammed through me, urging my legs to move faster.

I threw myself around another corner and collided with a door. The impact sent me ricocheting and I ended up on my butt on the floor.

I tried to push myself up, but it was too late: a figure was already stepping around the corner, Taser drawn.

I cringed against the wall as the redheaded guard— Tanner—came into sight.

When he saw me on the floor, he let out a deep breath. He lowered his Taser but didn't reholster it. "Are you going to make me use this?"

I shook my head. My heart hammered so hard that black spots filled the hallway and hovered in front of my eyes like swarms of flies.

The other guard hurtled around the corner, Taser drawn, finger poised over the trigger.

"She's fine," said Tanner, eyes locked on the Taser. "She's not putting up a fight."

Was he *helping* me?

"She ran," spat the guard. "Threw herself at me and ran. And she's covered in blood."

I raised a trembling hand to my forehead. The skin was tacky. *Kyle's blood*, I realized. I had gotten it on my face in the infirmary. The guard's fear suddenly made a little more sense.

"I didn't . . ." I swallowed and glanced at Tanner. He had taken Serena, but he was definitely the more reasonable of the two men in front of me. "My friend was hurt. I brought him to the infirmary. It's his blood. I stepped outside and got turned around." The words came out in a rush and I had to pause and catch my breath. "I only ran because I thought he was going to tase me."

"You'll be lucky if that's all I do." Turning beet red, the guard reached down and grabbed my arm. He pulled me up so hard and so fast that my shoulder popped and I had to bite back a gasp.

Keeping the Taser an inch from my face, he hauled me around corners and down hallways.

"You really think this is something to bother her with?" asked Tanner from somewhere behind me as I was yanked across a small waiting room and up to a gray door.

A receptionist froze in the act of hanging her coat on a hook. A purse and brown paper bag sat on the desk behind her. "She said she's not to be disturbed."

"She'll be disturbed for this." Still holding my arm, the guard holstered his Taser, then pounded on the door. The door, like the others, had a keypad next to the lock, but it also had something the others didn't: a small nameplate bearing fourteen letters.

WARDEN SINCLAIR

14

THE WARDEN WASN'T WEARING SHOES WHEN SHE OPENED the door. It was a ridiculous thing to notice, but it was the first thing I focused on. Her office had cream carpet—thicker, more expensive carpet than I'd ever seen in an office—and her nylon-clad feet sank into the pile.

I dragged my gaze upward. Sinclair was wearing a black suit with the blazer unbuttoned over a bloodred silk camisole. Her hair was pulled back in a twist, but strands had fallen free, especially around the white streak at her temple. She looked younger up close—maybe even as young as thirty—but fine lines had begun to appear at the corners of her eyes and around her mouth.

Her expression said she was a million miles away, but that lasted only until she took in the scene in front of her. The lines on her face stretched and deepened as her gaze slid over me and then locked on the guard holding my arm. Something dark shifted behind her eyes: a storm cloud passing over a blue sky.

"I told them you weren't to be interrupted." The

receptionist's voice, high and anxious, drifted across the waiting room. "I tried to stop them."

"It's all right, Sophie," said Sinclair. She arched an eyebrow and waited for the guard to explain.

He seemed to deflate slightly under her sharp gaze. "Found this girl wandering the corridors. Practically threw me through a wall before running."

I twisted and stared. *Through a wall?* I had barely touched him.

Sinclair turned her attention to me. "How did you get into the building?"

Like the guard, I could almost feel myself grow smaller. I had the sudden, irrational urge to tell her I was sorry, to apologize for everything and anything. I forced the feeling down. "My friend was hurt. The guard at the main door told me to take him to the infirmary. I stepped out into the hall to get some air and got turned around."

"Claims she was lost." The guard finally let go of my arm. "Biggest pile of—"

"Did you check?" There was a layer of frost in Sinclair's smooth voice that made things inside my stomach clench. "Did you call the infirmary?"

The guard's face flushed. "No . . . I . . . like I said, she attacked and—"

A barely perceptible sigh escaped the warden's lips. "Never mind. I'll handle it. Sophie, call the front entrance and find out who was on duty." The guard opened his mouth, but before he could say anything else, Sinclair ushered me through the door and into a windowless office that looked like it belonged to a principal and smelled like church.

The door clicked shut.

"Sit," she ordered as she crossed to her desk and picked up the phone. "Doctor LeBelle?" There was a pause. "Was a wolf taken to the infirmary a short time ago?" Another pause. "I see." Sinclair's eyes locked on mine. "There's a girl here. Mackenzie."

How did she know my name? The guards hadn't bothered asking. Shivering, I lowered myself onto one of two heavy wooden chairs as Sinclair listened to the voice on the other end of the line.

I scanned the walls. Framed diplomas and newspaper articles dotted seas of white to my left and right, but the space behind the desk was dominated by an enormous painting depicting a woman in a tattered Grecian dress. She knelt in the dirt, struggling to close the lid of a flaming box as shadows closed in around her.

It was beautiful. And creepy.

I frowned and squinted. Maybe it was my imagination, but the painting's heavy black frame didn't look like it was flush to the wall.

My attention was pulled back to Sinclair as she thanked the doctor and hung up the phone. She walked around her desk and sat in a massive leather chair. "Your friend was given permission to shift. His wound healed and he was sent to his morning class."

I started to breathe a sigh of relief but then thought about Serena and the graveyard in the woods. If Dex was right, Thornhill was a gallows and the woman in front of me was probably signing the execution orders. I couldn't let myself believe anything she said. "There was so much blood, though. . . ."

Sinclair's smile slipped, and my throat filled with dust. "Surely you know how much damage your body can heal?"

According to my father, the best lie was always the one mixed with the most truth. "I don't know many other were-wolves," I said, trying to keep my voice level as I forced myself to meet her cold blue eyes, "and all I've ever had were cuts and bruises."

Sinclair regarded me for a moment before seeming to accept the explanation. "I'm happy to hear that. Too much time spent among other wolves on the outside can make adjusting to a program like Thornhill's more difficult." I tensed as she reached into a drawer, but she only pulled out a container of aloe vera wipes. "For your face," she said, not unkindly, as she set them on the corner of her desk next to a container of hand lotion.

Hesitantly, I took a wipe from the package and passed it over my forehead. The white cloth came back tinged with Kyle's blood. Feeling slightly sick, I balled it in my hand.

"Blood bothers you?"

"Not because I'm a werewolf," I said quickly. "I've just always found it gross." My eyes returned to the painting behind the desk.

Sinclair glanced over her shoulder. "Pandora's box," she said, turning back to me. "I've always seen parallels between that particular myth and lupine syndrome. Some people see the disease as a gift without realizing how dangerous it is to lift the lid."

I swallowed. "And that's what Thornhill is? A way to help us keep the lid on?"

"For the wolves who commit fully to the idea of rehabilitation, yes."

With her dark skin and shoulder-length curls, the woman in the painting looked a little like Serena.

It gave me courage.

"I have another friend," I said, taking a plunge, "she was held back during admissions, but no one will tell me where she is or what's going on."

Sinclair plucked a file from atop a stack of papers. She opened the folder and glanced down. "Serena?"

I nodded even though she wasn't looking at me. "Yes," I managed, heart in throat.

Sinclair glanced up. "There were a few abnormalities in her blood. We want to make sure she isn't sick before putting her in with the general population."

"Sick?" I thought about the girl with the IV. Feeling like the ground was crumbling beneath me, I said, "How could she be sick? There's no way she has bloodlust."

Sinclair folded her hands on the desk, and I caught sight of a silver and garnet ring on her right index finger. Amy's mother had a ring like that, one with a garnet for Amy and a sapphire for her brother. A birthstone ring.

"Mackenzie, LS is a new disease. We barely understand how it works. We've recently found a virus—similar to the canine parvovirus, which affects dogs—in some cities where large numbers of werewolves tend to congregate. We believe Serena may have contracted it."

She's lying, I tried to tell myself, *there's no new disease. It's a trick*. But I remembered the way the girl had looked in the hallway. It was like something had been eating her from the inside out. I gripped the arm of my chair so hard that my thumbnail bent and snapped. When I spoke, I didn't recognize my voice. "Are you . . . are you sure she's sick?"

Sinclair stood and walked around the desk. She placed a hand on my shoulder and the scent of lavender wafted up from her skin. Her touch was heavy and stiff. When I glanced up, I spotted an HFD in her other hand. Trusting, but not that trusting.

"She may be fine. It's too early to tell."

"Can I see her?"

"We have to hold her in isolation for now."

I shook my head. "I don't understand. If there's this other virus out there, why haven't any of us heard about it? If there's a disease, why don't the other wolves talk about it when . . ." I trailed off and cursed myself. Fear for Serena had made me say too much.

"When wolves are held during admissions or removed from the dorms? When a few wolves start spouting conspiracy theories about disappearances?" Sinclair lifted her hand from my shoulder and stepped back. She perched on the edge of the desk. "Mackenzie, Thornhill is my first post as warden, but I've worked at three other camps. Each place is the same. Anytime anything happens to a wolf, conspiracy rumors swirl."

She crossed her arms. "As to why the disease hasn't been made public, I suspect the LSRB is waiting until they have enough information to assure the reg population that they're not at any risk from this new condition. No one wants a return to the riots we had when lupine syndrome was first announced."

But wouldn't the packs have noticed people getting sick?

Sinclair picked up on my uncertainty.

"The LSRB aren't evil, Mackenzie. We're not bogeymen. I applied for a job at the camps right after college. Do you know why?" She didn't wait for me to answer. "Because I wanted to help people. Infected people."

A short, skeptical noise escaped my lips before I could stop it.

"It's true." Something passed underneath Sinclair's perfect facade, something that was sad and a little messy and maybe slightly damaged. Something that was full of regret. It was a look I sometimes saw in the mirror after I had been dreaming of Amy. "My sister was infected. I joined the LSRB because I wanted to make things better for people like her. After I saw how horrible the other camps were, I lobbied for Thornhill. I wanted to create a place that was more than just a dumping ground where the infected were left to die." She paused for a long moment. "No one chooses infection."

I swallowed. "Your sister is in a camp?"

"No. Julie died when I was seventeen." Sinclair twisted the garnet around her finger, and I wondered if the ring had belonged to her sister.

"I'm sorry." The words weren't a lie, but they weren't quite genuine: I wanted to feel sorry for her, but I didn't trust her. She was the person keeping us here. For all I knew, everything she had just said was a lie. "Why tell me?" I asked hesitantly, trying to figure her out. "The disease? Your sister? Any of it?"

"Because I want the wolves in Thornhill to understand that I have their best interests at heart. I don't want what I'm trying to accomplish here being undermined by fear and rumors." She leaned forward. "I receive daily reports on the self-control class. Do you have any idea how remarkable what you did yesterday was?"

A lump rose in my throat. "I didn't do anything."

It was like I hadn't spoken.

"Part of the reason we restrict shifting to a single area is that, over time, people associate the pain and rush they experience with that environment. It eventually becomes harder to shift in other places and helps improve control. If you repeated the same exercise your class underwent yesterday in two months, fewer people would transform. In six months, almost none of them would." She gave her words a moment to sink in. "For a wolf to resist shifting on the first day is rare. You're already ahead of the curve when it comes to control. You can be an example to your peers."

A bead of sweat rolled down the back of my neck. I didn't want to be an example; I wanted to be invisible.

A sharp crackle emanated from the phone. I breathed a sigh of relief at the interruption as Sinclair reached behind her and pressed a button.

"Warden? There's been a code twelve. He's in the building, but he's panicking."

Sinclair inhaled sharply. "I'll be right there. Tell them not to agitate him." She stood and quickly retrieved a pair of heels from underneath the desk.

I started to rise.

"Stay here." She shoved her feet into her shoes. "I'll be back in a minute." The warden I had glimpsed flashes of over the past few minutes—the one who seemed sympathetic and concerned—had been replaced by the woman I had seen at orientation.

She crossed the room. The door closed behind her and there was an electronic beep as the lock engaged.

Silence.

I counted to ten and then darted for the phone. I punched in Jason's cell number. There was a click and then an automated voice told me to enter my phone code.

My vision swam and my ears filled with a faint buzzing sound as a wave of frustration rose up. I started to slam the handset down before checking myself at the last instant. With a deep breath, I slowly set it into the cradle.

I shot a nervous glance at the door and lifted Serena's file. The only thing inside was her admission form. There were no test results or doctor's notes—nothing to indicate there was anything wrong with her. The only thing out of the ordinary was a red circle around the age she had been when she became infected.

If Serena really was sick—if there really was a new disease—could it have something to do with age? No one knew why, but people who contracted LS before fifteen only had a 40-percent chance of surviving their first shift. Serena had been infected when she was eleven.

I closed the folder.

There was a laptop on the desk, but it displayed a login, and the stack of papers underneath Serena's file were just class schedules and budget sheets—nothing that would help me figure out what was happening to her and nothing that might help us plan a way out of this place.

Quickly, I moved on to the desk drawers. Only the top one was unlocked. When I opened it, I saw why: all it contained was a pen, three paperclips, and a box of meal replacement bars. I guess being a prison warden didn't leave a lot of time for balanced nutrition.

I closed the drawer and turned.

The painting filled my vision.

What I had taken for shadows behind the woman were smokelike men, contorted and screaming as though they were damned. This close, I could see that her dress wasn't tattered; it was scorched.

Not exactly something I'd want hanging in my office.

I frowned. The painting really wasn't flush with the wall. I ran my fingers over the frame and jumped back as the whole thing swung out and revealed a touch screen almost as large as the TV Jason had in his bedroom. A list of names filled the screen.

The list was broken into two sections, "assets" and "raw," and there were twenty names under the first category. My stomach lurched as I realized that Serena's name was third and that my name and Kyle's—each followed by a question mark—appeared near the bottom.

I tapped Kyle's name and an image filled the screen. It was a black-and-white shot of him in the cage yesterday morning. I was just visible behind his shoulder. I touched the photo and it closed.

Now I knew why Sinclair had known my name without being told.

I touched Serena's name. An image of her slumped behind a steel table filled the screen. She stared at the camera, eyes horribly blank. Underneath the photo was a small info icon. When I tapped it, the information from Serena's admission form overlaid the photo in a pop-up.

I reached out to close the info window and froze. It was like I had suddenly been dropped into a tank of ice water. All the air was pulled from my lungs and everything seemed to slow down as I read the last line of text:

Candidate for Willowgrove.

15

WILLOWGROVE. IT EXISTED. ACCORDING TO THE URBAN legends, it was a mystery camp. According to Dex, it was a death sentence. Whatever it was, it was real. It was real and Serena was caught up in it.

Muffled voices drifted through the door and jolted me out of my shock. I jabbed the touchscreen—once, twice, until it was back the way I had found it—then swung the painting into place.

Faint electronic beeps sounded from the keypad outside as I threw myself around the desk and into my seat. My butt barely had time to touch down before the warden opened the door.

Anger filled her eyes. For a heart-stopping moment, I was certain she knew what I had seen, but she simply said, "Mackenzie, it's time you headed to class."

I rose unsteadily and crossed the room. A dozen questions fought to get free, but I held them back. It wasn't like I could just tell Sinclair I had been snooping around her office and then casually ask what Willowgrove was.

She placed a hand on my arm, palm over the scar Derby had left, as she ushered me into the waiting room. My skin crawled until the touch fell away.

"Elliott, would you mind escorting Mackenzie to the remainder of her morning class?"

"Sure," said a voice capable of seducing an angel out of her halo, "I can make sure she gets there."

I *knew* that voice.

"Thank you, Elliott." Sinclair withdrew into her office.

I barely registered her exit.

"Whoa. . . ." Familiar hands were on my arms, steadying me as the room spun. Tan uniform. Blond hair. Green eyes. The colors swirled as I struggled to make sense of the person in front of me.

Jason shot me a tight, guarded grin. "Hi, there. I'm the new intern counselor."

I just blinked.

He shifted his grip so that one hand rested just underneath my elbow and drew me across the room. "They just had a code twelve—it's not a good time for you to be in here."

We stepped into the hallway and then hugged the wall as two program coordinators rushed past. "What's a code twelve?"

"A guard was scratched."

Jason guided me down halls and around corners. He released my arm as we approached the entrance where a guard—a woman instead of the man who'd been there earlier—was on duty.

She nodded and Jason returned the gesture, exuding strength and experience and looking years older. There was no way anyone would ever guess he was seventeen.

Outside, guards were milling in the courtyard. There was nothing I could do other than follow Jason and bottle my questions—at least temporarily. I glanced up at the sun, trying to gauge the time. Late morning.

I expected Jason to take the path that led to the classrooms and dorms, but he veered right and headed for an older path that hugged a small rise. The pavement was cracked and crumbling; I had to watch my step as we crested the minuscule hill and passed a long one-story brick building that almost looked like row houses.

"Original staff quarters for the sanatorium," Jason muttered absently, even though I hadn't asked. "They're tearing it down next month."

Sure enough, the windows were boarded up and yellow caution tape had been strung across the doors.

I stopped in the middle of the path. *"Jason, what are you doing here?"*

He turned and stared. The expression on his face was equal parts frustration and incredulity. "What do you think I'm doing here? I came to get you out." He turned and started walking again. "Come on. We need to talk."

I shook my head, even though his back was to me. "Later. Kyle had an accident"—no way did I feel up to telling Jason just what that accident had entailed—"but the warden said he was sent back to class. I need to make sure he's okay."

The lawns bordering the path were overgrown with

grass that was almost knee high, but cutting across them would be faster than doubling back and taking the path. Trying not to think about rodents and snakes, I stepped off the crumbling pavement and pushed my way through, skirting an abandoned pile of bricks and an old, dilapidated greenhouse.

I heard Jason follow. "Mac . . ."

"Later, okay? I promise." I couldn't believe anything Sinclair had said—especially after seeing that list. Until I saw Kyle for myself, I couldn't be sure he was okay. And until I was sure he was okay, I couldn't deal with anything else. Not even Jason.

"I've got a letter from your father."

My step faltered and I turned.

Jason crossed the distance between us and wrapped a hand around my arm. Before I could ask what he thought he was doing or why he had a message from Hank, he pulled me toward the greenhouse.

I tried to break his grip, but Jason was the only seventeen-year-old I knew whose house had a live-in physical trainer and a full-sized gym. He might not be a werewolf, but he was still above average in the strength department.

"Kyle's fine," he said, letting go of me so he could force open the greenhouse door. "I saw him leave the sanatorium from across the courtyard."

He managed to get the door open.

Before he could turn or step aside, I shoved him through, slapping my hands against his back so hard that I felt the sting in my palms. "Why the hell didn't you tell me that in

169

the first place instead of just grabbing me?"

Jason stumbled over the threshold. "Might have if you had slowed down for two seconds."

Of course. Stupid me. I followed him inside, resisting the urge to strangle him.

The greenhouse's tinted glass walls were caked with decades of grime, and the light that managed to filter through was almost murky.

It felt like we were standing in a dirty fishbowl. I pulled in a deep breath and immediately regretted it. "Ugh. It smells like something died in here."

Jason glanced at the corner and frowned. "Something did."

"Oh, ewwww." I turned back for the door, but he got there before me and blocked my way.

"Sure. Sneaking into a rehabilitation camp? No problem. One dead gopher? She runs for the hills." He reached into his pocket, then held out a folded sheet of paper. "From your father."

I ignored the snark and snatched the letter.

An old wooden counter ran the length of one wall. I walked over to it and leaned against the edge as I turned the letter over in my hands. I glanced up. Jason was watching me with an expression I couldn't read. It almost looked like hunger, but that didn't make any sense.

"How did you get in here?" I asked, shaking my head. "What happened to you after the raid and"—I stared at his neck and frowned—"where's your tattoo?"

He started with the last question first. "One of the local

guys was a makeup artist in Hollywood. Supposedly it's the same stuff Johnny Depp uses to hide his 'Wino Forever' tattoo on shoots."

"Local guy as in werewolf or local guy as in Tracker?"

Jason just looked at me and I knew it was the latter. "They got you in." My throat constricted. "Why would they help you?"

"Money, mostly." There was a small crate near his feet and Jason stepped on the edge, flipping it over onto its side. "Plus, being the last person to speak to Derby before his death comes with a weird sort of prestige. Thornhill's hard up for counselors and guards. It wasn't too difficult for them to get me in."

I shook my head. "But why would they think you wanted in? Someone doesn't just wake up one morning and decide they want to see the inside of a rehabilitation camp."

"Kyle. I told them I followed a wolf from Hemlock—one I thought might have killed Amy. Trackers are big on revenge."

I stared at him, horror-struck. "You told them Kyle might have killed Amy? *KYLE?*"

"I needed an excuse. That's all it was."

"And what happens when we get out of here? Don't you think they'll want to hunt the wolf they think killed both the granddaughter of a senator and Branson Derby?"

"I didn't give them Kyle's real name or age or anything that would lead them to him. Give me some credit." Jason ran a hand over his face. "Look, I had to tell them something. I had to get in here long enough to get you out."

"What about Kyle and Serena?"

"They're werewolves, Mac."

I pushed away from the counter. After everything that had happened in Hemlock . . . After everything he'd seen . . . "So, what? They deserve to be in here? They're infected so just write them off?"

Jason's eyes narrowed and his face flushed. Just for a second, he looked like a man who desperately wanted to hit something. "Of course not. But they can take care of themselves. They're not going to get electrocuted by a souped-up Taser or gutted by someone who doesn't know what they are. You need to get out of here. Once you're outside the camp, we'll figure something out. They'll be safe until we do."

A harsh, bitter laugh clawed its way out of my throat. "They're not safe," I said miserably. "They're probably in more trouble than I am." Briefly, I recounted what had happened since we arrived: Serena being taken and maybe being sick. Dex and his theory about Willowgrove. The graveyard. Sinclair and her sister.

When I was finished, Jason frowned and tugged on his shirt collar. "I've never heard anything about a secret camp or anything called Willowgrove. And I've heard a lot over the last few days."

He nodded at the letter I still held clasped in my hand. "It was your father's idea for me to use the Trackers to get in. Don't get me wrong, I would have thought of it on my own, but he suggested it before I had a chance."

"Why?" I unfolded the paper. A set of instructions and

172

a time were scrawled in my father's looping handwriting. I turned the page over. There was nothing else. Not even his name. Either name.

I scanned the instructions. "Western fence. Unscrew casing. Cut white wire. Replace casing. Test with reader." I glanced up. "Jason, what is this?"

He reached into his back pocket and pulled out a slim black case. He held the case out to me, and I set the letter down on the counter before taking it.

Inside were two screwdrivers, the smallest pair of wire cutters I had ever seen, and an electronic device the size of an iPhone. I pulled out the device. It was black with a yellow power button and a small digital display on the front. There was a volume wheel on the side. I turned it over. A label reading *Property of Thornhill* was plastered on the back.

"They use them to check the HFDs," explained Jason. "It picks up the frequency they emit and converts it to a sound regs can hear. No sound and the HFD is down—usually because of weather or animals."

I remembered that Eve and I had seen that guard, Tanner, checking the HFD in the woods.

"That's why Hank wanted me to get in," Jason added. "He needed someone to give you or Eve the letter and to get you one of those readers."

I frowned. "Me or Eve?"

Jason nodded. "Whichever one of you I saw first."

I glanced at the letter. I tried to tell myself that it was stupid to feel hurt and rejected over a folded sheet of paper, but part of me wondered how Eve and I could be interchangeable. How, between us, we hadn't warranted a single "be careful."

"He'll meet the two of you tonight along the western edge of the fence at two thirty. Just pick a spot and disable any HFDs in the way. It should be pretty easy—though I didn't have a chance to test the instructions. We can do a trial run before curfew. If you want."

I slid the device back into the case, then slipped the whole thing into my pocket. "How did he know any of this? How did he know there were HFDs in the camp or how to disconnect them?"

"Apparently, one of the women who designed Thornhill's security system was laid off. Without severance." A slight smile tugged at the corner of his mouth. "Revenge really does make the world go round." He glanced down at his watch. "Ten minutes until lunch. I guess I'd better walk you back in case Sinclair checks up on me."

He headed to the door and pulled it open.

I grabbed Hank's letter and shoved it into my pocket. "Jason?"

He turned in the doorway.

I swallowed. "What now?" He stared at me, confused, and I elaborated. "You want me to go, but I'm not leaving without Kyle and Serena. Where does that leave us?"

He stepped outside. I followed.

"What class do you have?"

"The Impact of LS on Society. Classroom D." He started walking. Uncertainly, I fell into step beside him. "Jason?"

He sighed. "You were right. We can't leave them here.

We have to find a way to get them out."

"A Tracker who cares about two wolves." I meant it as a joke, but the words came out soft and without a trace of humor.

"Yeah, well . . ." Jason suddenly had that deer-in-head-lights look all boys got when you asked them about their feelings. Staring straight ahead, he said, "Kyle's my best friend. And Serena . . . Don't tell anyone, but I'd be kind of pissed if anything happened to her. She's a pain in the ass, but she grows on you after a while. Like a tumor with really bad fashion sense."

A small smile crossed my lips at the thought of what Serena would say to the uncompliment. But just as quickly as it came, the smile vanished. *She'll be okay*, I told myself, trying to ignore the hitch in my chest. "Jason . . . what if she really is sick?"

"Then we'll figure something out. We'll find some way to fix it." His voice was so confident and matter-of-fact that I almost believed him.

We walked in silence for a moment.

Hank's letter felt heavy in my pocket and made me think of the one family member who mattered. Who was probably worried sick about me. "Have you . . . did you . . ." My cheeks flushed with guilt as I thought of how I had just run out on my cousin. "Did you call Tess? Does she know where I am?"

"There wasn't time, and I wouldn't have known what to say. Sorry," Jason added, even though he had nothing to apologize for. "Cells are jammed inside the camp and they monitor the calls we make on the landlines, but if I'm here more than a week, I'll have an afternoon pass. I can call her then. Kyle's folks, too, if he wants."

Given that Kyle hadn't told his parents he was infected or where he was going when he left Hemlock, I was pretty sure he'd be vaguely horrified at the idea of Jason calling them.

We reached Classroom D just as the bell rang. Wolves streamed out of the building, and Jason slipped a hand into his pocket as we were engulfed by the crowd. With a lurch, I wondered if they had given him an HFD. I wondered if he would ever use it.

Before I could figure out how to ask, Kyle stepped outside.

For a second, everything seemed to slow down and a weight was lifted from my chest. He was all right. The late morning sun edged the planes of his face, and the relief in his eyes was so raw it was almost staggering.

Then his gaze slid to Jason and the relief bled away, replaced first by shock and then by something darker. With a pointed glance at me, he turned and walked around the side of the classroom.

"Why do I get the feeling he's not happy to see me?" asked Jason.

Apprehension coiled in my stomach as we headed after Kyle. Just before rounding the corner of the building, I glanced back. I thought I caught a glimpse of Dex, but then a pair of girls blocked my view—just for a second. When they passed, he was gone.

"Great," said Kyle as we caught up with him. "I leave Hemlock to keep the two of you safe and now she's in here pretending to be a wolf and you—what? Beat up a counselor and stole the uniform?"

"I'm actually on staff," retorted Jason. "They make you buy the outfit, but the benefits include dental."

I shot him a reproachful look and he shrugged. "I didn't start it." To Kyle, he said, "Look, I couldn't go home knowing Mac was in here. Don't pretend you wouldn't have tried to get inside if you were in my shoes." He stared at Kyle, waiting for his anger to crack. When it didn't, he muttered, "Fine," and glanced at his watch. "I'm supposed to meet my mentor. If I keep her waiting, she'll rip me in two without breaking a sweat."

"Please tell me you're not talking about Langley," I groaned.

"Don't worry. She likes me. She's cute. Like a pit bull." He shot an unhappy, frustrated look at Kyle, then glanced back at me. "I'll try to find you after supper. We can see if Hank's instructions work."

Before I could say anything, he was gone.

Kyle shot me a confused look. "He's been with your father?"

"Apparently, Hank told him how to disable the HFDs and wants me to meet him at the fence tonight with Eve." I hesitated. "You know it's good that Jason's here, right? We have a better chance of finding Serena with him."

"I know," Kyle conceded. "I just wasn't expecting it. I just—why does your shirt smell like lavender?"

I frowned and pressed my nose to the fabric. Great. I smelled like Sinclair. "It's the warden's hand cream." I tried not to shiver. The whole werewolf-sense-of-smell thing still kind of freaked me out. Kyle would probably notice if I changed deodorant brands. "What were you going to say?" I asked in an effort to refocus.

"Nothing."

"You said, 'I just . . . ?'"

"It's nothing, Mac." A sharp note entered his voice, and I had the sudden feeling that I might not want to know what he had almost said. My gaze dropped to the Thornhill logo on his shirt.

The four of us—me, Jason, Kyle, and Amy—were as knotted and twisted as the vines circling the name of the camp. We were so entwined that it was sometimes hard to know where one of us left off and the others began. Even in death, we couldn't break free—Amy was proof of that.

I looked up. I used to take comfort in the fact that we were so tangled—it was like a promise the four of us would stay together—but staring into Kyle's dark eyes and remembering the things Jason had confessed to me in Hemlock, I wondered how much those ties and tangles had changed. What if, instead of merely holding us together, they were choking us? Choking them.

Would I be strong enough to let them go? If I had let Kyle go when he had wanted me to, would any of this be happening now?

For a moment, I could see another Kyle just under the surface: a fourteen-year-old boy who was all elbows and awkward angles with a voice that hadn't broken yet. Always quiet and often worried. The boy I could tell anything to—memories I'd rather forget and fears I could barely acknowledge.

I would do anything to hold on to that boy. I didn't think I was strong enough to let him go. "Kyle . . ."

"Of course—because 'meet behind the auditorium' is too complicated an instruction." Eve's voice fell between us like a blade.

I stepped back and tried to rein in my thoughts so they wouldn't show on my face as I turned and watched her stride toward us.

On the surface, she looked confident, like every worry would bounce off her skin. But her eyes were pinched and she kept rubbing her scarred wrist, circling it with her thumb and forefinger.

"So," she said, gaze darting between Kyle and me. "What happened?"

16

I SHOVED THE WIRE CUTTERS INTO MY POCKET AND SLID the plastic casing of the HFD back into place.

A sweep of light pierced the darkness in the distance: the flashlight from a guard on patrol. It looked like it was headed away from us, but the sight still sent a trill of fear through me. We had already dodged two patrols on our way here.

I started to climb back down. When I was halfway to the ground, I remembered the reader. I slipped it out and managed to hit the power switch while keeping a grip on the pole with my other hand. Silence. The HFD was down.

"Eve?" My voice was barely a whisper, but I knew she'd hear. "It's clear."

I reached for the next rung. My hand, slick with sweat, slid against the metal, and I lost my grip.

The ground and pole blurred together as I fell. I hit the hard-packed earth and all of the breath was forced from my lungs in a whoosh. Dazed, I stared up at the sky. The clouds and stars swirled together like the Van Gogh poster Tess had in her bedroom—what was that painting called?

Eve was speaking to me, but she seemed far away.

Starry Night, I remembered. *That's the painting.*

I forced myself to a sitting position.

"I'm not sure you should be moving. You hit the ground like a sack of cement."

I ran a hand over my skull. Nothing seemed to be dented or leaking. Unsteadily, I climbed to my feet. A sharp burst of pain radiated through each vertebra, but it faded after a moment. I was pretty sure nothing was broken. "I'm okay," I lied.

I turned to the fence. There was no sign of life on the other side. Hank's only instruction had been to pick a spot somewhere along the western edge of the camp. We'd headed to the shifting zone and then walked along the fence until we found a spot that seemed like it would be outside the areas the guards patrolled. "How long do you think we'll have to wait?"

Eve shrugged. "As long as it takes." I shot her an exasperated look and she sighed. "He'll be here. Curtis doesn't say things without following through."

My laugh was so sharp and sudden that it was out of my mouth and bouncing off the fence before I could even think about holding it back.

"And here I thought 'Don't draw attention to yourselves' was obvious enough that I didn't need to include it in the instructions." Hank materialized out of the darkness on the other side of the fence looking for all the world as though he had recently thrown himself down a ravine. He was wearing a black denim jacket over a ripped black shirt and his black jeans were caked in mud and shredded at the knee.

I almost asked if he was all right, but the words stuck in my throat.

"Curtis!" All of Eve's swagger and bravado fell away, leaving her looking oddly awkward and young. Words tumbled from her mouth as she approached the fence. "Is the rest of the pack safe? Did you find the Trackers who did it? Please tell me you tore them to pieces."

Hank ran a hand over what had to be at least two days of stubble. "The club burned to the foundation. Most of us who got out headed for Briar Creek."

I frowned. "Briar Creek?"

"Ghost town about an hour and a half from of Denver," explained Eve. "Just a few foundations."

"Only way there is an old unpaved road," added Hank. "Harder for anyone to get the drop on us." The lines on his face deepened as he stared at me. "You shouldn't be on that side of the fence, kid."

I shrugged and the gesture elicited a small twinge of pain in my back. "They have my friends. It's not something I would expect you to understand."

I could practically feel Eve shoot me a dirty look, but all Hank said was, "Fair enough."

The words took me aback. The old Hank wouldn't have let the implied criticism slide.

He slipped something from his pocket and drew his arm back. A small black shape went sailing over the fence. It bounced off the razor wire and landed at Eve's feet.

A plastic film canister—like the ones that were always lying around the art room at school.

She picked it up and popped the lid. Two pewter charms, each attached to a small length of twine, fell into her palm. She lifted one of the charms and dangled it from her fingertips. It was round and unadorned save for a strange symbol that looked like three interlocking teardrops etched onto the front.

"Keep those on you at all times," said Hank. "There's a truck heading into Thornhill tomorrow night. At one thirty a.m., it'll deliver a load of lumber to a construction site on the east side of camp—dorm fourteen. The guard escorting the truck and the driver will let you stow aboard—after you show them those charms. When the truck leaves, the two of you leave with it."

Neither Eve nor I spoke. The hum coming off the fence seemed to grow louder, filling the silence until I could feel the vibration in my chest.

Hank wanted to get us out. Both of us. It didn't make sense. He hadn't cared about me three years ago, so why care now? Out of the corner of my eye, I saw Eve drop the charms back into the canister. I shouldn't have been able to hear the sound they made as they hit the bottom, but I did.

"I'm not going anywhere without Kyle and Serena."

Eve stepped closer to the fence. "What about the pack? They're counting on you. I told"—she flexed her hand around the film canister—"I've *been telling them* that you'd think of some way to get us out."

"I had to practically sell my soul just to make

arrangements for the two of you," said Hank. Then, in a tone that was chillingly matter-of-fact, he added, "They'll be looking for two girls with those charms. Anyone else approaches that truck and the guard will shoot."

Eve didn't back down. "You don't understand. There are things going on here. Kids are missing—including Eumon kids. Wolves are getting sick and maybe dying. You can't leave them in here."

Hank's eyes flashed. "Even if I could get them out, what do you think would happen if every Eumon disappeared from Thornhill? How long do you think it would take the Trackers or the LSRB to figure out which pack was behind it?" He paused, letting her think it through. Then, each syllable the lash of a whip, he said, "They would wipe us out."

"So that's it?" I asked. This side of Hank was familiar. He had stopped pretending and was back to being someone I understood. "You don't care what happens to them in here."

He turned his gaze on me. His eyes burned like blue flame, and even though he had never raised a hand to me, I was suddenly glad he was on the other side of a very large, very deadly fence. I had seen my father look at other people that way; the results were never good.

Eve, meanwhile, seemed to disappear inside herself. She stood eerily still, like a living statue. Finally, she said, "You could work with the other packs. The Carteron leader's daughter is here. If she knew, she'd join with you. The Portheus pack might follow. You could try to take out the whole camp. If you did that, they wouldn't know who to strike back at. Even the Trackers wouldn't be crazy enough to retaliate against all three packs."

"No."

That was it. One word without explanation or apology.

"The pack will mutiny if they find out you got me out and left the others in here."

Something shifted behind my father's eyes. He looked at Eve the way he had looked at me three years ago when he told me he was going out for a pack of cigarettes.

"He's not going to tell the pack, Eve."

"They're not stupid," she said, and I wasn't sure if it was me or Hank she was addressing. "They'll figure it out. They'll know I didn't get out on my own."

Despite the start we had gotten off to, I suddenly felt sorry for her. I had never had any illusions about my father, but I knew how painful it was to discover someone you trusted was a stranger. "He'll get you out of here, but you won't be going back to the Eumon." I glanced at Hank. "Right?"

"There's a pack in Atlanta. They're expecting her."

"I won't go."

"Atlanta is nonnegotiable."

Eve stared at my father as though seeing him for the first time. "I'm not talking about Atlanta. I won't leave Thornhill knowing I abandoned the others."

Hank clenched and unclenched his right hand. It was too dark to see the network of scars crisscrossing his knuckles, but for a second, I imagined they shone white. "Do you think this chance is going to come again? Half the wolves in there would—" He suddenly turned.

A half second later, I heard the unmistakable sound of an approaching engine.

"Patrol's early." Hank cursed and glanced back at us. "Get to your dorm. Both of you will be on that truck tomorrow. One thirty a.m. No discussion."

A jeep roared into view. Instinctively, I dropped to the ground, trying to make myself as small as possible as headlights swept the air. Next to me, Eve had the same idea.

After a handful of seconds, I raised my head just enough to see what was going on. Hank was running away from the fence. As I watched, he crumpled and began to shift.

I wanted to look away, but I couldn't.

Hank's bones shattered and his muscles snapped. His spine bowed and his mouth opened in a silent scream.

Time slowed down as his body tore itself to pieces. When it was over, a wolf with fur the color of ash mixed with snow stood in his place and everything became a thousand times more real: My father was infected.

Bullets sent up a spray of dirt near the wolf's paws and time snapped back.

My stomach lurched, but the wolf was a faster and smaller target than the man had been. It—Hank, I reminded myself—dodged the jeep and raced into the night.

The jeep careened recklessly in an attempt to follow as someone yelled what sounded like GPS coordinates into a radio.

Hank was a speck of gray and then he was gone.

I raised myself to a crouch. I could see pinpoints of light in the distance—headlights on our side of the fence.

"Eve."

She stood and stared at the spot where Hank had disappeared. I pushed myself up and then reached for her arm. "Eve!"

She shoved me away, and I barely kept from landing on my butt. "How could he make a deal to save the two of us and leave the rest of them behind?" Her voice was loud. Too loud.

I glanced nervously in the direction I had last seen the headlights. They had disappeared behind a building, but I had no doubt they were headed this way. Eve was staring at me, waiting for an answer. "I don't know," I said. "But we can't stay here."

She pulled in a deep breath and then nodded. "Come on," she said before breaking into a run.

I struggled to keep up. I knew she was slowing her pace for me, but before long I began stumbling over my own feet. It felt like someone had slashed my chest with a knife, and I was concentrating so hard on forcing my legs to keep moving, that I didn't notice or question where Eve was leading me.

She came to sudden stop. Half blind with exhaustion, I collided with her back. It was like hitting a concrete wall. And, like concrete, Eve didn't budge when I slammed into her.

I wiped the sweat from my face as I tried to relearn how to breathe. I looked up, expecting the dorm. Instead, I saw red bricks covered in ivy: the sanatorium.

We were near the rear of the building. We stood in the

shadow of a shed that was half rotted and looked about a century old. It had probably been here when the first TB patients arrived.

Eve stared up at the former hospital. All of the windows were dark, and the only light came from a small orange-tinted bulb hanging above a steel door. "What do you think happens to them? To the wolves who go missing?"

I swallowed and thought about Serena. "I don't know."

"He expected me to leave. To just forget about them. *Atlanta.*" She uttered the word like a curse as she ran both hands through her hair. "I'm not going. When that truck leaves, I won't be on it."

"I'm not going anywhere without Serena and Kyle," I said with a shrug. "If Hank knew me at all, he would have known that."

"You weren't surprised. You really never thought he'd help, did you?"

With a small sigh, I slipped a finger under my wrist cuff and ran it along the edge of Amy's bracelet. "When Hank left, it took me three days to realize it was permanent. I spent the time huddled in a motel room. Waiting. It wasn't until the manager kicked me out that I accepted he wasn't coming back."

The gray in Eve's eyes swirled like fog. "Hank told me he left you with relatives."

I noticed her switch from "Curtis" to "Hank" but didn't point it out. "Then he lied. I remembered the name of a cousin and found her number in the phone book."

"He's not the person I thought he was," she said softly.

"Maybe," I conceded. "But I'm not sure he's the person he used to be, either." Hank might have been willing to turn his back on the other Eumon, but he had tried to get Eve and me out. He had even tried to find a new place for her.

Maybe the real Hank wasn't the selfish, callous man I remembered or the leader Eve wanted him to be. Maybe the real Hank was somewhere in the middle.

I flashed back on an image of a gray wolf dodging a hail of bullets. He had risked his life to come here.

"Do you think he got away?"

Eve gave a small, angry shrug, followed by a grudging nod. "He's fast—even by werewolf standards. It would take more than a single jeep to catch him." She gave me a long, evaluating glance. "I figured you wouldn't care, one way or the other."

I didn't want to care. I *didn't* care. Curiosity wasn't caring.

Eve could have pushed. She didn't. Instead, she slipped the film canister from her pocket and held it between her thumb and forefinger. "So what the hell do we do with these?"

I let out a deep breath. "Hank said the guard will be expecting two girls with those charms, but he didn't say anything about the guard knowing what we look like."

"So someone else could use them. . . ."

I nodded. "I think we should try to get into the main building tomorrow night. If we can find Serena before the truck leaves, she can use my charm."

Eve thought it over. "Makes sense. And we might find something useful while we're at it. The packs don't get

189

along, but I know a couple of girls in Carteron and Portheus who are decent. I can give my charm—along with anything we find—to one of them. If Hank won't do anything, maybe the other pack leaders will."

She so wasn't going to like my next suggestion. "I think it should be you," I said. "I think you should use the charm."

She stared at me in disbelief. "Are you *insane*? After everything you heard me tell Hank? After everything we just talked about?"

I shot a quick glance at the sanatorium. It was still dark. "Hank wanted to get you out of here. He even made arrangements so you'd have someplace to go after leaving Colorado. That's a lot more than he ever did for me. He cares about you—enough that you might actually stand a chance at changing his mind about helping the others."

Eve crossed her arms. "And if he doesn't listen to me?"

"Then you can try and get some of the other Eumon on your side. There must be some of them who've lost people they care about to this place. And you could try approaching the other packs."

"While everyone else stays in here." She scowled. "I use that charm for myself and it's like I'm turning my back on them and running away."

I shook my head. "Don't think of it as running away from a problem. Think of it as running toward a solution."

A look of complete disgust swept her face. "That is the lamest thing I have ever heard."

"My cousin listens to old self-help books from the eighties on tape."

She twisted the cuff on her wrist. "All right. Say I agree to use the charm. What happens next?"

A light flickered on in one of the sanatorium windows, and we eased farther back into the shadows.

"We convince Kyle and Jason that we need to break into the building tomorrow night, and we do it without telling them about the charms or Hank's offer—otherwise, they'll try to make sure I'm on that truck when it leaves."

A knot formed in my chest.

Up until now, the biggest secret I had kept from Kyle was the time I had lied about scratching his car. He'd be furious if he knew what Eve and I were planning—so unbelievably furious—but he would eventually get over it. He'd have to.

There was no way I was using that charm for myself.

17

I TURNED IN A SLOW CIRCLE ON A DESERTED STREET. THE restaurant where I worked. The shops that had closed up after the attacks last year. Riverside Square in the distance and the tang of the water on the breeze.

Hemlock. Home.

But there wasn't a single person or car in sight. It was like the Rapture had come for everyone and left me behind.

"No piles of clothes." Amy stepped out from a doorway. She wore a white T-shirt that clung to her curves and made her skin look even paler than usual. "If it was the Rapture, there'd be little piles of clothes everywhere. I saw it on one of those *Predictions of the Bible* shows." Her footsteps didn't make a sound as she walked toward me. "Besides, you wouldn't be the only one left."

I swallowed. "Because I'm not that bad?"

"Because the rest of Hemlock isn't that good." She took my hand. Her skin was cold and clammy: a corpse's grip I couldn't break. "Come on," she said, tugging me down the street and around the corner.

"This is all wrong," I murmured. We were on Windsor even though Windsor wasn't anywhere near the river. And instead of a paved street, the road was rough gravel.

When I realized where she was leading me, no amount of force could pull me forward. I stared at the alley where Ben had killed her. "I can't go in there."

"You can't avoid it forever."

I finally wrenched my hand free. "Why are you still here? Is it because I let Ben get away? Because I let them take Serena?"

Amy pulled a piece of bloodred candy out of her pocket and popped it into her mouth. "Maybe I'm here because I'm lonely and you're my bestie, ever think of that?" She sighed and kicked at the stones beneath her feet. "You don't really believe that stuff you told Eve, do you? About how maybe your father isn't the person he used to be?"

I shrugged uncomfortably. I had always avoided talking about my pre-Hemlock life with Amy—at least as much as I could. There was no way she would have understood what it was like to grow up with nothing and to have a father who put you—your safety, your well-being, your everything— dead last.

There was something in Amy's eyes that looked horribly close to pity. "You had it right the first time. People don't change. They let you down and betray you. You can't count on anyone."

"I'm not counting on Hank."

"I'm not talking about just Hank."

A chill swept down my spine. "Whatever happens, I'll deal with it."

She shook her head. "You're not ready for this. None of you are."

She started to walk away.

"Amy, wait!" I ran after her and tripped. I fell to my hands and knees and the gravel dug into my palms. I looked down. What I had taken for ordinary rocks were shards of bone.

"Three blind mice," whispered Amy. "See what happens when they run." She glanced over her shoulder as someone called my name. "There's never enough time," she said sadly. As she turned back to me, bloodstains blossomed across her T-shirt and darkness swallowed the street.

"Mac!" someone hissed.

I opened my eyes, and Eve's red hair and slight frame came into focus.

"Look," she whispered, nodding across the room.

I rolled over as quietly as I could. It was sometime before dawn, but Eve and I weren't the only ones who were awake. Halfway across the room, two guards quietly stripped one of the beds and emptied out a dresser. Moments later, a counselor led a new girl to the bunk.

"Orientation will be in an hour," said the counselor, voice pitched low. "Try to get some rest until then."

The mattress groaned as the girl sat on the edge. She didn't lie down. I flashed back on what it had been like—the blood test, the haircut, the shower—and couldn't blame her for not wanting to sleep.

"Whose bed was that?" I whispered, once the counselor and guards were gone. Eve and I had claimed the last two bunks when we arrived. Someone had gone missing in order for this girl to have a place.

"Shayla House. The one who tried to start something with me the other morning."

The girl with the foxlike face. The one whose mother ruled one of the other Denver packs. My throat suddenly went dry. In Thornhill, who you were really didn't matter.

The noonday sun filtered through the dirt-caked roof of the greenhouse. Dust motes hung in the air and left a dry taste on my tongue. The smell was just as bad as it had been yesterday—though continued exposure did seem to make it slightly more bearable. Emphasis on slightly.

I stared at Jason. "What do you mean Serena doesn't exist?"

The four of us sat around a rickety table—Eve across from Jason, Kyle across from me—with stacks of guard rosters and delivery schedules spread out between us. While we had been stuck in class, Jason had spent the morning gathering information on anything and everything that might help us get Serena out of the sanatorium.

We had to assume she was there. Any alternative was unbearable.

Jason reached up to scratch his neck, but caught himself before he could chip away the makeup covering his tattoo. "The LSRB keeps tabs on every wolf in every camp. There are four Serenas in their database. None are at Thornhill and none are the right age. And that's not all." He glanced at Eve. "The Trackers told me they delivered fifty-seven wolves in September. The LSRB only has forty-three Thornhill registrations on record for that month."

"They don't want anyone—not even the LSRB—knowing how many heads are really coming in." Kyle's brown eyes darkened until they were almost black. "It makes Dex's theory sound a lot less crazy."

A chill swept through my body. "That means . . ." I had to swallow and start again. "That means anything could happen to Serena and there would be no record of it. Sinclair could do anything to her"—*could kill her*—"and no one but us would ever even know she had been here."

"We'll get her out," promised Kyle. "We'll get her out of the sanatorium before anything can happen to her."

A flurry of "what-ifs" flew to my lips, but I held them back. *What if something's already happened to her? What if we're too late? What if Sinclair was telling the truth and Serena really is sick?* They were questions we didn't have the answers to and asking them would only make us go in circles.

"We have to get her out tonight," I said as I picked up the delivery schedule for the week. Thanks to Hank, I already knew what I would find, but I studied the sheet of paper for a moment before saying, "There's a delivery coming in tonight at one thirty a.m. If we time it right, maybe we can get Serena on the truck and out of the camp before anyone realizes she's missing."

"Getting her on board and through the gates without

anyone noticing . . ." Jason shook his head. "It's a long shot."

"You have a better idea?" asked Eve.

Jason scowled, but didn't reply.

After a moment, Kyle reached for the schedule and broke the stalemate. "A long shot is better than nothing. The rest of us can try and come up with a plan for ourselves after Serena's safe."

He shot me a small, tight smile. Hank's charm—tied to Amy's bracelet and tucked under my wrist cuff—suddenly felt hot against my skin. I hated lying to Kyle and Jason, but I was too worried they'd insist I use the charm to get myself out—especially since a girl had gone missing from my dorm just hours ago.

I needed their help too badly to risk an argument. If I had to, I'd tell them the truth after we got Serena to the truck.

Jason flipped through papers until he found a blueprint. "The sanatorium had a psychiatric ward in the basement. When they renovated, they turned it into the detention block. Odds are, that's where Serena will be. It's the only part of the building—other than the offices—counselors don't have access to."

"Mental patients and werewolves in the cellar," muttered Eve. "It's almost a cliché." She tucked her feet up underneath her and raised herself to a sort of crouch, perching on her stool like a crow on a wire.

"A very secure cliché," said Jason. "The elevator goes down to the lower level, but you need a key to access that floor and Sinclair has the only copy. There is a stairwell, but it's behind a door requiring a six-digit code that only the warden and the program coordinators have. Even guards need an escort to go in."

My heart sank. The warden and program coordinators rarely ventured into the main part of the camp. And even if we could get to one of them, it wasn't like they'd just give us the code.

There are always ways to make people talk. My father's voice seeped through my mind like a drop of ink spreading through a glass of water. I would do anything to get Serena and Kyle out of Thornhill; suddenly, though, anything was a frightening thought.

With a deep breath, I pushed Hank's voice aside. My stomach rolled as the smell of decay tried to slither down my throat. I wondered how Kyle and Eve, with their were-wolf-sharp noses, could stand to be in here. I was just a reg and it—*smell.*

"Sinclair's hand cream!" The idea hit me so hard that I almost fell off my stool. "You said I smelled like lavender," I said to Kyle. "That's how we get the code!"

Eve and Jason stared at me blankly, but understanding flashed across Kyle's face. "You want a werewolf to sniff out her hand lotion on the keys she's pressing."

"Would it work?"

He thought it over. "Maybe. That stuff does reek."

Eve shook her head. "Even if you could pick out the numbers—and that's a big if—six digits equal a lot of combinations. We'll need time." She glanced at Jason and her eyes narrowed. "Are you even listening?"

He obviously wasn't. All of his attention was focused on the wall behind Kyle even though you could only make out the vague suggestions of shapes and colors through the grime on the glass.

I opened my mouth to ask what was wrong just as one of the shapes moved.

Kyle and Eve were through the door in an instant, Jason fast on their heels.

"Stop!" Jason's voice boomed out as I crossed the threshold.

I rounded the corner of the greenhouse in time to see Kyle and Eve hit the ground. I caught a glimpse of a small black object in Jason's hand: his HFD.

Twenty feet away, a boy in an olive uniform froze. He turned, eyes darting from Kyle to Eve.

Dex.

On his feet. Completely alert. Standing there as though the HFD didn't have the slightest effect on him.

He stared at me in shock for a moment—the same shock, no doubt, that was on my own face—and then his gaze dropped back to Eve. The scars on his cheek twisted as he scowled. "Let them up. I won't run."

Jason hesitated.

I went to Kyle and crouched at his side. "Do what he says, Jason."

"Mac . . ."

I glared at him over my shoulder. I couldn't believe he had just used one of those things with Kyle and Eve in range. For a horrible second, Jason didn't move. I held my breath, letting it out only when he finally slipped the remote back into his pocket.

Kyle recovered first. He eased me away, refusing my offer of help as he climbed to his feet.

I straightened and watched Dex help Eve up. "Why didn't you go down?"

Dex raised an eyebrow. "I could ask you the same question, but I think I know the answer." He nodded at my arm and I glanced down.

At some point, I had been less than careful and pushed up my sleeves. Derby's cut was visible on my arm. Jagged and pink and new.

"You're not past the incubation period."

"She's not infected," corrected Eve as she slipped out from the support of Dex's arm. "What did she mean you didn't go down?"

Jason spoke before Dex could. "Is anyone else immune? Have any of the other flea—wolves figured it out?"

Kyle glanced at him. "What are you talking about?"

"Trackers developed the first HFDs four, maybe five years ago." Though he spoke to Kyle, Jason's gaze remained locked on Dex. "They don't use them because wolves develop a tolerance and the amount of time it takes varies. A few wolves aren't affected at all. Ever."

Eve stared at Dex. "When did they stop affecting you?" There was a vague note of accusation in her voice, as though she were really asking why he hadn't told her.

"About three weeks ago. After they took Corry but before I found the graveyard." Dex paused and swallowed.

"Do you know about the restricted zone in the woods?" Eve and I nodded and he kept going. "Until I saw that, I thought there was still a shot of finding Corry and getting out. I kept testing the HFDs by the fence, hoping I'd find one that didn't work—not that I had a plan for getting over the fence. After a while, setting off the HFDs hurt less. Then it stopped hurting at all. I can still hear them, but it's like my eardrums have adjusted to the sound."

Jason scrubbed a hand over his face. "The Trackers don't use them because they're unpredictable—they'd rather stick with Tasers and guns. When they found out Sinclair had designed most of her security system around the things, they assumed she had found a way to perfect them." He shook his head; he looked ill. "She hasn't. She's playing Russian roulette with the staff. Guards don't have the devices and counselors have to fill out a report every time they use one. Everyone thinks it's because Sinclair has a soft spot for the wolves, but she's trying to keep them from getting exposed too often and building up a tolerance."

There was an upturned, broken wheelbarrow a few feet away. Eve sat on it and twisted the cuff around her wrist. "It's Pavlovian. They scare us to death in the first self-control class, probably figure we'll go near the fence at least once on our own, and then rely on the memory of pain to keep us in check."

"The counselors, the guards, hell, the lunch ladies, and the orderlies . . ." Jason ran a hand through his hair. "If they knew the risks they were taking . . ."

"The risks they're taking?" I stared at him in disbelief.

"Jason, all those people signed on to work at a rehabilitation camp."

"That doesn't make them bad."

"It sure as hell doesn't make them good."

He tried to stare me down. It didn't work.

"That's why the Trackers got you in." Kyle's voice was sharp enough to draw blood. "They wouldn't have done it unless they were getting something in return, and they would have wanted a hell of a lot more than just money. They thought Sinclair had figured out how to fix the HFDs and wanted you to get them one."

Jason swallowed. "It's not as bad as you think."

In a blur, Kyle grabbed him and thrust him against the wall of the greenhouse. The glass shook and a web of cracks spread out from the spot where Jason's shoulders had hit.

"Kyle!" I rushed forward and grabbed his arm, but he shrugged me off.

"What did you promise them?"

Jason's cheeks flushed bright red and his words came out a choked rasp. "An HFD and dirt on Sinclair."

Kyle let go, stepping back so quickly that Jason lost his balance and slid to the ground.

"I wasn't actually going to get them one," he said, staring up at Kyle. His green eyes were dark, like the ocean at twenty thousand feet.

"Why spy on Sinclair?" asked Dex. "She's a warden in a rehab camp—shouldn't she be on the Trackers' list of BFFs?"

Jason pushed himself to his feet. He glowered at Dex, not making any attempt to hide his distrust. "Why don't you tell us what you were doing sneaking around and eavesdropping before you start asking questions?" His hand strayed toward his pocket before he seemed to remember that Dex was immune to the HFDs.

Dex shrugged. "I saw you and Mac yesterday. You were standing awfully close for a werewolf and a counselor. It made me curious."

It wasn't enough for Jason. "Why'd you run when I told you to stop?"

"Habit."

For a second, I thought Jason would continue to push, but he accepted the explanation. "She's paying the Trackers to bring wolves in. Paying them a lot. It's making some people suspicious—especially when she could just get wolves from the other camps. Since her sister was infected, they think maybe she's some sort of wolf sympathizer, that maybe she's trying to create Thornhill as a safe haven for wolves."

"If they're suspicious," said Eve, "why keep bringing her wolves?"

"Greed." Jason shrugged. "Not all of the Trackers think it's strange and not all of the ones who do care. The ones who want to know what's really going on are the ones who got me in." His gaze shifted to Kyle and a look that was painfully earnest crossed his face. "It was the only way I could get inside. I didn't tell you because I knew you wouldn't like it."

For a moment, Kyle didn't react, then he inhaled deeply as though reining in suspicion or anger. "All right. How do we storm the castle?"

18

I pushed back a heavy plastic sheet and peered out into the camp. Flashlight beams pierced the night in the distance. Lots of them.

Eve had slipped away from the dorm just after curfew, leaving a note that said she'd meet us—as planned—at eleven. With no idea where she had gone or why, I'd had little choice but to wait until I met the guys at the half-constructed classroom we had agreed to use as a staging point.

When Eve still hadn't shown after twenty minutes, Kyle and Dex had gone looking for her. That had been fifteen minutes ago, and every additional second made the silence heavy and the air harder to breathe.

"You ever hear that expression about a watched pot?" Jason's voice cut through my thoughts.

I glared over my shoulder.

Moonlight filtered through the plastic, but his face was in shadow. He leaned against a support beam, bottle in hand, not drinking, just twisting the cap on and off. "I'm just saying that driving yourself crazy won't make them show any faster."

"Aren't you even a little worried?"

Jason shrugged. "Kyle and Dex can take care of themselves." But he fumbled the cap and took a swig from the bottle.

He was just as worried as I was. Maybe it should have been reassuring to know that someone felt the same way. It wasn't.

Wearily, I walked away from the side of the building and snatched the bottle from Jason's hand. The last thing we needed tonight was a Sheffield with lowered inhibitions. I debated taking a drink—God knew I could use something to slow the synapses firing in my head—but I capped the bottle and stashed it behind a stack of drywall.

Rough-hewn letters caught my eye as I straightened. Someone had carved *Thornhill Sucks* into a two-by-four. For some reason, the tiny act of rebellion made me feel braver.

The floor creaked behind me, but I just stared at the letters and tried to tell myself that everything would be all right.

"Are you okay?"

Jason was so close that his breath ruffled my hair.

"Yeah," I lied.

"Mac . . . about tonight . . . if anything happens . . ."

I turned. "What is it?" Jason almost never had trouble with words. Whether they were the right ones or the wrong ones, they usually came easy to him.

Before he could reply, the rustle of plastic came from the edge of the construction site. A knot loosened in my chest as Kyle climbed into the building.

He held the sheeting aside, and Dex helped Eve through the gap. My eyes widened as the three of them drew near. Eve's face was so pale that it practically glowed and she leaned on Dex as though her legs were shaking.

"We found her near the restricted zone in the woods," explained Dex. "It took me weeks to build up a tolerance to the HFDs, but genius here thought she could do it in a couple of hours."

"Was worth a shot," muttered Eve. She pushed Dex's hands away as he tried to steady her. "I'm fine, Dexter. I just need to shift. Besides, we're already behind schedule." She glanced at me. "Sorry about slipping out. And about being late."

I shrugged. "It's okay." It wasn't, but I probably would have tried the same thing in her place.

Dex walked to one of the far corners and hauled off his shirt. I quickly looked away as he reached for his fly. After a lot of debate that afternoon, we had agreed that Eve and Dex would cause a distraction to draw some of the guards out of the sanatorium. Then Jason, Kyle, and I would go in after Serena.

Eve shot Jason a glare as she headed for one of the other corners. "Sneak a peek, Tracker and I'll gut you."

"I could be infected with LS and dumped in an all-male rehab camp for a decade, and I still wouldn't be desperate enough to look."

I dropped my gaze to the floor—the safest place—as the room filled with a ghoulish cacophony of breaking bones and tearing muscle. It sounded like a slice of hell, and my fingers twitched with the urge to cover my ears.

A prickly sensation crept down my spine. I glanced up. Kyle was watching me, his face carefully blank. Was it hard for him not to shift? Did part of him want to?

When the noises stopped, I turned to face two wolves. One, Eve, was a rich silver. The other was pure white.

My heart lurched. *Dex*, I told myself. *It's just Dex.*

The white wolf jumped gracefully to the ground, the silver wolf right on its heels.

Kyle followed, then turned to help me down. The feeling of his hand in mine was warm and familiar. Reassuring.

I glanced over my shoulder as my sneakers hit the ground. Jason was watching us—was staring at my hand in Kyle's—with an expression filled with too many emotions to read, but entirely too easy to understand.

Wondering why things had to be so complicated, I eased my hand out of Kyle's and put a fraction more space between us. I didn't feel guilty—I couldn't help the way I felt about Kyle and I wouldn't want to—but I also didn't want to hurt Jason. Not any more than I had to.

Love's a game where the odds are permanently fixed. The house always wins, and anyone stupid enough to sit at the table is lucky if they walk away with their soul intact. Amy's voice echoed back through the fog of memory. At the time, I had assumed she and Jason were in the middle of one of their usual fight–make up–make out cycles. Suddenly, though, I wondered if

I had been responsible for those words, if Amy had known about—and been thinking of—Jason's feelings for me when she uttered them.

I forced thoughts of Amy away. There wasn't anything I could do to change things—no matter how much I wished I could.

Eve let out a small yelp as she and Dex circled us. The wrist cuffs had stayed in place through the transformation, and they threw the gait of each wolf slightly off.

Kyle crouched down so he could look her in the eye. "We'll meet back here in an hour. If you get cut off, head for the dorms. We'll try to get Serena to the truck."

Eve's wolfish gaze slid to me, and I gave her the slightest nod. No matter what happened to us, she had to make it to the truck. She had to get out of the camp for everyone's sake. She tossed her head and then took off running, Dex following right behind.

Kyle, Jason, and I made our way through the camp. Three times, we had to hide from patrols. There were definitely more guards out than there had been last night, and most of them were heading to and from the fence—a fact I took as confirmation that Hank had gotten away. Even as a reg, he'd always had nine lives.

I didn't want to care, but like it or not, he was the only father I had.

We reached the sanatorium and ducked into the shadows along the side of the building just as dueling howls split the night.

Every inch of my body hummed with adrenaline as a

group of guards—six, maybe seven—thundered past. The howls came again, drawing the men farther into the camp.

"Stay here," whispered Jason before disappearing around the corner.

A minute later, a low whistle cut through the air.

Kyle and I raced for the door at the front of the building.

Jason held it open, then slipped in behind us. "This way," he said, taking the lead. We headed down a maze of gray hallways, taking so many twists and turns that I was certain I'd never remember the way back. All of the corridors looked the same, and I wondered how Jason could possibly know where he was going.

We rounded another corner and I froze at the sight of a security camera. Of course. Why hadn't I realized there would be cameras? Why hadn't I noticed them the last time I was here?

Jason paused and glanced back when he realized I had stopped. He followed the direction of my gaze. "Don't worry. The night shift is too short staffed for anyone to watch the footage."

Hoping he was right, I focused on the rest of the hallway. It was different from the others. My pulse skipped a beat as I recognized the white tile and the keypads next to the doors. We rounded another corner and there it was: the steel door I had found the last time I was here.

"The stairs are right on the other side," said Jason. "I got a glimpse of them when I was scoping out the hallways this morning."

Kyle headed for the keypad next to the door, and Jason

slipped a notebook and pen out of his pocket. "I was a Boy Scout for six months," he said, catching my flicker of surprise. "Being prepared was a whole thing."

"It was Cub Scouts," corrected Kyle, "and you got the both of us kicked out after three weeks." He leaned down and put his face near the keypad.

Please, I prayed. *Please let this work.*

"Well?" asked Jason.

"Hang on. There are a lot of different scents on this thing."

My heart plummeted. It had been a stupid idea. It had—

"Nine . . . three . . . two . . ." Kyle turned his head and sneezed. "Four and eight."

Jason glanced at his notebook. "That's only five numbers."

Kyle checked the keypad again, then straightened and shook his head. "All the buttons smell, but it's strongest on those five."

"Maybe one number is in the code twice." I walked forward and nudged Kyle aside. "Read me them?" I asked Jason.

"Nine, three, two, four, eight."

I repeated them softly and began punching in different combinations as quickly as I could. Each time I entered a code, a small red light flashed for half a heartbeat.

My fingers started to cramp and the taste of copper flooded my mouth as I bit my lip. How many strings had I tried? Fifty? A hundred?

Footsteps and the sound of someone whistling echoed down the adjacent corridor. For a horrible second, I froze, then my fingers flew over the keypad in a blur.

"Mac . . ."

I blocked out Jason's sharp whisper. I blocked out everything but the keypad and the small flash of red.

Suddenly, there was a soft click and the light turned green. I threw open the door and the three of us tumbled inside seconds before the footsteps reached the corner.

I blinked in the too-bright light at the top of a too-white stairwell. Before my eyes could adjust, Kyle's hands were on my back. "Move!" he hissed as he herded Jason and me down the stairs.

We reached the bottom and hurtled through another door only to find ourselves in a hallway just as sterile as the stairwell. White doors lined both sides of the corridor and each had a keypad.

We were trapped. No better than rats in a maze.

"Back," snapped Jason, grabbing my arm and tugging me behind him before wedging us both in the small space to the left of the stairwell entrance. To Kyle, he said, "If it's just one, you can grab him when he comes through."

My mind full of Tasers and guns and HFDs, I started to object, but I could hear steps descending the stairs.

My heart thudded in my chest—so fierce and fast that I was sure Jason would feel it despite the layers of clothing between us.

With a soft *whoosh*, the door swung open, hiding Jason and me from view. I heard something shatter followed by a strangled cry and a loud thud.

I pushed past Jason as the door swung shut.

Kyle held a program coordinator pinned—face-first, arms behind back—to the wall. Shards of a broken mug lay in a puddle of coffee on the floor. The man tried to twist away and I caught sight of a birthmark on his cheek: it was the program coordinator I had asked about Serena that first morning in Thornhill.

"How did you get in here?"

Kyle glanced at me and there was something cold and a little inhuman in his eyes—it was almost like the wolf was peeking out. "Go check for Serena."

I nodded, but before heading down the hall, I stepped up to the coordinator and checked his pockets.

"Do you have any idea how much trouble you're in?" asked the man as I took his HFD. His voice was steady and laced with authority, but his face was beet red and sweat dripped off his brow. "When the warden gets her hands on you . . ."

In response, Kyle pulled the man's arms sharply back, eliciting a ragged grunt of pain. "Don't look at her. Don't talk to her. Forget you've even seen her."

"Kyle . . ."

"Check for Serena." His voice came out with the hint of a growl.

I shot a worried glance at Jason, but did as Kyle said.

The first two doors were plain and unbroken, but every door after that had a slitlike window at eye level. Each window looked in on sparsely furnished rooms lit by rectangular yellow lights over narrow bunks. The wolves in rooms one and two looked emaciated and sick—like the girl I'd seen that morning in the hall. And, just like the girl, both were hooked up to IVs.

Shayla, the missing girl from my dorm, was in the third room. Her body sprawled bonelessly on her bunk and she looked so out of it that I wondered if she had been drugged. Could you drug a werewolf?

Room four was empty, and rooms five and six both held boys.

I peered through the slit into room seven. For a moment, I thought it, too, was empty. Then I caught sight of the small figured huddled at the head of the bed.

Serena.

19

SERENA HAD WEDGED HERSELF INTO THE SPACE WHERE the corner of the mattress met the corner of the room. Her legs were drawn up to her chest and her forehead was pressed to her knees. Her hair had been cut short and left in unruly tangles.

I couldn't see her face, but I knew it was her.

"Serena?" I called her name through the glass. She didn't react. I tried the handle, but of course the door was locked. "Guys, she's here."

"What's the code?" Jason's voice, hard edged with threats, filled the hallway. Through the window, I saw Serena flinch.

"I don't have it."

The sharp snap of breaking bones echoed in the air and the program coordinator let out a strangled cry.

I whirled and then froze. The breaking bones had been Kyle's. His hand was changing. As I watched, his fingers lengthened, the tips turning long and deadly. He met my gaze and quickly looked away, almost as though he suddenly couldn't stand the sight of me.

"Think carefully," Kyle said, voice rough, as he lifted a hand that was no longer human and placed it on the program coordinator's shoulder. "I'm guessing life in a camp would be especially bad for someone in your position."

I knew Kyle wouldn't really infect him—he couldn't really infect him—but looking at the expression on his face, it was almost easy to believe the lie.

For a moment that seemed to stretch without end, the only sound in the hallway was the program coordinator's labored breathing. "All of the codes are in the control room," the man said, finally. Moving as little as possible, he inclined his head toward the first door on the right.

Kyle steered the man to the door. "What's the code to get in?"

Instead of answering, the coordinator glanced at Jason. "Who sent you to Thornhill? Was it the RfW? You know you won't get away with any of this."

Kyle twisted the coordinator's arm. "The code. Don't make me ask again."

"Seven-six-one-three-eight-two."

Jason entered the numbers and the light on the keypad flashed green. He slipped into the room, followed by Kyle and the program coordinator. I shot a nervous glance at the stairwell door and the broken coffee mug before following.

The room we found ourselves in was dark save for the glow from a bank of computer monitors. All but one displayed a screensaver of the Thornhill logo rotating in 3D.

"Late-night sugar high?" I asked, eyeing the pile of junk

food wrappers surrounding the one computer in use.

The coordinator shot me a disgusted look. "The codes are next to the door."

Jason slipped a gray binder from a rack bolted to the wall. He flipped through it and then tore out a hole-punched page. "Got it." He glanced at the coordinator. "Now what do we do with him?"

"Tie him up? Lock him in a closet?" I bit my lip and tried to think of options.

"He knows Jason isn't really a counselor and he's seen our faces. We can't just leave him here." Kyle shifted his hold on the man. One hand was still clawed and deadly. I tried not to look at it too long or too hard.

He was still Kyle. No matter what happened, he would always be Kyle.

"We have to take him with us." Jason ran a hand through his hair and over his neck. "We can stash him in the old staff quarters or something—just for a few days."

He kept talking, reasoning it through with Kyle, but their words ceased to register as my eyes locked onto the monitor across the room. Though my gaze had passed over it moments ago, I hadn't really noticed what was on the screen.

I walked forward, heart in throat.

A spreadsheet filled the screen, but over it was an open video file. The clip had been paused on the image of a girl sitting behind a table. A girl with shoulder-length curls and a torn shirt.

The computer was only ten steps away, but those ten

steps felt like ten thousand. In the video, Serena sat behind a heavy metal table—the same table I had seen in the picture of her on Sinclair's touch screen. Only this time, Serena's arms were in restraints and there was an IV stand behind her.

"Mac? What are you—" Jason sucked in a sharp, audible breath as he drew closer and realized what I was looking at.

I had seen Serena moments ago and her hair had been cut even shorter than mine. "This was shot the night we arrived." My voice came out high and thin. "That's the shirt Serena was wearing during the raid."

I glanced over my shoulder. "What is this?"

The coordinator didn't answer. Hand shaking, I grabbed the mouse and clicked play. Serena shrank back as a woman in a tan counselor's uniform, Langley, entered the room. The counselor carried some sort of metal rod in her hands. Before I could process what was happening, she brought the bar down on Serena's fingers.

Serena's scream burst out of the computer's speakers and echoed in the room. In the video, a large digital clock flickered to life on the wall behind her. Jason made a grab for the mouse as I backed away. He shut the video player and the sudden silence was deafening.

Another open video lay underneath the first. Jason dragged the cursor toward the red *X* that would close the file, but I shouldered past him and took control, clicking play before he could stop me.

Serena's hair was short in this one, but unlike in the cell, it was neat and combed. A woman in a white coat stepped into the frame and faced the camera. She adjusted a pair of tortoiseshell glasses. With a jolt, I recognized her as the woman who had signaled out Serena during admissions.

"One-five-six-seven's transformations have slowed since she began phase two. Longest delay: four-minutes-sixteen-seconds between stimulus and shift."

Serena turned her head. "Please," she begged, her voice so broken that things inside my chest snapped, "I can't do it again."

She's talking to someone off camera. The thought hit me just as I noticed a human-shaped shadow shift slightly on the wall with the clock.

The woman with the glasses held up a syringe and approached the table. Tears coursed down Serena's face, but she was powerless to resist as the needle pierced her arm. The clock flickered to life once more.

Jason reached for the mouse when Serena's body began to tear itself apart. "Wait!" I clicked pause as the mystery figure crossed the room. Warden Sinclair.

Tears burned at the corners of my eyes and my throat constricted. So this was her idea of helping the wolves in her care. This was rehabilitation.

"They're actually doing it." Kyle's voice was thick with a bass growl. "They're actually working on a cure."

"That's not a cure," snapped Jason. "That's torture."

The room blurred. "There was never any new disease." A rush of anger filled me, and I had to clench my hands to keep from grabbing the monitor and hurling it to the ground. "They made them sick. They made them sick to keep them from shifting."

"What did you give her?" Kyle's voice raised the hair on the back of my neck. He tightened his grip on the program coordinator and the man's face twisted in pain.

"If I tell you, they'll kill me."

Jason swore and headed for the door. He paused on the threshold and glanced back at Kyle. "We don't have time for this. You stay with him while Mac and I get Serena." His gaze dropped to the coordinator. In a voice that hinted at blood and pain, he said, "We'll take him with us and get answers out of him later."

I knew what Jason was implying, and I knew I should care—we were supposed to be the good guys—but right now I didn't. I couldn't. All I could do was follow him into the hall and to Serena's cell.

"Are you okay?" he asked.

"Not even a little."

Jason checked the paper he had pulled from the binder and punched the code into the keypad. The light flashed green and he pulled open the door. I slipped past him and into the cell.

The room was plain and white and smelled of bleach and copper. Its one yellow light cast a jaundiced glow over the tile walls. A toilet and sink occupied one corner, while the other played host to the bed.

Serena was still curled in on herself. It was like she hadn't moved the entire time we had been in the control room. She was dressed in white clothes that hung off her small frame. Her skin—what little of it was visible—was covered in a sheen of sweat.

"Serena?" I stepped forward and she curled up even tighter, almost as though she were making herself as small a target as possible.

I glanced at Jason; he looked as lost as I felt.

I turned back to Serena and frowned. Her hands were bound. Steel manacles connected by a foot of chain encircled each wrist.

Slowly, I took a second step toward the bed and then a third. "Serena? It's me. It's Mac. . . ."

She lifted her head. Awareness bled into her eyes. "Mac?" Her voice was a rasp. She gave her head a small shake and squeezed her eyes shut. "Go away."

I flinched, assuming she was blaming me for everything that had happened. "Serena . . ."

"You're not real. You all keep coming, but none of you are ever real." She tapped the side of her head against the tile wall. One. Two. Three. "You're not really here." Tap. Tap. Tap.

Each tap was a spike to my chest.

"Look at her wrists." Jason had eased farther into the room. He touched my elbow. "Mac, look at her wrists."

I had already looked. I had already seen the cuffs. I . . .

The realization slammed into me, and my knees threatened to buckle. Impossible. It wasn't the cuffs that had Jason staring at Serena like she was something amazing and terrifying, it was the skin around them. It had been rubbed raw from straining against the restraints, so raw that strips of flesh seemed to half hang off her wrists. Blood trickled out in a slow but constant flow, dripping onto the bed.

Serena hadn't struggled while we had been in the cell. Her wrists should have started to heal, but they hadn't.

With a sick lurch, I noted bloodstains on the blankets— easy to miss because the fabric was a dark russet-brown. *That's why the room smells like copper,* I thought. *It's Serena's blood.*

Jason edged closer to the bed, trying to get a better look at her hands.

Serena seemed completely oblivious to his presence, but she stopped tapping her head against the wall and uncurled herself by small fractions as he slowly advanced.

Her entire body tensed as Jason took another step.

He held up his hands, trying to convey that he wouldn't hurt her. "Serena?"

She suddenly bolted from the bed, knocking him off balance and sending him crashing onto his butt.

"Serena!" I stepped toward her, but she shoved me away. My palms and forearms slapped the tile wall, and I just managed to keep from dashing my brains out. It hurt, but not nearly as badly as it should have.

I spun in time to see her lift her manacled hands and fling the chain around Jason's throat.

She's going to kill him. For a horrible second, the thought paralyzed me, then I raced forward.

"Stop it, Serena!" I screamed for Kyle as I tried to force her arms up. Her muscles were rigid with strain and her

221

skin was scorching to the touch.

Jason managed to get his fingers under the chain and pushed against it in an effort to keep her from crushing his windpipe. When that didn't work, he threw his weight back, trying to knock her off balance.

Serena let out a horrible sound—like a cornered and wounded animal—and pulled the chain tighter.

Jason made a gurgling, choking noise as his oxygen was cut off completely.

A string of swear words emanated from the doorway, and I glanced over my shoulder as Kyle shoved the program coordinator into the room.

Kyle's eyes widened as he took in the scene. His nostrils flared and his gaze darted to the bloodstained blanket before locking on Serena. "Watch him," he ordered me as he circled to approach Serena from behind.

I placed myself between the program coordinator and the door. The man took a step to the left. "Don't even think about it." I wasn't infected, but you'd never know it from the growl in my voice.

Kyle grabbed Serena from behind.

She let out a wordless howl as he forced her hands up and away from Jason's neck. He moved back, hauling her with him, folding his arms over her chest like a straight jacket.

He was too late: Jason had already passed out. Without the chain and Serena's body to hold him up, Jason crumpled. I dove forward and barely managed to keep his head from splitting open against the tile floor.

Too late, I realized my mistake as the program coordinator darted past me and out into the hall. An alarm sounded before I could so much as think about going after him.

Hands shaking, I checked Jason's pulse: weak but steady. We had to get him out of here. We had to get them both out of here.

Serena stopped struggling and sagged in Kyle's arms. *Bloodlust.* The thought ricocheted through my head like a bullet. Whatever they had done to her, it had left her rabid and out of control.

We had to get them out of the room and up the stairs without Serena losing it again. If we could manage that, then maybe we'd have a chance. If we could get her out of the building, we could sort out whatever was wrong with her afterward.

There was a loud thud—audible even over the alarm— and then shouting filled the corridor outside the cell.

Kyle let go of Serena and pushed her behind him, putting his body between her and the door. His gaze darted to mine.

Looking into Kyle's eyes, I saw fear and desperation— not for himself, but for the rest of us. He knew there was nothing we could do. We were out of time and luck.

I glanced down at Jason. His chest rose and fell steadily, but there was a ring of red around his neck where the chain had pressed against the skin. I pulled his head onto my lap.

It was over. All over.

Guards flooded the cell.

Two pulled Jason away from me and dragged him into the hallway. I surged to my feet only to be forced to the nearest corner. My shoulder blades collided with the tiles as I heard Kyle shout my name.

He and Serena were rushed by another group in blue.

Kyle tried to protect her and collapsed as a Taser took him full in the chest.

A scream shredded my throat. I tried to move forward, but the guards blocked my way and penned me in.

The electricity coursing through Kyle's body stopped. He tore the darts from his chest and staggered to his feet.

The voice of a female guard rang through the cell. "Keep resisting, and we'll tase the girl."

Half the Tasers in the room swung in Serena's direction.

Kyle didn't have a choice: wordlessly, he held up his hands in surrender.

We were both herded into the hallway. There was no sign of Jason, and instead of turning toward the stairs, guards forced us in the opposite direction.

Serena started screaming and her cries chased us down the detention block. I covered my ears, desperate to block out the sound.

It wasn't until we were shoved through a door and into an old, untouched part of the psych ward that the cries fell away.

I shivered and tried not to stumble over the debris covering the floor.

Here, there were no white tile walls or rooms that smelled of bleach. Instead, the corridors reeked of mold and looked like the setting for one of those shows where B-list celebrities went ghost hunting. Half the doors were off their hinges, offering glimpses into abandoned rooms filled with broken furniture, shredded paper, and graffitied walls.

Kyle and I were flung into the last room on the left: a cell with peeling green paint and a single lamp that hung down from the ceiling like a flying saucer. There was one window above the door; all of the other walls were solid.

The door slammed shut. For the second time since leaving Hemlock, we had been locked in a room without hope of escape.

20

SOMETHING SCURRIED IN THE CORNER AND DARTED behind a mildew-stained mattress. With a small shudder, I moved a little farther down the wall. I wasn't sure how long we had been in the cell—long enough for my legs to ache from standing—but there was no sign that anyone was coming for us anytime soon.

"Why a camp?" Kyle paced the room. "If the government was working on a cure, they'd do it at the CDC or some secret lab. There are better ways. Easier ways." He shook his head. "And they wouldn't need to pay the Trackers to bring wolves in—not when the camps are full of them. Sinclair has to be doing it on her own."

I bit my lip and chipped flakes of paint off the wall with the edge of my thumbnail. "Finding a cure for LS would take way more resources than a warden and a handful of program coordinators. You'd need labs. Doctors. Money."

Kyle paused. "So maybe she's working with someone?"

"Or found out what someone else was doing and stole it." Industrial espionage. That was a thing, wasn't it? I scrubbed a hand over my face. In a way, it didn't matter. We were trapped; even if we knew exactly what was going on at Thornhill, there wasn't anything we could do to stop it. Our only hope was that Eve had made it to the truck, that she had gotten out of the camp and would somehow be able to stage a rescue.

I considered telling Kyle about the charm and the deal my father had made, but instead I asked the same question I had asked seventeen times before. "What do you think's happening to them?"

Kyle didn't say anything; I knew he didn't have an answer any more than I did, but I couldn't stop asking. Every time I closed my eyes, I saw Serena attack Jason. I saw her face as Kyle pulled her away. Feral. Wild. Not a trace of my friend inside.

And it was my fault.

Shivering, I pushed myself up onto an old wooden dresser and scooted back until my shoulder blades rested against the wall. "Kyle?"

"Yeah?"

"I'm sorry." I dropped my gaze to my knees because that was easier than looking at him. "This is my fault. All of it."

"Don't be stupid." He started pacing again. He was like one of those animals you saw at the zoo—the ones that walked the length of their cage until they collapsed.

"I'm not being stupid." All of this had happened because I had tried so hard to hold on, because I hadn't let go when Kyle had wanted me to. "If I hadn't followed you to Denver . . ."

"The raid would still have happened. It didn't have anything to do with you."

"But you might have gotten away. And Jason and Serena wouldn't have been there. They . . ." A lump rose in my throat and I couldn't finish the sentence.

Kyle crossed the room. He placed his hands flat on the dresser, one on either side of me, close enough that his thumbs grazed my legs. "Mac. Look at me."

I shook my head. I couldn't.

"*Mac.*"

I forced myself to meet his gaze. His eyes were dark and earnest without a hint of the blame I knew I deserved.

"All of us made choices. Including Jason and Serena."

"But they made them because of me. Jason came to Denver to help me find you, and Serena came because I called her."

"Serena wanted an adventure, and Jason . . ." Kyle pulled in a deep breath. "Jason's in love with you." He reached up and brushed the hair back from my face. "Neither of them had entirely selfless motives. You can keep blaming yourself, but it's a waste of time and energy."

I shook my head. "You sound like my father."

Kyle raised an eyebrow. "Gee, thanks."

"I just meant you sound practical," I elaborated. "Hank has a lot of flaws but he's always been very good at practical. He used to say guilt was a useless emotion." I slipped a finger under my wrist cuff and ran it along the charm. I hoped Eve had acquired that same practical edge. I hoped she had gone for the truck even if she realized we were trapped in the sanatorium. It was what Hank would have done.

Silence filled the room like the tide coming in.

"What do you think is going to happen to us?" I asked, when I couldn't take the quiet any longer.

"I'm trying not to think about it, actually." Kyle leaned forward. He didn't tell me that everything would be all right or that things weren't that bad. He didn't lie.

I brushed my lips against his.

It was a soft kiss. Gentle and comforting.

After a moment, Kyle pulled back. "Promise you'll tell them that you're a reg."

"Do you really think it matters now?" It couldn't—not after I'd been caught sneaking into the sanatorium.

He frowned and ran his hands lightly over my legs, letting his palms come to rest on my knees. "Maybe not."

I pressed my forehead to his. "Kyle?"

"Yeah?"

"I'm really scared." Saying the words made the fear seem more real, but it also eased some of the pressure in my chest.

In response, he kissed me again. Like before, the kiss started off gentle and comforting, but this time, it quickly plunged into something distracting and desperate.

I tried to bury everything in the kiss—all of my guilt and anger and fear—as Kyle's hands slid up my back and knotted in my hair. I clung to him with every inch of every limb and kissed him like it was the last time I'd ever get the chance.

After a while, Kyle's hands slid to my shoulders and he eased me away. "Mac, there's something I have to tell you . . . about what happened in Denver. . . ." His voice held a jagged edge that had nothing to do with his being infected and everything to do with the fact that I had just spent the last several minutes trying to devour him.

He pulled in a calming breath as he searched for words. "Is this something that's going to upset me?"

"Maybe," he admitted.

"We're stuck in a dilapidated cell in an evil rehabilitation camp awaiting possible death, torture, or insanity. Maybe you could hold on to whatever you have to say until after we figure out if we're going to survive?"

Despite the situation, a small smiled tugged at the corner of his mouth. "Okay." He leaned in for another kiss, but suddenly stopped. His brow creased as he tilted his head to the side.

"What is it?"

"Guards, I think."

Kyle tugged me off the dresser and then carried it over to the door as though it weighed nothing. He placed it underneath the window and then hopped up effortlessly. "It's Dex," he said as he peered out into the hall.

"What about Eve?" A knot formed in my chest as I scrambled up after him.

Kyle shook his head. The dresser wobbled under our combined weight and he reached for my arm to steady me. "Just Dex."

I pressed my face to the dusty glass.

Dex stood between two guards, his back to us. He was shirtless and his skin was covered with dark patches. He hugged his chest—hugged it so tightly that his fingers dug into his sides and his shoulders shook. Bile rose in my throat as I realized the patches on his skin were dried blood.

"Dex?" Kyle's voice was too low for the guards to hear, but loud enough for a werewolf.

Dex swayed slightly on his feet, but showed no sign of hearing.

One guard unlocked the cell across from us. As soon as the door swung open, the other pushed Dex inside. Dex stumbled forward and crashed to his knees.

Without a word, the guards pulled the door shut and left.

"Dex?" Kyle called, louder this time. There was no answer.

"What if he's passed out?" I thought of internal injures and those stories you heard about people choking to death on their own vomit.

"He'll be okay," said Kyle, the words automatic and without strength behind them.

"What if Eve . . ." I couldn't bring myself to finish the question. If Eve wasn't with Dex, did that mean she had gotten away? Or did it mean something really bad had happened?

"Eve is probably laying low." Kyle stepped off the dresser and landed lightly on the balls of his feet. "And Dex . . . Dex will be fine." But he didn't sound convinced and he avoided meeting my eyes.

I lowered myself to a crouch and then eased down to the floor. As I did, my fingers grazed a thin, brittle piece of paper glued to the side of the dresser. An inventory label. I peered at it, curious. It was yellow with age and it took me a moment to decipher the faded lettering.

My breath caught in my throat and my heart raced.

"What is it?" asked Kyle.

I shook my head, unable to string syllables together. The label read: *Property of Willowgrove.*

It was here.

Willowgrove wasn't a secret camp or some trick to balance the books as they killed off wolves. It was the name of the old sanatorium. The name of the place where they were testing Sinclair's cure.

Time was hard to gauge when you were locked in a dilapidated cell with no hope of escape. We ended up sitting with our backs against the wall. Sometimes we talked or held hands. Other times we stayed silent, each lost in dark thoughts.

Eventually, exhaustion caught up with me, and I found myself slipping in and out of that space between waking and dreams. In those moments, it was like Amy was in the cell with us, whispering things that Kyle couldn't hear.

"You're going to get him killed, you know," she said, crouching next to me and leaning in close.

I jerked awake with enough force that I slammed the back of my head against the wall.

I blinked, for a moment disorientated.

Kyle was no longer beside me. He was standing near the door.

"What is it?" I climbed wearily to my feet and rubbed my aching skull.

Instead of answering, he backed up, placing himself between me and the entrance a handful of heartbeats before the door swung open.

Two guards shoved the dresser aside. They stormed into the cell and three more followed in their wake. Four of the men held Tasers, the other gripped a gun.

All five trained their weapons on Kyle.

I expected them to yell or give us an order, but they just stood there. Waiting.

The sound of high heels echoed down the hall. My pulse pounded behind my ears and my legs felt suddenly shaky. I could think of only one person who would wear heels in a place like this.

Warden Sinclair stepped through the doorway. She slipped her hands into the pockets of her slacks as she surveyed everything and everyone in the room. Her suit looked freshly pressed and her hair and makeup were both immaculate. She was a surreal contrast to the decay and grime surrounding us.

A small smile—one without an ounce of kindness or sincerity—curved her mouth. No sooner had it appeared than Kyle fell to his knees.

I reached for him, but one of the guards trained his Taser on me. I wasn't a wolf: if they tased me, I might not get back up.

"So it is true." Sinclair slipped her hands from her pockets.

An HFD was nestled in her palm. "You really are just a human."

I started to ask how she had known, but I was certain I already knew the answer. Jason. He had told her—either willingly or because she had forced it out of him. Serena was incapable of making sense, and Eve . . . Eve was like Hank. Even if Sinclair had gotten her hands on her, Eve wouldn't have broken.

The warden slid the HFD back into her pocket.

Kyle shook off the effects of the device, but before he was fully on his feet, one of the guards grabbed my arm and pulled me away from him.

I tried to twist free and came face-to-face with Tanner. The last time I'd been caught in the sanatorium, the red-headed guard had seemed almost sympathetic. This time, he was cold and impassive. His grip was like a vise as he pulled me to the warden.

"Let her go." Kyle's voice was a barely recognizable growl.

"I don't think so." With a wave of Sinclair's hand, the other four guards in the room converged on Kyle.

I hadn't thought it was possible for me to hate anyone as much as I hated Branson Derby and Ben, but in that moment, I would have traded my soul for the ability to hurt the woman in front of me. "What did you do to Serena?"

Ignoring my question, she said, "I took you into my confidence, gave you a chance to prove yourself, and you've been lying since the moment you entered my camp." Something that looked like disappointment passed behind her eyes. "I misjudged you."

I'm not the one torturing people and burying them in the woods. The words flew to my lips but I bit them back. The less the warden thought we knew, the safer we'd probably be.

"How did you get inside Thornhill?"

I swallowed as Tanner tightened his grip on my arm. The girl I had switched vials with was long gone. There was nothing Sinclair could do to her. "I swapped samples with one of the wolves. Where's Jason?" I knew he had used an alias, but I couldn't remember it and it didn't matter now.

The small creases around Sinclair's mouth deepened. "Tell me what you were doing last night. The boy's a Tracker, but who sent you? The RfW? No, they're too spineless. One of the Colorado packs?"

I shook my head. "Does Serena have bloodlust? Did you give it to her?"

In a blur, Sinclair's hand shot out. She grabbed my chin and gripped it so tightly that her nails dug into my skin. She glanced at Kyle over my shoulder. "Take another step and I'll have the guards tase her instead of you." She was using me against him just like they had used Serena back in the detention block. The threat was as effective now as it had been then.

The warden's gaze shifted back to me. "What were you doing last night? How many others are involved?"

The radio at Tanner's waist crackled to life with a burst of static. At a nod from Sinclair, he let go of my arm and stepped into the hall. He closed the door behind him, making it impossible to hear whatever was said—impossible for a reg, at least.

Sinclair's eyes bore into mine as her fingers continued to dig into my skin. I was too scared of what they might do to Kyle to struggle. "I am not toying with you," she said. "I am not about to let one stupid girl jeopardize Thornhill and everything I've worked for."

"You mean Willowgrove?" Fear and exhaustion made me slip, and even though I knew the words were a mistake, I felt a brief surge of satisfaction as Sinclair released her hold on me and stepped back.

The satisfaction lasted only as long as it took for her palm to connect with my cheek.

Sinclair hit me with enough force that I reeled and stumbled back several steps. Kyle's arms locked around me, steadying me. "Are you all right?"

I tried to nod, but my ears were filled with a ringing sound and I felt like I might vomit. How could one slap hurt so much? Did she practice? I blinked and the ringing and nausea receded—at least marginally.

Sinclair was staring down at her hand as though she couldn't quite believe she had hit me. It didn't make sense. She had an entire block full of werewolves she tortured and a graveyard in the woods where she dumped the bodies. Why was she was acting like hitting me was a shock?

The cell door opened and Tanner reappeared. "Warden?" He went to her side and spoke in low tones.

I buried my face against Kyle's neck, mindful of the four guards still watching us. "Can you hear what he's saying?" I whispered.

Kyle's arms tensed around me for a second, then he eased me away. "Mac, listen. . . ." He gripped my shoulders and shot a nervous glance at the men in the cell. "Whatever happens, promise me you won't fight. Just do what they say and don't give them a reason to hurt you." The look in his eyes scared me more than the warden or the guards. It was horrible and final, like a door slamming irrevocably shut.

"What did he say?" I started to turn my head, but Kyle tightened his grip, forcing my attention back to him. "Kyle?"

"Just promise me."

Sinclair's voice filled the cell. "Take her upstairs and take him to the detention block."

"What? No!" I struggled as Tanner pulled me away from Kyle for the second time. He was bigger and stronger than I was, but I made him fight for every inch he dragged me back.

Another guard entered the room. He squeezed past us, a heavy pair of manacles—restraints like the ones Serena had been wearing—in his hands.

Kyle stood completely motionless, eyes locked on me, as his wrists were bound. The muscles in his forearms and jaw tensed, but he didn't object or resist.

I was sure Sinclair wasn't a woman who responded to begging, but I still tried as I was wrenched past her. "Please don't hurt him. *Please.*"

For a split second, I could have sworn I saw pity in her eyes, but Tanner forced me out of the cell before I could be sure.

The iron grip Tanner kept on my arm left me no choice but to stumble along at his side. He didn't speak or look at me as he dragged me down the corridor and into the detention block.

I tried to dig my heels in as we passed Serena's cell, but he just kept pulling me forward until we reached the stairwell to the upper levels. As he shifted his hold to open the door, I managed to twist and look back.

Kyle had been led into the detention block. Guards unlocked one of the empty cells and ordered him inside.

My breath hitched in my throat as he turned to look at me. The rest of the corridor fell away and all I could see were his eyes. He stared at me the way I stared at photographs of Amy—like he was trying to memorize every detail before they faded. Like I was someone he had lost.

I opened my mouth to say his name, but before I could, I was forced into the stairwell. Just before the door slammed shut behind me, I thought I heard Kyle say he was sorry.

The journey through the rest of the sanatorium was a blur. Even Tanner's grip became a distant pressure as my mind raced.

I had to find a way back to Kyle. A few days in the detention block had stripped Serena of all but a shred of her humanity. I couldn't let the same thing happen to him.

I *wouldn't* let it happen.

We rounded a corner and the doors to the courtyard loomed ahead.

"No." I shook my head and stumbled. This wasn't right. Sinclair wouldn't let me go—not with everything I had seen—and she wouldn't throw me back in with the rest of Thornhill's population.

The graveyard. Every muscle in my body tensed as Tanner forced me through the doors and out of the building. He was going to take me to the middle of the woods where I would never be able to cause trouble again.

Whatever conclusions Kyle had drawn in the cell—whatever he had heard that made him think I'd be safe if I didn't resist—had been wrong. He'd gone to the detention block without a fight and it had all been for nothing.

I blinked in the morning light. Remnants of dawn still streaked the sky and a faint breeze rustled the ivy on the sanatorium walls. It was going to be a beautiful day—not that I would live to see it.

Pain split me like a knife. *I'll never know,* I thought. *Kyle, Serena, Jason—I'll never know what happened to them.* Tears filled my eyes and I furiously blinked them back. For all I knew, the warden was watching from somewhere inside; I wouldn't give her the satisfaction of thinking she had broken me.

"Are you all right?"

The familiar voice filled me with dread as Tanner yanked me to a stop.

I turned to Jason. His face was pale and drawn. There were dark shadows under his eyes and a collar of bruises around his neck. Gone was the tan counselor's uniform and in its place were designer jeans and a wrinkled polo shirt. His tattoo was completely visible, the black ink stark against his skin.

Pressure built inside my chest. Twenty seconds ago, I had been convinced I would never see Jason again, but that was preferable to seeing him here. My gaze slid to the two men in blue standing on either side of him.

Three guards to dispatch of two teenage regs.

Jason's gaze swept my face. He frowned. "Unhurt. That was one of the conditions."

Tanner shrugged. "It's just a bruise. Feel free to stay and take it up with the warden."

I raised a hand to my cheek. It was still tender where Sinclair had hit me. My eyes darted from Jason to Tanner and then back as I wondered what the hell was going on.

Before I could ask, a grinding noise—a thousand times worse than nails on a chalkboard—filled the air. The gates leading out of the camp rolled open and a black Lincoln Town Car drove through. It pulled a U-turn in the courtyard and then came to a smooth stop forty feet away.

Tanner shifted his grip to my forearm as he pulled a strange clamplike device from his pocket.

Instinctively, I flinched.

"Relax." He slipped the device over my wrist cuff and rotated it ninety degrees. The cuff sprang open with a click and Tanner slid it off. Only then did I think of my contraband bracelet.

A curious expression crossed his face as his eyes roamed over the coins. His gaze seemed to linger a fraction longer on Hank's charm, but he stepped away without comment.

Two men climbed out of the car. The driver was pudgy and balding while the man who stepped out of the passenger side had thick dark hair and a runner's build. Both carried guns in shoulder holsters and each had a black dagger tattooed on his neck. I had spent enough of my childhood around violent men to read body language; these two were career bad guys.

My gaze darted to Jason. He didn't look surprised to see the Trackers. If anything, he looked . . . *relieved*?

He met my stare with a dark expression I couldn't fathom as he strode to my side and took my arm. The guards didn't stop him.

What had he done?

His grip just shy of painful, Jason herded me to the car.

"What did you do?" I choked out the words as panic clawed at my throat. We couldn't leave. Sinclair had Serena and Dex. *She had Kyle.* She was going to put him in a room with a digital clock. They would break every bone in his body while cameras rolled, and when it was over, he'd be like Serena—barely reachable.

One of the Trackers pulled open the back door of the car.

"Get in," snapped Jason, momentarily letting go of my arm.

"What? No!" I shook my head and retreated a step.

"Get in, Mackenzie." Jason's voice was cold and dismissive. Almost unrecognizable. In three years, I couldn't remember him ever using my full name.

I started to take another step back, but he was too fast.

Before I knew it, I had been forced into the Town Car and the door was slamming shut.

It was a car for the wealthy and powerful—all-leather interior with a sheet of dark glass dividing the back from the front—but the details barely registered as I grabbed the door handle. Locked.

Jason slid into the other side of the car.

Desperate, I threw myself across his lap, scrambling for his door before he could haul it shut.

Too late.

He grabbed my wrists and pushed me back. "Sinclair knows you're a reg," he hissed. "What do you think you can do for them by staying?"

Tears—hot and angry—filled my eyes and distorted Jason's face as I struggled against him. Even as some part of me knew he had a point, my fear for Kyle and Serena left me wild. Almost rabid.

He used his body to pin me to the seat. For a second, I had a flashback that it was Ben on top of me, forcing me to the floor in his bedroom.

My knee connected with Jason's leg just below the groin. He let out a strangled groan but didn't relax his hold.

I didn't want him touching me. I didn't want him touching me ever again. "Get off of me," I snarled. I sounded crazed. Infected. "Don't touch me."

"Not until you calm down."

"You had no right—"

Jason cut me off. "I promised Kyle."

I froze. "Promised Kyle what?"

"That I'd get you out if I had a chance. So many strange things were happening at the camp that he worried Sinclair wouldn't let you go—even if she found out you were a reg."

"You're lying. He would have told me." But even as the words left my mouth, I knew they weren't true. Kyle had kept things from me before—like his infection and leaving Hemlock. All of the fight drained out of me and I sagged against the seat.

Slowly, cautiously, Jason let go of my wrists and eased his body off mine.

Kyle must have heard Tanner tell Sinclair the Trackers were nearing the camp. He must have known they were coming for Jason and me. That was why he had told me not to resist.

The tears I had barely managed to keep in check finally spilled over. It felt as though something had punched through my breastbone and was prying my ribs apart.

Jason reached for me—comfort, not restraint—but I edged away. "I told you not to touch me." The words were raw with the strain of not sobbing.

I wiped my eyes with the edge of my sleeve and turned to stare out the back window.

Thornhill was already gone. The only thing behind us was empty road.

Sinclair had broken Serena and she would break Kyle and Dex. For all I knew, Eve hadn't made it out and was either dead or in her grasp as well.

The warden held all of the cards. Everything that mattered. I didn't have so much as a shred of proof about what was really going on beneath the sanatorium. Beneath Willowgrove.

Fresh tears blurred my vision.

Whatever game we had fallen into, Sinclair had won.

21

AFTER AMY DIED, I HAD SPENT SLEEPLESS NIGHTS WON-
dering what falling into a black hole would feel like.
Everything that made you up—every atom, every thought—
would be pulled apart in a moment where time had no
meaning.

I don't know how or why that specific thought had
started. Maybe it was because Amy was our center; without
her, everything seemed to collapse.

Sitting in the Town Car as we got farther and farther
from Thornhill, I didn't have to wonder what being torn
apart would feel like: I knew.

Slowly, every muscle aching, I turned my back on the
empty road.

I reached out and ran a finger over the tinted glass separating us from the Trackers. "Can they hear us?" I tried to
look at Jason. It took me two attempts to manage it.

"No." He nodded as he said the word.

Yes, then. I started with the question that seemed safest.
"What are they doing here?"

"I called them." Jason swallowed and my eyes were drawn to the ring of bruises around his neck.

It struck me, suddenly, how lucky he was. How lucky we both were. A werewolf should have been able to snap his neck like a twig, and there was no way I should have just walked away after one shoved me into a wall. Not any time soon. Either some part of Serena was still capable of holding back, or whatever they had done to her had left her with little more strength than a reg.

Ben had been able to control his own version of bloodlust—not much, but a little. Enough that he had tried to fight the urge to kill me.

I pushed the thought away. I didn't want to believe Serena had bloodlust or anything like it. "How did you call them?" I asked, forcing myself to focus back on Jason. "You told me cells were jammed inside the camp."

"They are." He gave me a long, searching stare. "Mac, I . . ." He glanced at the smoky glass and cut himself off from whatever it was he wanted to say. "The doctor stepped out of the infirmary to talk to the guys who brought me upstairs. I used the phone on his desk to call my contact in Denver. With all the extra guards on patrol, I figured there might not be anyone monitoring the outgoing calls. I was right."

He ran a hand through his hair, leaving it sticking up in an unruly halo. "I told the Trackers that Sinclair was hiding wolves from the LSRB and putting their welfare above the safety of the regs on staff. I didn't have time to tell them much, but it was enough for them to want a full report. Enough for them to get me out."

I stared at him skeptically. "And, what? They asked nicely and she just let us go?"

"They threatened to tell the LSRB about the discrepancy in her registration records. You know how much government agencies like audits. They'd send agents to Thornhill before Sinclair could say 'investigation.'"

And if she was working on some crazy cure in secret, an investigation was the last thing she'd want.

I sank back against the seat and pressed the heels of my palms to my eyes until starbursts fired behind my closed lids. "She'll take it out on Kyle and Dex," I said, slowly lowering my hands. I wanted to throw up. "She'll make the two of them pay for the fact that we got out—that's if she doesn't just make them crazy like Serena."

"I didn't have a choice, Mac."

I didn't say anything. There was nothing I could say without completely losing it and saying too much. What had given them—both him and Kyle—the right to go behind my back and make secret plans to get me out whether I wanted them to or not?

A small voice in the back of my head pointed out that I wouldn't have survived one day of Sinclair's torture. *Besides,* it whispered, *you kept secrets from them, too. You didn't tell them about the charm or your plan to get Serena and Eve out.*

As hard as I tried, I couldn't completely tune out the voice.

I let out a shaky breath. Being angry at Jason might be temporarily satisfying, but it wouldn't help anything in the long run. "I get why the Trackers would come to your rescue, but why am I here? Why would they bother with me?"

He shrugged. "I told them you were an undercover reporter who had seen a lot more of the camp than I had."

It beat telling them who I really was. If the Trackers found out they had the reg daughter of a pack leader . . .

Bait or blackmail: those would be the best-case scenarios.

The thought hit me a nanosecond before the car swerved.

I was thrown against Jason so violently that I ended up half in his lap.

"What the hell are they doing?" The words had barely left Jason's lips when the car put on a sudden burst of speed.

I pushed away and then froze. A sliver of white and chrome was visible through Jason's window for a split second before it fell back.

My pulse jumped as I strained to catch a glimpse of the other car. There were white jeeps at Thornhill—a whole row of them next to the admission building. Had Sinclair changed her mind about letting us go?

Jason tried to lower the partition separating us from the Trackers. It wouldn't go down. "Hey!" He hit it with his fist, splitting his knuckles and leaving a dark smear against the glass.

The car swerved again, this time throwing both of us to my side of the seat as gunfire erupted behind us.

"Down!" I yelled, grabbing Jason's arm and rolling us both to the floor.

His breath came out in a whoosh as I landed on top of him, but his arms strained around me, holding me tightly as another round of gunfire split the air.

There was a bone-jarring impact from behind. The Town Car put on a second burst of speed, but it wasn't enough. A scream ripped from my throat as the car was hit again. The sound of groaning metal filled the air, and with a third hit, they managed to run us off the road.

The car bounced over uneven ground and then pitched sharply to the left. We tilted onto two wheels. For a horrible moment, I thought we were going to flip, but then the other wheels crashed back to the ground and we came to a shuddering stop.

Jason's heart pounded against my chest. My own matched it beat for beat.

The sudden stillness was almost surreal.

"Are you all right?" His voice was a rough whisper against my cheek.

I nodded and a wave of dizziness made everything spin as bile rushed up the back of my throat. I struggled to speak. "Think so. You?"

"So far."

There was a shout from outside. The Town Car shook as one of the front doors was wrenched open, and there was a jagged scream that abruptly cut off.

Everything went horribly quiet.

Voice raw, I whispered, "If you're carrying any sort of weapon, now would be a really good time to tell me."

"Only my razor-sharp wit."

We were so dead.

Fear flooded Jason's eyes and I knew he was thinking the same thing.

We were going to die.

We were going to die far from home and everyone who cared about us.

We were going to die, and no one would ever know what had happened.

I choked back a sob.

Outside, there were more shouts followed by the sound of an engine—the jeep, probably. A single gunshot rang out.

"Mac . . . I . . . if . . .Oh, what the hell." The space we were wedged in was barely wide enough for Jason's shoulders, but he somehow flipped us so that my back was pressed to the floor and his body was covering mine.

My hands were trapped against his chest. "Jason, what—"

Before I could finish the question, his lips crashed against mine.

I went completely still as the kiss stole the breath from my lungs. I should have pushed Jason away—I knew that—but I was scared. So scared. If these were our last minutes on earth—if this was the end—wasn't it better for a kiss to be the last thing I remembered?

My lips parted under Jason's and the kiss deepened. It wasn't fierce and desperate; it was sad and lost. I managed to get my hands free and slipped my arms around him, holding him close as I tried to block out the sound of more gunshots.

Jason pulled back a fraction of an inch. "I love you." The words were a shaky whisper against my lips.

I held him tighter because it was the only thing I could do.

The door behind Jason was yanked open and light flooded the back of the car.

"No!" My scream echoed in my ears as he was pulled outside.

I started to scramble after him, but the other door was wrenched open and strong arms locked around my waist. They pulled me back, into the bright sunlight.

As soon as my legs cleared the car, I fought. I kicked and yelled and scratched with my nails. I caught flashes of movement—other people in a barren field along the side of the road—but they were only impressions.

They could kill me, but I was going to inflict as much damage as humanly possible first.

"Jesus Christ, kid."

I froze and glanced down at the hands holding me.

Familiar spiderwebs of scars across the knuckles and a silver ring—a ring, I realized, that bore the same symbol as the charm on my bracelet.

For the second time—third if you counted his attempt to get me out of the camp—my father had come to my rescue.

No sooner had the details clicked into place than Hank's hands fell away. I stumbled and caught myself against the open car door as Jason came to my side.

The rest of the field slowly came into focus.

A handful of men and women milled around, all of them looking more than capable of taking care of themselves. Since their presence didn't seem to bother Hank, I assumed they were part of his pack.

A white jeep was parked fifty feet away, its hood crushed

like a tin can. A body was slumped over the steering wheel.

One Tracker—the one who looked like a runner—was lying dead on the ground halfway between the jeep and the Town Car. He had taken a bullet to the head. The bodies of two men lay crumpled not far away. I walked over to them and stared down at what I could see of their faces. Though they were wearing plainclothes, I recognized them as guards from Thornhill.

My stomach flipped. "Did you kill them?" I asked, looking up.

"Didn't have much choice. They started firing as soon as they saw us." The stubble Hank had been sporting the other night had filled out into the beginnings of a full beard. His battered leather jacket bulged slightly on the left side, a sign he was carrying at least one gun. He raised an eyebrow. "Any objections?"

"None," I replied, my voice flat and hard and unfamiliar to my own ears. The guards had fired on the car and run us off the road. I had no illusions about what they would have done to Jason and me.

"Did you kill the Trackers?" Jason's voice was carefully blank.

The look Hank shot him was long and appraising. After a moment, he shook his head. "They hauled that one out and shot him before they saw us. The other one is in the car. Looks like he was hit and bled out just after the crash." It was clear he didn't consider the two deaths a loss.

I stepped away from the bodies at my feet. "These ones are guards. From Thornhill." I swallowed and glanced at the

Town Car. It was riddled with more spots than a Clearasil ad. If Hank and his wolves hadn't shown up when they had . . .

I shook my head. "How did you find us? How did you know we were in trouble?"

Hank's gaze drifted down to my bracelet. "There's a tracking chip inside the charm. That way, if the men I bribed to get you out had gone back on the deal, I would have at least known where you were."

A voice called him over to the jeep. "Stay here," he ordered, striding away before I could respond.

"What men? What bribe?" Jason's voice was sharp. His eyes narrowed in suspicion.

"Nothing," I said quickly as I started after Hank. If he had known where I was, then he'd be able to track Eve. He'd know if Sinclair had her.

I had barely gone three feet when I caught a glimpse of red out of the corner of my eye.

"Impressive." Eve stood where I was certain there had been empty space just a moment before. She rocked back on the heels of a pair of cherry-colored Doc Martens. Gone was the gray Thornhill uniform; in its place was a baggy flannel shirt knotted over a black tank top and jeans. There was a tired, pinched look around her eyes, but otherwise she looked fine. Better than fine. "I leave you on your own for less than a day and you piss off the warden so bad that she sends a hit squad after you."

"You know what they say," muttered Jason absently as his gaze swept the field. "If you don't have at least one person out to kill you before breakfast, you're not living up to your potential."

Eve ignored him. "Dex and Kyle?"

I shook my head. "Sinclair has them. Last I saw, Dex was pretty out of it." I couldn't tell her about Kyle. Not until I trusted myself to do so without breaking.

She glanced away as she ran a hand through her hair. "There were too many guards. Dex and I split up. And then, with the truck . . . I wanted to go back and make sure he was okay, but Tanner said there wasn't time."

"Tanner?" I frowned and rubbed my arm where the red-headed guard had gripped it. "What does he have to do with anything?"

"He was the guard Han—Curtis paid off. Turns out he's actually RfW."

Suddenly, the way Tanner had tried to calm the other guard that first time in the sanatorium made sense. As did the way he had looked at my bracelet. He must have known who I really was the second he had seen it.

Eve scowled. "I shouldn't have listened to him. I should have gone back and helped Dex."

Hank reappeared. He placed his right hand on her shoulder—a gesture that would have felt alien and uncomfortable to me but that didn't seem to faze her. His other hand was clenched in a fist at his side. "You made the right choice. Out here, you're useful."

"Yeah, well, it doesn't feel right." Eve pulled in a deep breath and dug the heel of her boot into the ground.

I frowned and shot a glance at Jason. His eyes were locked

on my father and there was a crease just above his brow; Hank's choice of words hadn't slipped past him, either.

I cleared my throat. "What do you mean 'useful'?" I asked, not daring to let myself hope. "Useful for what?"

"Getting him out."

Eve recovered first. She stepped away so she could study Hank's face. "You changed your mind? You're going to break the Eumon out of Thornhill?"

I held my breath. Without Hank or the Eumon, the plan had been to approach one of the other packs. But even if they agreed to help, that would take time—time Kyle and Serena didn't have.

I stared at Hank, waiting for him to give Eve a yes or no. Instead, he said, "That depends."

"On?" asked Jason, the single syllable as sharp as a blade.

My father's eyes—every bit as icy and blue as Sinclair's—fell on each of us in turn. "On you." He opened his fist and held up a flat metal circle, like an oversized coin. It bore the same symbol that was etched on the charms he had given Eve and me. The same symbol on his ring.

"The guards left one on the body of each Tracker. It's the symbol of the Eumon," Hank added, glancing at Jason and me. "If the Trackers had come looking for their men and found it here, they'd assume the pack had put out a hit. Probably as a message in retaliation for the raid."

"Sinclair couldn't just kill us in the camp," I said slowly, "not without going against the Trackers and pissing them off. But they wouldn't suspect her if we were killed on the road—not if she made it look like we were caught in the crossfire during an attack."

I shivered. The sun was warm—unseasonably warm—but I was suddenly freezing.

Jason glanced back at the body of the Tracker. "I got those men killed."

"Sinclair got those men killed. Not you." I reached for his hand, but he brushed the touch aside. Unable to say or do anything to comfort him, I shifted my attention back to my father. "You said your help depended on us. Why?"

He flexed his hand around the piece of metal. "Because I want to know what was so valuable that the good warden would send a hit squad after my daughter and try to pin it on my pack."

22

"Take me through the videos again." Hank stared at the three of us—Jason, Eve, and me—from across a scarred breakfast table.

We were in a single-wide trailer—one of thirty—in an abandoned trailer park about forty minutes from Thornhill. The avocado-green appliances and yellow cupboards screamed 1970s, but according to Hank, the place had only been vacant a few years.

I didn't ask how he'd known. Guys like my father always had a dozen places where they could lie low. If the empty beer bottles and food wrappers on the floor were any indication, this place was on more than one person's list.

I sighed and scrubbed a hand over my eyes. "We've already told you everything about them. Twice." The adrenaline had worn off ages ago. My nerves were frayed, my body ached, and I was hyperaware of the fact that each second we spent talking was a second Sinclair was probably hurting Kyle and Serena. "All we're doing is wasting time."

Eve shot me a warning look. We needed Hank—I knew

that—but I was seriously starting to suspect that nothing we said or did would convince him to risk his neck or the pack.

Still, we had to try.

I steeled myself to describe the videos again, but Jason saved me. "Serena was hooked up to an IV in both clips. In the first, they broke her hand. In the second, they injected her with something. The way she reacted when she saw the needle"—he shook his head and a dark look passed through his eyes—"it wasn't the first time. That's it. They hurt her, then waited to see how long it took for her to lose control and shift."

Hank twisted the silver ring on his right hand. "And she seemed more alert in the videos than when you saw her in the cell? More aware of her surroundings and what was going on?"

"Yes," said Jason, a note of frustration creeping into his voice. Like me, his patience had worn thin, but he was doing a better job of keeping his emotions under the surface. It was like our normal roles had flipped. "Serena knew where she was and what was going on. In the cell, she was completely out of it. She recognized Mac—but only for a second."

Hank turned his gaze on me. "Did she say anything to you?"

"This is such a waste of time," I muttered, pushing my chair back and standing.

"Mackenzie . . ."

There was a small window across the room—a patch of

bright blue against the dingy, decrepit kitchen. I walked to it and folded my arms over my chest. Eve had found me a clean shirt in the trunk of her car—a guy's sweatshirt that was two sizes too big—but I was freezing. I stared at the abandoned trailer park without really seeing it. "She said something about how I wasn't real. How we all kept coming for her, but none of us were ever real." The words were a knife between my ribs. I pictured Serena waiting in that cell, praying we would come for her and eventually giving up hope.

"Nothing about Sinclair?" prodded Hank. "Nothing about what they were trying to do or if they had succeeded?"

"Nothing." Tears blurred the scene outside the window, and I hastily brushed them away. Hank had always said crying was for the weak; I was certain he wouldn't appreciate it now.

I turned and leaned against the windowsill. "What does it matter? We know Sinclair's trying to cure wolves. Obviously, she hasn't been successful."

The blue in Hank's eyes—normally so flat and empty—darkened and swirled. "What makes you so sure?"

Eve leaned forward with a frown. "What do you mean?"

Hank continued to stare at me. "I mean maybe their cure is working exactly as intended."

I shook my head. "No. No way." I flashed back on Serena's face as Kyle hauled her away from Jason. It had been twisted and bloodthirsty. Almost unrecognizable. "She was more violent, not less."

259

"Did she shift?"

I opened my mouth, then snapped it shut. It was Jason who answered. "No."

Hank gestured at Jason's neck and I knew what was coming. After all, hadn't I thought the same thing? "Why didn't she break your neck? Whatever they did kept your friend from shifting or using her full strength."

"Maybe part of her was still in enough control to hold back," I countered, trying not to look at the bruises on Jason's skin. "But even if they did find a way to keep her from shifting, it's a complete failure as a cure. It made her crazy and violent, not better."

"What makes you think this was ever about making wolves better?" asked Hank.

All three of us stared at him as though he'd lost his mind.

"It has to be about making wolves better," said Eve. "What good is a cure, otherwise?"

"What would you rather deal with?" Hank asked her. "Three hundred people in straitjackets who could be contained or three hundred wolves who were each capable of tearing your throat out the second you let down your guard?"

I glanced at Jason as a horrible feeling of coldness spread through my chest. The idea that Serena could be considered a success—that what had happened to her might be the end goal rather than a horrible, unexpected side effect—wasn't just immoral or sickening. It was evil.

"If the change was permanent," continued Hank, "you wouldn't need rehabilitation camps anymore. If wolves can't shift, they can't infect. You could put them in hospitals and mental wards with reg patients."

Permanent. The room dimmed around the edges as Jason stood and came to my side. "But wolves can heal almost anything." A high, panicked note entered my voice. "Once we get Serena away from that place—"

The screech of metal against linoleum cut me off as Eve pushed her chair back and surged to her feet. "Dex is in the sanatorium and there are dozens of Eumon in the camp." She leaned forward and gripped the table. "Curtis, you have to do something. If you don't . . ."

"Do you hear that?" muttered Jason, gently nudging me away from the window.

I edged over, barely registering his words. I was too focused on my father and Eve. A week ago she had worshipped him; now she stared at him as though desperately hoping he could be the man she once thought he was.

She swallowed. "Please, Curtis."

"Mac . . ." Jason tugged on my sleeve.

Annoyed, I opened my mouth to ask what was so important, but then I heard it: engines. What sounded like an entire caravan. I spun to the window just in time to see the dust kick up as dozens of cars and motorcycles flooded the park.

"The pack?" I turned and stared at my father. Jason and I had driven to the trailer with Eve, but Hank had followed in his own truck. "You called them before we got here. You already made the decision to hit the camp." My voice was soft, wondering. I was used to people surprising me, but the surprises were rarely good.

The slam of car doors filled the air as Hank met my gaze. "Sinclair brought the fight to me when she tried to kill you and frame my pack. Even if she hadn't, what she's doing at Thornhill is too dangerous to go unchecked."

He stood and headed for the door.

"Thank you," I said, throat tight, as he reached for the handle. "Thank you for helping us."

Hank pushed open the door. "Not necessary. But there is no 'us,' Mackenzie. You're staying here."

In an old, cobweb-filled community center in the middle of the park, twenty werewolves—along with Jason and me— had gathered to plan a mass prison break. After four hours, three arguments, and one fistfight, we had come up with something that might work. If we were lucky.

I tried not to think about how seldom luck had been on my side.

Hank hadn't wanted me at the meeting—as far as he was concerned, the less I was involved, the better—but I had seen parts of Thornhill Eve had never gotten near. Jason could have filled in those blanks, but Hank didn't entirely trust him and the other wolves didn't trust him at all.

Unfortunately—at least from their perspective—they needed him.

Jason had managed to memorize an incredible amount of information about Thornhill's security systems and protocols during his short time behind the gates. Guard rotations, the number of staff who carried HFDs, even how and under what circumstances the camp would contact the

LSRB for help—all details the wolves needed to strengthen their strategy.

If he applied that same focus to school, he would save his father tens of thousands of dollars in future Ivy League bribes—assuming he lived long enough for college to be an option.

Given that he had just pissed off a room full of were-wolves, that might have been a big assumption to make.

"I didn't say not to defend yourselves." Jason pushed himself to his feet and stared down the length of the long table.

Actually, he had. Three minutes ago, when he had reminded one of the wolves that she could survive a Taser to the chest and warned her against "overreacting" and "retaliating" against the guards if she was hit.

"Shut up, Jason." I hissed the words out of the corner of my mouth and tugged on his sleeve, trying to get him to sit back down as twenty wolves—including Eve—stared at him with open hostility.

He pulled free of my grip and ran a hand through his hair. "Look, I'm just saying the fewer the casualties, the better. The counselors and the orderlies—hell, even most of the guards—don't think they're doing anything wrong. They've always been told the camps were a solution, not a problem. Most of them don't know what Sinclair is really doing. They don't deserve to get annihilated."

"Do you have any idea how many people their 'solution' has hurt?" demanded a man sitting at Hank's right hand. With a thick red beard and massive forearms, he looked like he'd be most at home swinging an ax at a redwood. "Do you know how many wolves are trapped in the camps?"

"Sixty-three thousand one hundred eighteen." Jason didn't even need time to think about the answer. "Officially, at least."

The man crossed his arms and glanced at my father. "We're wasting time here. We don't need anything else from him. There's no reason for him to stay."

Hank didn't reply. He just stared at Jason, waiting to see what else he'd say or do as though this was some sort of test.

Jason pulled in a deep breath and sat back down. He started to reach up and scratch his tattoo, but caught himself and put his hands flat on the table. "For the last twelve years, the LSRB and the Trackers have been doing everything they can to convince the rest of the world that werewolves are all time bombs waiting to go off." He spoke slowly and distinctly, with way more care than I had ever heard from him. "If you swarm Thornhill and don't do everything you can to limit the number of reg deaths, you'll be doing them a favor. You'll give them all of the ammunition they need to convince every last reg that locking up wolves is the only way to keep the public safe. They'll call it the Thornhill Massacre. It'll be on the news all day, every day, for months, and by the time it falls off the front page, the damage will be irrevocable."

I stared at Jason in shock. I hadn't thought beyond getting the wolves out. I had known the LSRB would try to find them—that was a given—but the idea that the agency could spin the breakout to gain more public support had never crossed my mind.

A quick glance at Eve's face and open mouth showed that it hadn't occurred to her, either. In fact, almost every wolf around the table was staring at Jason in stunned silence as they absorbed the full implications of his words. A few were even nodding in agreement.

The Trackers had recruited him, in part, in the hope that he would become a poster boy for the group. I suddenly understood why. When Jason wanted to, he was capable of exuding the sort of magnetism shared by really good politicians and cult leaders. In just a handful of sentences, he had taken a room of angry werewolves and thrust them so deep in thought that they heard his words without seeing the tattoo on his neck.

Only one person around the table remained completely unfazed.

Hank didn't look at all surprised by Jason's words. After a long moment, he pushed his chair back and stood. "We've got six hours. I suggest you each try to find a quiet space and rest up. Those of you on the recon team: meet me back here in four."

"Curtis . . ." Eve tried to get his attention as he walked past, but Hank didn't spare her so much as a glance as he strode across the room and out the door.

The gathering began to break up. A few wolves left while others lingered and talked in small groups of twos and threes. Jason was pulled into a debate about whether a guard could tase a wolf moving at full speed. It no longer looked like he was in immediate danger of being torn apart, and for the moment, he wasn't paying attention to me.

No one was.

I slipped out of the community center and went looking for Hank.

He wasn't hard to find.

I stepped into the trailer we had used earlier. Twilight was falling outside, but two Coleman lanterns lit the interior with a soft glow.

"Guess I didn't teach you to knock." Hank popped the cap off a bottle of beer and took a seat at the table.

I closed the door and leaned against it. "You never used to drink before a job."

"I didn't always have a werewolf metabolism."

"Fair enough." It was just one more thing that seemed to have changed. I pulled in a deep breath. "That stuff Jason said—about how the LSRB and the Trackers would use a breakout—it didn't surprise you, did it? You already thought of it."

The lines on Hank's face deepened, leaving him looking tired and older. He toyed with his beer without taking a drink. "When you and Eve first asked me to break all of the wolves out of Thornhill, why do you think I said no?"

I thought back to the night at the fence and shrugged. "Potential payout minus probable cost." It was the formula he used for everything.

Hank nodded. "But not for me. There are dozens of

packs across the country. Did you honestly think you and Eve were the first to consider taking down a camp? Did you think you were the first to want to?"

Before I could say anything, he added, "Other packs have thought about it. No one's tried because doing so is tantamount to declaring war on the LSRB."

War? I swallowed, throat suddenly dry at the enormity of the word. "It's just one camp. Not even a regular-sized one." Thornhill had a few hundred wolves. The larger rehabilitation camps had close to eight or ten thousand.

"One camp is enough to give people hope. No one has ever stood up to the LSRB before. Not like this." Hank's gaze carried so much weight that I felt somehow smaller under it. "Even if we fail, wolves in other camps will hear about what we tried to do and they'll fight back—first in small ways that won't seem to matter, and then in larger ones that will add up. Soon, other packs will start resisting instead of hiding."

"But that's good, isn't it?" I shook my head. "If no one ever fights back then nothing will change."

"Do you remember what happened to Leah?"

My breath caught, and I knew Hank could read the memory on my face.

Of course I did.

Leah had lived down the hall from us in Detroit. She'd been kind and smart and had tried to look out for me. She had also been a werewolf—though I hadn't known it at the time. After people found out she was infected, a group of

Trackers had dragged her into the street and beaten her to death.

Instead of trying to stop them, our neighbors had cheered and watched.

"What happened to her will happen in every city, every day. If we take down a camp, the backlash against wolves will be worse than it was when the epidemic broke." Hank watched me, gauging my reaction.

Fear settled in my stomach like lead, and the urge to throw up rose in my throat. Suddenly, everything seemed too big, and I felt exactly like what my father probably saw: a naïve seventeen-year-old who was way out of her depth.

It took me a moment to find my voice. "Why, then? Why didn't you say anything before? If you're so sure that'll be the result, why do it?" He had wanted to get Eve and me out. We were out. What else did he have to gain?

Hank shrugged and finally took a swallow of beer. "I told you this morning: what she's doing is too dangerous to go unchecked."

I bit my lip. I knew I shouldn't push, I knew I should just be grateful he had changed his mind, but for some reason I needed to understand. "But it doesn't affect you. Not directly."

Hank's eyes narrowed and I knew he was starting to lose patience. He had always hated questions. "If what they did to your friend is considered a success, then it will affect me. And every other wolf in the country. Sooner or later, the LSRB will come after us. This way, we're taking the fight to them instead of just waiting."

"There's no reason to think the LSRB knows what Sinclair's doing," I reminded him. "She's been falsifying the admission records."

"Maybe," he conceded. "Or maybe they're just covering their tracks in case it ever comes out. Either way, after tonight, things are about to get a whole lot darker for any wolf and anyone suspected of having werewolf sympathies."

He shook his head and stood.

"You need to go home. You need to pick up your life, and forget about the wolves and Thornhill."

"I can't do that." I took a deep breath. "Serena and Kyle are my friends. I won't just turn my back on them. I'm coming with you tonight."

Hank's response was instant. "Absolutely not."

"You need regs in case anyone uses an HFD against your wolves. You know you do. You can shoot out the big ones on the poles, but you won't know who has a handheld one until it's too late."

"I've got the Tracker."

"And if something happens to him? If he gets shot or hurt or someone on your team decides trusting him is too big a risk?" Hank scowled and I knew I had him. "I know my way around the camp, I've been in the sanatorium, and HFDs don't affect me. You need me. Whether you like it or not."

I turned and pulled open the door.

"You don't have a future with that boy. You know that. Sooner or later, every wolf turns their back on their old life. If he's the reason you're insisting on throwing yourself into harm's way—"

"Maybe you turned your back on your life," I said, "but Kyle's not you. And he's not the only reason I'm going. Even if he was, you don't have the right to give me advice."

Before Hank could say anything else, I stepped out of the trailer and strode away.

23

I found Jason stretched out on a broken porch swing that someone had dragged under a cluster of trees. He stared up at the branches, too lost in thought to notice me. A low fire burned in a circle of stones a few feet away, casting him in an orange glow.

He cut his hair. My step faltered as the thought brought me up short.

Jason's blond locks—practically worshipped by every girl back home—had been trimmed to Thornhill regulation length.

On Kyle, the cut worked. It made him seem older and harder in a way that could make a girl's knees go weak. On Jason, the look had the opposite effect. He appeared younger. Less like a soldier and more like a refugee. Without thick waves to draw your eye away, his face gave up the illusion of perfection. His nose was just a little too big and his mouth was just a little too full. He was still handsome—no haircut could change that—but it was the kind of handsome that snuck up on you.

A twig snapped underfoot as I took a small step forward.

"Hey," Jason said, sitting up.

"Hey," I mumbled, oddly embarrassed to have been caught watching.

"I was going to wait for you back at the community center," he said, "but Eve offered to cut my hair. I figured it might make me less recognizable." He ran a hand over his head. "How bad is it?"

"Not that bad." I walked over to the swing and flopped down next to him. Not until I was sitting did I realize just how tired I was. Suddenly, my entire body felt heavy, like my limbs were encased in concrete, and it was all I could do not to close my eyes.

We both fell quiet, but the silence wasn't uncomfortable. Around us, members of Hank's pack moved through the trailer park—some preparing for the assault on Thornhill, others hanging out in small groups around campfires or looking for quiet places to catch a few hours of sleep. Twenty wolves had planned the breakout, but close to a hundred would be involved.

"I'm going with you," I said after a while. "Tonight."

He nodded as he reached down for a half-full bottle of beer that had been left next to the swing. It was the same brand Hank had been drinking.

Jason took a swig and then offered me the bottle. I shook my head and he finished it.

"You're not going to try and talk me out of it?" I asked.

"Would there be any point?" He tossed the bottle lightly onto the grass.

"No," I said—or tried to say. As soon as I opened my mouth, the word turned into a yawn.

"You're exhausted." Jason reached out and ran his knuckles—still raw from punching the glass divider in the Town Car—against my cheek. The gesture was strangely gentle and entirely unexpected.

A blush started in the center of my body and quickly worked its way up to my face as I remembered the kiss in the back of the car. I tried not to think too long or too hard about the taste of his lips or the way his body had covered mine.

"Jason . . ." I swallowed. "About what happened this morning. After the crash."

He shook his head. "Just leave it."

"But . . ."

He dropped his hand and gave me a small, forced grin. "If we survive the night, then you can tell me it was a mistake, deal?"

The words were similar to something I had said to Kyle back in the sanatorium, and the memory made things twist inside my chest. "Okay."

"We've got a few hours," said Jason, trying to cover the awkwardness of the moment. "You should try and get some sleep."

It was tempting—so tempting—but I was too scared to let my guard down. "Hank really didn't want me going. I don't want to give him a chance to leave me behind."

"I'll stay up and wake you when things start to happen. I managed to get a couple of hours of sleep when they had me locked in the infirmary."

Still, I hesitated.

"You can't run on willpower and snark indefinitely." Jason shifted farther down the bench, making a little more room. "I promise I'll wake you up."

"Even after you went to all that trouble to get me out of the camp?"

"Even after."

I didn't think I'd be able to sleep, but I slid down and curled up on the end of the swing. If I just closed my eyes for a while, maybe it would take the edge off the horrible feeling of heaviness.

After a few minutes, Jason gently tugged my legs onto his lap. "Do you think we're doing the right thing?"

I opened my eyes. A lump rose in my throat and I had to swallow past it before I could speak. "I thought you wanted to help Kyle and Serena. And Dex is only in the sanatorium because we got him involved."

"I do—it's just . . ." Jason drummed his fingers on my shin as he tried to find the right words. "There's a difference between breaking out three wolves we know and a few hundred we don't. What if some of them hurt people after they get out?"

"Pick three hundred regs at random and not all of them are going to be gems," I said.

"It's not exactly random if they're in prison."

"You can't compare a camp and a prison." I shivered and huddled in my sweatshirt. "Most of the people in Thornhill aren't there because they committed some sort of crime—unless you count not reporting their infection. They were caught in raids. They were in the wrong place at the wrong time."

"Like Kyle and Serena," he said grudgingly as he moved his hand away from my leg.

"Exactly."

Silence stretched between us and this time it was uncomfortable. The fire was almost out, but neither of us got up to do anything about it.

"Jason?"

"Yeah?"

"Why are you so worried about the regs at Thornhill? You were right—if the wolves don't try to limit causalities, the LSRB and the Trackers will use it against them—but that wasn't the only reason you said what you did, was it? You said something else back at the camp, once. Something about how working at Thornhill didn't necessarily make people bad."

He let out a deep breath. "Some of them are bad—I'd like to kill the ones who hurt Serena—but I think a lot of them have never stopped to wonder whether or not the system they're part of is wrong."

"They remind you of yourself," I said slowly. The tattoo on his neck was just visible in the dying firelight.

Jason nodded.

Neither of us spoke for a long while. Eventually, my eyes

started to flutter closed again.

"Jason?" His name came out a near-unintelligible mumble as I fumbled weakly for his hand.

"Yeah?"

"Thank you."

"For what?"

I tried to say "for choosing us," but the tide carried me away.

A layer of decaying leaves covered the water in the fountain.

"Gross," muttered Amy, wrinkling her nose as she stepped up onto the ledge encircling the basin. Her gray high-tops slapped the concrete as she walked around the water.

It was dark—the sky completely devoid of moon and stars—and the only light came from the windows of the sanatorium. "This isn't right." I knew this fountain: it was the one from Riverside Square. It should be back in Hemlock, not in the middle of Thornhill.

Amy completed the circle and hopped down. Her shirt—one of Jason's Italian dress shirts—flapped in the breeze.

"You're always so stuck on landmarks and geography. Places are more than just GPS coordinates. Sometimes, they overlap."

She sat on the edge of the fountain. "Like you. You take pieces of Hemlock with you wherever you go, so parts of it exist even inside a place as bad as this."

"Very deep," I said.

"I have a lot of free time on my hands. It leads to moments

of self-reflection and philosophy. And memory." She leaned back and stared up at the empty sky. "I finally remembered the story. The one my grandpa told us."

"Okay. . . ."

"Once upon a time—"

"That's for fairy tales, not ghost stories," I pointed out as I sat next to her.

She rolled her eyes. "Fine. *Once* there was a woman who owned a doll shop. She was obsessed with making a doll so lifelike that people would forget it was just fabric and porcelain."

"Seems like a lame obsession."

"Shut it."

"Sorry. It's a brilliant obsession. Please continue."

Amy mock-glared. "One day, a small girl was run over by a horse and carriage just outside the shop. The doll maker ran out to help, but the girl was dead by the time she reached her. As the woman watched, a puff of air the color of sunset passed through the girl's lips—the child's soul carried on her last breath.

"The doll maker began visiting hospitals and gutters, catching the last breaths of dying children in glass bottles and then sewing those bottles into dolls."

"Let me guess," I said, "the dolls looked more lifelike." Now that Amy was telling it, I did sort of remember listening to the story while toasting marshmallows in her grandfather's fireplace.

She nodded. "But no one would buy them because when they looked into the glass eyes, they swore they heard the echo of screams." She stretched. "Trapped in a bottle and sewn inside a doll for all eternity? Who wouldn't be scream-ing?"

I shivered.

"You do know why I'm really here, don't you?"

I shook my head. I didn't. Not anymore.

Amy looked at me sadly, then glanced over her shoulder at the fountain. Something churned the leaves and gave off a sharp, metallic scent. With horror, I realized the liquid in the basin was blood.

I scrambled to my feet, but Amy stayed sitting as though nothing were wrong.

She dipped her finger in the fountain and it came back coated in red. "Things are about to get so interesting."

24

A THIRTY-FOOT-TALL ELECTRIC FENCE WAS INTIMIDAT-
ing no matter which side you were on. After all, a fence
couldn't distinguish between someone trying to break in and
someone trying to break out, and it wouldn't discriminate
between reg and wolf. It was an equal-opportunity killer;
everyone who had gathered in the narrow space between
it and the concrete wall that would eventually encircle the
camp was at risk.

It was a risk I was all too willing to take.

I stared at the handful of lights that were visible in the
distance. It was impossible to know whether they came from
the dorms or the sanatorium, but the sight was a hook in
my chest. Anything could have happened to Kyle and Serena
after Jason and I had left the camp. Anything could be happening to them right now.

I crossed my arms and shivered.

The gesture didn't slip past Hank, though he mistook
the cause. "It's not too late to go back to the park. One of
the wolves can take you."

I was struck, again, by how little my father knew me. I was afraid—of course I was afraid—but that wasn't going to stop me. "I already told you: I'm staying. Besides, you can't afford to be a man down."

The recon team consisted of ten werewolves—including him and Eve. There wasn't a single one to spare.

For a second, I was certain Hank was going to argue, but he let it drop and walked away.

A hand skimmed my temple and I jumped.

"Your hair was coming loose," said Jason as he tucked a lock underneath my cap.

He was wearing an outfit identical to mine in every way but size. Everyone was dressed in the same all-black ensemble: black cap, black long-sleeved shirt, black jeans, and black boots. We looked like a gang of cat burglars. Or mimes.

"Thanks," I mumbled, trying to ignore the blush that rose to my face. I had promised Jason we wouldn't talk about the kiss, but I could still feel it between us. I knew I didn't have anything to feel guilty about—we had both been positive we were going to die—but this close to the sanatorium, this close to Kyle, it seemed like a betrayal.

"Outer patrol!" hissed a female voice. "Hit the dirt!"

Along with the wolves, Jason and I dropped to the ground and crouched behind the wall. A moment later, I heard the low roar of an engine. A spotlight swept the fence to the left and right of our hiding place. I held my breath, but the guards didn't bother getting out to check behind the concrete barrier.

The sound of the engine faded, and people slowly got to their feet.

"All right," snapped Hank. "They're running extra patrols. We've got thirty minutes at the most. Let's get this done."

Construction crews working on the wall had erected scaffolding on the outward-facing side. Hank leaped onto the first platform and began climbing. He scaled the rigging easily, his movements infused with a wolflike grace he hadn't possessed a few years ago. Two of his men followed in his wake.

Eve wandered over to Jason and me. Lines creased her brow as she stared up at the top of the wall. "This is insane."

"It was your idea," I pointed out, trying to ignore the way my stomach churned.

"It didn't seem so crazy when we were just talking about it."

"A jump over a razor wire–topped electric fence from forty feet in the air without a safety net below," said Jason, "what could possibly go wrong?"

In unison, Eve and I told him to shut up.

One of the wolves handed Hank a backpack—black like our outfits. He hurled it over the fence. It cleared the top wires easily and landed with a soft thud several feet inside the camp. I tried to tell myself it was a good sign as Hank hurled a second bag over, but there was a world of difference between a pack and a man.

"At least the wall is higher than the fence," said Eve. "Ten feet, easily. That's a huge advantage."

I didn't see how ten feet was a huge anything—especially not when there was almost twice that much space between the wall and the fence—but I didn't say so. Pointing out the obvious wouldn't be good for anybody's nerves.

There were only two ways into Thornhill: through the gate or over the fence. We could have waited a few days and hijacked a delivery, but no one wanted to risk leaving the wolves in the detention block that long. By now, Sinclair would know that the hit she had put out on Jason and me had failed and there was no telling what she might do to Kyle, Serena, and Dex as payback.

Unfortunately—short of driving a tank through it—there was no way to disable the fence from outside the camp.

The zip line had been Eve's idea. She was the one who had remembered the ancient water tower near the fence. If a wolf could survive the drop to the ground, they could run a line to the tower from the wall. Then the rest of us could propel across.

"I still don't understand why your father is doing it," said Jason as we watched Hank gauge the distance he'd have to clear to make it over. "Shouldn't they have picked someone who's not completely indispensable?"

"You don't get to be the head of a werewolf pack without being insanely tough," said Eve. "There are two, maybe three wolves who are stronger than Curtis, but not by much and they don't heal nearly as fast. We need someone who can recover quickly."

"And you're sure he'll be able to? Recover quickly?" I didn't ask what would happen if he hit the fence. No werewolf, no matter how tough, would survive that.

Eve pressed her mouth into a thin, hard line and didn't answer.

She has no idea.

I peered up at the top of the wall, trying to ignore the sudden lump in my throat. An old, familiar feeling settled over me as I watched Hank back to the very edge of the concrete. It was the same knot of uncertainty and fear I used to get when he left on jobs.

Hank shook the tension out of his arms and said something to the other wolves on the wall. Then, without warning, he ran the three steps to the edge and launched himself out into space.

For a horrible second, I thought he wasn't going to make it, but then he twisted in midair and cleared the razor wire with just inches to spare.

Relief sparked in my chest. Before it could take hold, Hank plummeted to the ground like a bag of bricks.

He hit the earth with a horrible thud. Clouds of dust billowed around him, and when the air cleared, he wasn't moving. He lay half-sprawled on his back, arms and legs twisted at unnatural angles.

"Get up. *Get up.*" Eve's voice was low and urgent, half command, half plea. She approached the fence. "C'mon, Curtis. Get up."

He didn't move.

I reached for Jason's hand and squeezed, squeezed so tightly that I was probably hurting him.

Kyle had once fallen from a second-floor window, but

those had been residential stories. And as badly hurt as he'd been, he hadn't looked nearly as broken.

The minutes dragged on. Eventually, Jason detangled his hand from mine. "Eve . . ."

"He'll be all right," she said. "Just give him time."

But her voice shook with uncertainty, and around us, the other wolves had begun exchanging nervous whispers.

Years ago, I had convinced myself that I was fine with never seeing Hank again, but there was a difference between a world in which Hank chose not to be part of my life and a world in which he simply didn't exist. The first I could handle, the second I wasn't ready for.

I stared at Hank, willing him to get up. I stared so long and so hard that when his arm twitched, I was sure I had imagined it.

But Eve had seen it, too. "Curtis? Can you hear me?"

In response, my father's body tore itself apart. Muscles shifted and the few bones that hadn't shattered on impact snapped with the sound of a dozen cracking whips. When it was over, a massive wolf with fur the color of ash and snow rose to its feet.

The wolf—I still had trouble thinking of it as "Hank"— tossed its head and took a few experimental steps before breaking into a slow run.

Eve stumbled back a half step in relief. She shook her head, grinned, and then glanced up at the two wolves on the wall. "You're good to go!"

As they began assembling and positioning equipment, the gray wolf circled back and sniffed one of the packs. It lifted its head and the air around it seemed to shimmer before fur flowed into skin and my father was left kneeling on the ground, his back to the fence.

I quickly looked away as he pulled clothes from the backpack and dressed.

"It's safe to look," said Jason drily, a moment later.

I turned as Hank grabbed both bags. He jogged to the water tower, scaled the ladder on the side, and then tied a white cloth around a rung near the top. I wasn't normally scared of heights, but seeing him climb so high on the rickety structure made my stomach flip.

Jason glanced at his watch. "We're cutting it too close."

"They're going as fast as they can." I glanced back at the wall. The wolves had assembled a tripod. On it was a contraption that looked like the misbegotten offspring of a telescope and a fire extinguisher.

They waited until Hank climbed down to the ground and then adjusted their aim. With a small blast, a grappling hook shot through the air and sailed over the fence. It hit the water tower with a metallic clang and snagged the rung Hank had marked with the cloth.

Everyone seemed to collectively hold their breath.

The water tower was far from the center of camp, but if a guard had heard and decided to investigate, everything we had planned would fall apart.

The night stayed quiet.

Gradually, in small increments, the muscles in my chest unclenched.

Hank scaled the tower again. After pulling the cord taut,

he slipped the grappling hook free and then secured the line using a series of intricate knots. When finished, he raised a hand to signal that everything was ready.

Eve arranged the team in order of importance. Jason and I ranked low; there were only two wolves behind us. The men on the wall would stay and protect the line on this side of the fence. If things went wrong, it might be our only way back out.

Eve started up the scaffold. As the smallest and lightest, she had the dubious honor of being the group's guinea pig.

"Be careful," I called up to her.

When she reached the top, she paused and pulled on a pair of heavy black gloves.

There was no harness or safety gear: Eve simply lowered herself to the edge of the wall and grabbed the rope with her gloved hands. She crossed her ankles over the line and began shimmying across. She moved impossibly fast, using the strength and speed that came with lupine syndrome.

I bit my lip as she neared the fence. There were just a few feet between her back and the top of the razor wire.

Eve made it over, but she wasn't in the clear, yet. The wall was seven yards from the fence; the water tower had to be at least twice that.

After another few moments, she reached the tower. In an impossibly graceful move, she swung off the rope and onto the ladder. She climbed partway down, jumped the last eight feet to the ground, and then held up her arms in a Rocky pose.

The other wolves crossed the line just as quickly. There

was a tense moment when one man looked down and almost lost his grip as he was passing over the fence, but he made it.

Then it was Jason's turn.

He shot me a cocky grin as he pulled on his gloves. "See you on the other side." He ascended the scaffold so quickly and lithely that it was almost possible to mistake him for one of the werewolves.

I glanced at the line and frowned. Was it my imagination or was the rope hanging a little bit lower? Before I could ask the woman behind me, Jason started across. All that time he spent working out definitely had benefits: He wasn't quite as quick as the wolves, but most regs would never have been able to keep up with him—not unless they were professional athletes or members of Cirque du Soleil.

Even so, I didn't blink until he reached the other side.

My turn.

I climbed the scaffold, slipping on my gloves as I went.

"It's easy," said one of the wolves with a small, slightly flirtatious smile as I reached the top. "Just hold on and don't look down."

"Right," I bluffed. "Piece of cake." I sat on the edge of the wall and grabbed the rope. It didn't look like it was hanging low at all now. *Just my imagination*, I told myself as I hooked my ankles over and gracelessly half squirmed, half flopped off the concrete.

The others had made it look easy. It wasn't. Within minutes, my arms were shaking and my legs were cramping.

I kept pushing myself. I could see the fence out of the corner of my eye. If I could reach it, I would be a third of the way across. *Don't think about how far it is to the tower,* I told myself. *Just concentrate on getting to the fence. Focus on that first third.*

Almost there . . .

My muscles were on fire.

One hand over the other. That's it. . . .

I made it past the fence and felt a ridiculous swell of pride that I hadn't lost my grip and barbecued myself.

See? Not so bad.

The rope suddenly shook beneath me and dropped an inch.

I yelped and stopped moving.

"Mac!" Jason yelled my name as the line dropped again.

The bottom fell out of my stomach as I held on for dear life.

"Mac, you have to keep going! You have to get to the water tower. Now!"

Jason's voice came from almost directly below me. I turned my head.

I had never seen him look so scared—not even in the car when it seemed certain we were both about to be killed. "The ladder is coming free—the tower's too old. There's no way to hold it. When the line goes down, it'll hit the fence. You can't be holding it when that happens."

There was wire in the line: If I was still holding it when it fell—*Oh, God.* I'd complete the circuit. Even if I survived the fall, I'd be fried.

I started moving again. This time, my arms shook from fear as much as strain, but adrenaline masked the pain.

"You're doing fine, Mackenzie." Hank's voice came from somewhere below, but I didn't slow to look. "Just a little farther."

The rope dropped another five inches—all at once—and a small scream escaped my throat.

"It's all right," said my father. "Just keep moving." There was a note in his voice I had never heard before. It took me a second to realize it was fear.

I tried to move faster, but adrenaline could only do so much, and because the rope had dipped, I was now forcing myself up an incline.

As I neared the water tower, I could hear the groan of metal. It sounded like the ladder was peeling away bolt by bolt. I didn't dare look to see how far I had left to go.

Suddenly, strong arms grabbed me and pulled me off the rope. I expected Jason and was dumbstruck as I started into my father's blue eyes.

"You okay?"

I managed a nod as we raced down the ladder.

Jason swept me into a hug as soon as my shoes touched the ground. I let him hold me for a few seconds and then gently pushed him away. "I'm okay, Jason, I'm fine." I was superconscious of the group of ultratough werewolves standing a few feet away, and I didn't want Hank to think that bringing me had been a mistake, that I'd fall apart every time there was trouble.

"The hug was to reassure myself, actually," said Jason.

I was about to retort when Eve shouted to get back. Grabbing Jason's hand, I ran from the tower.

With the tortured sound of twisting metal, the ladder gave way and crashed to the ground where we had just been standing.

I glanced at the fence. Sparks lit the night where the cable had become tangled in the wire.

Now there was no way out except through the main gate.

Eve turned to Hank. "Do you think they'll send someone to check?"

He nodded. "Not right away—they'll probably assume an animal got caught—but eventually." He drew two of the wolves aside. "Stay here and watch the fence. If anyone shows up, keep them from contacting the rest of the camp and raising the alarm."

"Without killing them," added Jason.

Hank shot him the kind of look that said he might be tempted to do some killing of his own. "Without killing them—*if it can be helped.*"

Jason frowned but thankfully didn't push. The last thing we needed was for my father to lose his temper and leave us at the fence with a couple of werewolf babysitters.

Eve retrieved one of the black bags. "You heard him," she said as she unzipped the top flap and began handing out guns and magazines. "Bullets are a last resort. Don't shoot unless you have to or unless someone has an HFD."

Jason reached for a gun and she hesitated. She glanced at Hank. Only after he nodded did she hand one over.

"Smith and Wesson. Forty caliber." Jason turned the gun over in his hands. "Don't take this the wrong way, but I figured werewolves would pack something bigger."

"Not when we're hunting regs," said one of the other wolves.

Maybe it was my imagination, but Jason seemed to pale slightly. Without further comment, he loaded the magazine Eve handed him and then tucked the gun into the back of his waistband.

"Here," she said, passing him the toolkit and device for testing the HFDs. "I went back to the greenhouse and snagged these before I left last night."

She turned to me. "Gun?"

I shook my head. I knew how to shoot—I couldn't count the number of times Jason had dragged me to the shooting range to act as a buffer between him and his father—but I was scared of what I might do if I was let loose in Thornhill with a gun—especially if Sinclair had hurt Kyle and Dex or done anything else to Serena.

I glanced in the direction of the sanatorium and pressed my nails into my palm, pressed them so hard I broke the skin.

No, me loose in Thornhill with a gun would not be a good idea.

To my surprise, Eve didn't take one, either. "First thing we have to do is hit the laundry building," she said as she tossed the bag to one of the wolves staying behind. "We're not going to blend in dressed like this."

Hank shouldered the other backpack and began giving orders. I tried to pay attention, but the lights from the camp kept pulling my gaze. *Please be all right,* I prayed. *We're coming. Just hang on a little while longer.*

I tuned back in just as Hank finished. It didn't matter: I already knew my part in the plan.

Jason and I fell into step behind the wolves as we headed toward the center of camp. To my surprise, Hank hung back.

"That charm still on your bracelet?" he asked, shooting a glance at my wrist.

I nodded and pushed up my sleeve. "Yeah."

"Good. As long as you keep it on, I'll know where you are."

"I . . . umm . . . okay . . ." It didn't seem like the kind of statement that should require a "thank-you," but I felt like I had to say something. Maybe other daughters could take that sort of quasi-caring sentiment for granted—maybe Eve could take it for granted—but I wasn't used to it and I wasn't sure how to respond.

Hank seemed just as uncomfortable. He nodded once, and then returned to his place at the front of the group.

We left the fields and walked past the woods, then came to a stop as the camp loomed before us.

I took a deep breath and went to stand beside Eve.

We shared a brief glance—a second of perfect under-standing—and then both looked ahead.

The last time we had entered Thornhill, we had been scared, helpless.

This time, we were coming to tear it down.

25

"Something's not right." I stopped in the shadows next to a dormitory. "It's too quiet."

Jason glanced back at me. He had donned an olive uniform—the male equivalent of the outfits Eve and I had slipped into—and for all intents and purposes, he looked just like a Thornhill werewolf. "It's after curfew," he said, as if that explained everything.

It didn't.

"There should still be something. Voices coming from open windows. Toilets flushing. Guards on patrol. There should still be some noise."

But around us, the camp was as silent as a tomb.

Eve tilted her head to the side and frowned. "Mac's right. It's too quiet."

"We're wasting time." The wolf Hank had sent with us—a man with a gray handlebar mustache and the faint trace of an unidentifiable accent—eased around us. "Curtis gave us a job and we have to get it done."

We had split into two groups. The first—led by Hank—had headed for the sanatorium to take down Thornhill's communications system. That would keep anyone from contacting the LSRB and make it harder for the guards inside the camp to coordinate a response once they realized they were under attack. After the communications system was down, they would blow the gates, providing a way in for the dozens of wolves who were lying in wait outside.

Once they accomplished those two things, Hank's team would hit the detention block.

I hated that Serena, Kyle, and Dex came third, but I understood the reasoning: Without taking care of the communications system and the gates, we'd never be able to get them out of the camp. There was no way any of us would get out.

I had wanted to go with them, but I had convinced Hank he needed me to help combat the HFDs and he was holding me to that. The other team—my team—had been tasked with neutralizing the handheld versions of the device.

The HFDs were signed in and out at the beginning and end of each counselor's shift. Any not in use—including extras in the event they were needed by guards—were stored in the vault, a room in the basement of the staff quarters, which also housed the traditional weapons like Tasers and guns.

Most of the counselors would be off duty by this time of night, so most of the HFDs should be signed in. All we had to do was get into the staff quarters without anyone raising the alarm, get down to the vault, destroy every HFD we could find, get back out without getting shot, and then rejoin Hank's group.

Easy.

No problem at all.

Definitely not any sort of suicide mission.

The male wolf paused at the corner of the dorm. "Well?" he asked, shooting Eve an impatient look before rounding the building and disappearing from sight.

Eve hesitated, then shrugged. "He's right. No matter what's going on, the others are counting on us to hit the vault." She headed after him.

I glanced at Jason. "We haven't so much as seen a guard. Don't you think that's a little strange?"

He scanned the area around the dorm and frowned. He didn't tell me I was wrong. "C'mon," he said, after a moment. "If something is going on, we should stick close to the wolves."

Knowing he was probably right and unsure what else we could do, I followed him around the building.

Eve and the other wolf had already darted over an expanse of grass and were waiting in the shadowy gulf between two classrooms.

No sooner had Jason and I taken a step toward them than a voice split the night. "Stay where you are!"

I whirled. Two guards were racing toward us, their Tasers drawn.

They slowed to a walk when they were still a few feet away. One pulled a radio from his belt. "We've got a couple more stragglers near the dorms."

Wherever Hank's team was, it was safe to say they hadn't taken out the communications system yet.

I glanced over at the classrooms. Eve and the other wolf had disappeared. I couldn't blame them. There wasn't anything they could do. The guards had already radioed in. Knocking them out and running would just alert the rest of the camp to the fact that something was going on.

Next to me, Jason kept his head down and his eyes on the ground, trying to give the guards as little opportunity to recognize him as possible.

"Auditorium," snapped the one with the radio. "Now."

I saw Jason's fingers twitch out of the corner of my eye. I held my breath, praying he wouldn't do something stupid like go for the gun at his back.

I shouldn't have worried.

Jason was reckless, but smart. The guards hadn't hurt or threatened us. He left the gun where it was and started walking.

Stomach in knots, I fell into step next to him. First the trouble at the fence and now this—I fought back the thought that our plan had been cursed from the start.

The guards walked behind us. Neither holstered their Taser.

Why the auditorium? I wanted to ask, but I didn't want to say or do anything that would make the guards suspicious.

I tugged my sleeves down as far as they would go, making sure my wrists were completely covered. The last thing I needed was for either guard to realize I wasn't wearing a wrist cuff.

Amy's bracelet, though hidden, was a reassuring weight. *As long as you keep it on, I'll know where you are.* Hank's words echoed back to me.

The irony of counting on my father after warning Eve not to do the same was not lost on me.

We rounded a bend in the path and the auditorium came into view.

I stopped so suddenly that Jason's shoulder collided with mine.

I barely noticed. I was too busy trying to make sense of the scene in front of us.

Large spotlights blazed on each corner of the roof; they flooded the immediate area with light, obliterating any shadows someone might use to hide—but that wasn't the bad part.

A circle of guards—what looked like almost every guard in Thornhill—surrounded the auditorium like a living net. They faced the building, their backs to the camp and their weapons drawn. A few held Tasers but most held guns.

All of the air rushed out of my lungs with a single thought: *Sinclair knows we're here.*

I didn't know how—maybe someone had gone to investigate the fence and slipped past Hank's wolves—but why else would she gather every guard in one place?

One of the men behind us cleared his throat as a guard with a shaved head and a ridiculously thick neck strode up the path. "These are the two we found near the dorms."

The bald guard turned his gaze on us. My heart thudded in my chest as I waited for him to realize we were part of the group who had infiltrated the camp. Any second, he would give the order for us to be dragged to the detention block in shackles.

"Dorms?"

"Seven and four," I said, struggling to keep my voice blank.

He glanced at the men behind us. "We've got reports of a few more kids hiding in that old greenhouse. A couple of guards are already on their way, but they could probably use some help." He shifted his focus back to Jason and me. "You two, inside."

He didn't know who we were. Something inside my chest unclenched a fraction of an inch. Even if they knew a group had breached the fence, they didn't know we were part of it.

Jason tugged on my hand, urging me forward.

There were two guards covering the entrance to the auditorium. One stepped aside as we approached while the other pulled open the door.

. I slipped my hand out of Jason's: If there was trouble, I wanted him to have both hands free for the gun.

"Out of the frying pan," I muttered.

"And straight into hell," he finished.

The smell of sweat and an almost claustrophobic sense of mass hit me as I crossed the threshold. The number of wolves crammed inside the auditorium far exceeded the benches. Some sat in the aisles, others crouched between rows.

I glanced to my left and right. There were five guards on either side of the door. Unlike the ones outside, their weapons were still holstered—at least for now. Maybe they were worried about tipping a room full of anxious wolves from fear to panic.

And the wolves were frightened. It showed in the eyes of the ones who watched the guards and in the small noises some of them made as they cried. It was in the way most of them held themselves too still—as though they expected someone to strike or shoot them at any moment.

They're too scared to do anything; they're the perfect hostages. The thought was ice water dripping down my spine. What if Sinclair had been told about the planned breakout? Maybe there was a mole in Hank's pack who had tipped her off. Maybe she had gathered the wolves as collateral.

My eyes slid to the front of the room. The same black-and-white posters covered the wall—CONTROL OVER ANGER, CONSTRAINT IS FREEDOM, YOUR DISEASE IS NOT A WEAPON—but the podium and folding chairs had been replaced by a small platform that looked as though it had been hastily nailed together. On it stood two program coordinators and the warden, their backs to the assembly as they discussed something in low tones.

Jason clamped his hand around my arm. "Don't do anything," he hissed as he pulled me toward the nearest aisle.

"Why?" I asked as I sank to the floor next to him. "What would I do?" As much as I wanted to strangle Sinclair, it wasn't like I was going to rush the stage. Not with ten guards in the room and more waiting outside.

Jason didn't answer and he didn't relax his hold on my arm; if anything, he tightened his grip.

Two women joined the group onstage. One was Langley,

the other was the woman who had injected Serena with some unknown drug or poison in the videos. She adjusted her glasses and gave the crowd of wolves a nervous glance.

An echo of Serena's voice—shaking as she begged them to stop—filled my head. I thought of the gun hidden at Jason's back as a wave of anger swelled in my chest, so thick and black that I practically choked on it.

Jason swore under his breath as the group moved to the edge of the dais. Suddenly, I knew why he was gripping my arm, what he must have glimpsed when we first entered the auditorium. It wasn't Sinclair or even the women who had tortured Serena.

I started to rise, and Jason shifted his hand to my shoulder, forcing me back down while whispering a frantic stream of comfort and caution in my ear.

"You can't help him. If you draw attention to us, it'll all be over. It's okay. They'll be okay."

I shook my head and bit the inside of my cheek—bit it so hard I tasted copper—to stop the flood of sounds threatening to punch a hole through my chest.

Kneeling on the platform were Kyle and Dex. Thick manacles encircled their wrists and were connected by chains that were bolted to the stage. Kyle's eyes were locked on Sinclair, but Dex stared at the floor in front of the dais as though he didn't have the strength to raise his head. Someone had clubbed Dex's temple at some point; blood had run down his face and etched each of his scars in red.

Kyle's face was unmarked, but his shirt clung to him, the fabric darkened by stains. I tried to convince myself the stains were sweat—and some probably were—but most of the patches were too dark and had left the fabric too stiff to be anything other than blood.

How many hours? My stomach flipped and tears filled my eyes. Kyle and Dex were werewolves: as long as their captors paused to let them heal, their bodies would always be able to take more. Jason and I had been gone for nearly an entire day. Sinclair or Langley or the guards could have tortured them the entire time.

"Kyle . . ." The whisper was so low that it was barely more than my lips forming the shape of his name, but his body still tensed.

His dark eyes swept the crowd and then filled with shock and fear as they found mine. My pulse had been racing from the moment the guards had spotted Jason and me; now it climbed so high I felt like I was having a heart attack. For a moment, I worried surprise and confusion would make Kyle say or do something to give us away, but he buried his emotions as his gaze slid to Jason. The heavy chain tethering him to the dais had a slight amount of give and he wrapped the excess around his hand—almost like a makeshift knuckle ring.

Jason was still gripping my shoulder. He glanced from Kyle to me and then back. When he was certain that I wasn't going to do anything crazy, he dropped his hand and pulled slightly away.

"What are we going to do?"

He didn't answer.

Think. I had to think. But before I could come up with the slightest idea, Sinclair strode back across the stage.

Even at a distance, her blue eyes were too bright and the wrinkles in her suit seemed permanent. She looked like someone who had substituted Red Bull for sleep. But her voice, when she spoke, didn't sound tired. It was sharp and focused and filled with threats.

"I'll give you one more chance. Last night, three wolves were spotted outside after curfew. They led dozens of guards on an extensive chase and wasted *hours* of resources. Two of those wolves are behind me. I want to know where to find the third. Eve. Dorm Seven. ID one-three-four-eight. She wasn't in her bed this morning. She didn't report for class or her work detail. She is somewhere in this camp, and someone in this room had to have seen something."

I glanced at Jason and saw the same confusion on his face that must have shown on mine. This was all about *Eve*? The wolves weren't being held as some sort of bargaining chip against Hank and the pack?

That's why the guards are facing the building, I realized. If Sinclair knew an attack was coming—if she knew the camp had been infiltrated—the guards would be facing out, not in.

But why Eve? Why would the warden drag every wolf here over one girl?

Sinclair waited.

No one moved. No one spoke.

"Do you honestly expect me to believe none of you saw a thing? No one so much as noticed her slip out after curfew?"

Again, silence.

Sinclair's gaze swept over us—blue fire hot enough to scorch. I slouched down, praying to go unnoticed. After a moment, when no one came forward, she slipped an HFD from her pocket and pressed the trigger. Most of the wolves collapsed, including Kyle.

Jason and I quickly slumped to the ground as two of the guards broke away from the back of the room and began walking the edge of the crowd.

Aside from Dex, only one girl was unaffected. I couldn't see her, but I could hear her. Mystified and frightened, she didn't have the sense to play dead.

There were confused murmurs from most of the guards as they realized neither the girl nor Dex had gone down, but the two men sweeping the room didn't seem surprised at all. I listened, helpless to intervene, as they tased the girl, then dumped her with the guards outside.

The woman with the glasses crossed the stage to speak to Sinclair. "This is completely unnecessary. A total over-reaction."

"Don't tell me you've started to feel sorry for them." I watched from under my lashes as a look of disgust crossed Sinclair's face. "I've seen how much you enjoy your work."

"Don't be ridiculous." The woman pulled off her glasses and wiped them on the corner of her sweater. "They're just too valuable to play with—especially in this manner. If my superiors knew . . ."

Sinclair shook her head and slammed a door on the discussion. "I don't answer to your superiors, and I am not playing games." She stared levelly at the woman until she retreated to the side of the stage.

A few feet away, a boy turned his head slightly, trying to track the woman's movement. Jason and I weren't the only ones faking.

The warden slid her thumb off the trigger of the HFD.

Gradually, the other wolves came to. I sat up and watched Kyle shake his head and raise himself back to his knees. He wrapped the slack of the chain around his hand again. This time, there seemed to be more of it. I squinted at the dais as he leaned to the side in what looked like an innocent stretch. The bolt holding the chain to the stage seemed to lift slightly. He was breaking free in small increments that would go unnoticed until it was too late.

Frightened whispers filled the air, growing in intensity and pitch as the wolves realized one of their own—the girl—had just gone missing.

Sinclair held up the remote. "Until someone comes forward with information, this HFD will go off every five minutes."

It was complete overkill. I could understand why she had sent men after Jason and me, but she had no reason to think Eve had made it out of the camp; she had no reason to think Eve was in any kind of position to hurt her.

"Thornhill is a *choice*." A tired, frustrated note crept into the warden's voice. "If any of you would prefer to be elsewhere, I will *happily* put you on a truck to Van Horne and you can find out firsthand just how horrible a camp can be."

Find out.

It suddenly clicked. Eve hadn't been caught with us, but

that didn't guarantee that she hadn't seen or heard something about Serena or the detention block.

Thornhill worked because the things that didn't make sense or were too frightening to think about stayed under the surface. People whispered about the disappearances, but no one talked about them openly. If the inmates started questioning too much, cracks would form.

Sinclair would do anything to stop that from happening. She would do anything to protect her work. And right now, *anything* meant finding Eve before she could spill any of the camp's secrets—even if that entailed punishing an entire auditorium full of teens.

The brightness in the warden's eyes wasn't exhaustion: it was fanaticism. She was absolutely convinced that what she was doing at Thornhill was noble and right and worthy of protection.

Hank believed they were just looking for a way to make wolves easier to manage and control, that none of what was happening here was about finding a true cure. Looking at the way Sinclair's blue eyes gleamed, I wasn't so sure he was right. My gaze fell on the garnet ring she wore and I thought of the sister she had told me about. Everything Sinclair had done was horrible and twisted, but what if it hadn't started out that way?

I swallowed and leaned into Jason. "How long until Hank hits the gates?"

Surreptitiously, he pulled back the cuff of his sleeve and checked his watch. "Twenty minutes. At most."

Twenty minutes.

Even if Sinclair hadn't taken the wolves as hostages, she'd be a fool not to use them once she realized the camp was under attack. We had to come up with a plan before that happened.

My eyes locked on Kyle. "We'll find a way to get you out," I whispered. "I promise."

Just as the last syllable left my lips, an explosion ripped through the camp.

26

THE WINDOWS RATTLED AND THE WALLS SHOOK. PEOPLE
surged to their feet and bodies churned around us like water.
Jason and I were ripped apart and pulled to opposite sides of
the room. I fought against the sea of wolves and craned my
neck, desperate to get a glimpse of the platform.

Sinclair was shouting at the guards, but her voice was
lost under the roar of the crowd. Behind her, Kyle strained
against his restraints. The muscles in his shoulders and
arms writhed under the skin. I shouted his name, terrified
he would lose control and give the guards a reason to shoot
him.

He gave a final tug and the chain snapped. The end of it
whipped through the air and forced Sinclair to jump back.
In her haste not to get hit, she lost her grip on her HFD. The
small device went flying and landed harmlessly among the
wolves.

Kyle scanned the mob—checking to make sure Jason and
I were all right—before crouching next to Dex and working
to free him.

Langley turned toward them, HFD in hand. A chunk of the wall next to her exploded and she dropped the device.

My eyes found Jason.

He stood in the middle of the crowd, gun drawn, eyes darting between the two program coordinators and the woman with the glasses in case any of them went for their HFDs. A few people around him dove down and covered their heads, but most of the wolves were so panicked that they didn't realize where the shots had come from.

"Trackers." The word tore through the auditorium and grew in strength until it drowned out everything else. It made no sense—why would Trackers attack a camp?—but the wolves had lived under the threat of raids and attacks so long that it was the first conclusion they rushed to when things started exploding.

Faint gunshots could be heard outside, lending credence to the cries.

"It's the Eumon pack! It's not the Trackers! It's a rescue!" I couldn't make myself heard over the chaos.

The guards at the back of the hall didn't know what to do. One chained the doors shut while a few tried to make their way to the dais where Kyle and Dex had cornered Sinclair and the other four staff members.

One guard panicked and fired into the throng as wolves began losing control and shifting.

On the platform, Dex lunged for Sinclair. He pulled her arms behind her back with one hand as he thrust her in front of him. He put his other hand near her neck. "Stop!" he roared as the guards pressed forward. "Anyone else shoots at the wolves and you get the warden back in pieces." The bones in his hands snapped and lengthened, adding weight to the threat.

Looking at the barely controlled rage on Dex's face—an expression so far removed from the boy I'd gotten to know over the past week—I had a feeling he wasn't bluffing.

Kyle was on the same wavelength. He shot Dex a nervous glance as he confiscated HFDs from the woman with the glasses and the two program coordinators.

Dex's threat worked—at least temporarily. No more shots were fired on the crowd.

Unfortunately, the crowd was too far gone to notice.

Around me, more wolves lost control. We had to do something to stop the mass panic. Quickly. Otherwise—threat to Sinclair or not—the guards would open fire en masse.

A body crashed into me, hitting me so hard that I flew back and landed on the auditorium floor. I had to move or risk being trampled, but I spent a handful of seconds staring up at the latticework of pipes crisscrossing the ceiling as an idea took shape.

I had to get to Jason.

I pushed myself to my feet, but before I could take a single step, another hit sent me crashing back to the ground. A foot connected with my stomach as a wolf tripped over me. The wolf went sprawling, and I pulled my knees up to my chest and retched.

Suddenly, someone's arms were around me, lifting me and shielding me.

"Kyle!" I threw my arms around him and buried my face against his neck, for a second not caring that we were in the middle of a stampeding mob.

He eased back to check me for injuries. "What are you doing here?"

"Rescuing you."

He raised an eyebrow. "How's that working out?"

"This part wasn't in the plan," I admitted. I took a deep breath. "I need to get to Jason. I have an idea."

To Kyle's credit, he didn't argue or question. "Okay. C'mon." He grabbed my hand and fought his way to the center of the room, keeping me close and safe until we reached Jason's side.

"How many bullets do you have?" I asked, pressing my mouth close to Jason's ear.

The small, tight grin that flashed across his face was completely mirthless. "Three times as many as I intend to use," he said, quoting one of his father's many gun tips.

I glanced up at the fire sprinkler above our heads. It was hard to tell from the ground, but I was reasonably sure it was the kind with a bulb inside. Break the bulb, and the sprinkler would go off—not an easy shot, but Jason's father had been dragging him to target practice since he was a toddler. "I need you to take out some of the sprinkler heads."

He looked at me like I was crazy. "Do you really think this is the time for a wet T-shirt contest?"

A few feet away, a girl lost control and doubled over.

"Please, Jason!" Without waiting for a response, I turned and raced for the dais, trusting Kyle would follow.

There was a chorus of yelps behind me as the first sprinkler went off, but I didn't look back. I knew Jason would hit more of them and I had to get to the front of the room before the surprise wore off.

Sinclair's eyes widened slightly as I jogged up the three stairs to the platform.

"Decided to come back and visit?" asked Dex. His voice was steady, but his arms were shaking and his skin was covered in sweat.

"Something like that," I said, hoping he wasn't as close to losing control as he looked. I shot a quick glance at the staff members standing off to the side. None of them took their eyes off Dex. As long as he held Sinclair hostage, he held sway over them. Even, it seemed, over someone as brutal as Langley.

"You're making a huge mistake." Somehow, despite the fact that she was being held hostage by a werewolf she had probably tortured, Sinclair still managed to sound authoritative. "You're only chance is—"

Dex flexed his hand against her throat and she immediately stopped talking.

I turned to face the auditorium. The shock of the water seemed to have kept more wolves from shifting, but they were focused on Jason, not the front of the room. Low rumblings started as a few people recognized him from his short stint as a counselor.

I glanced at Kyle. "I need to get their attention."

Kyle cracked his neck and let loose a howl that no human throat was capable of.

Almost like a single unit, the wolves turned to the front of the room. Even the guards—who had regrouped near the doors—stared expectantly at the stage.

I glanced at Kyle. "Neat," I murmured. He blushed and then shrugged.

Focusing back on the crowd, I raised my voice until I was practically shouting. "The explosion was the gates being blown. The Eumon pack is breaking us out."

Some people looked excited and others relieved, but a lot of the faces in the crowd looked skeptical. "We have to get to the gates," I continued. "Once we get past them, the pack has escape routes and transportation set up."

Wolves shot questions at me—so many and so fast that they all blurred together—but I addressed the guards. "The blond gentleman in the olive uniform and the nice werewolf on my left are going to collect your Tasers and guns."

Kyle hopped off the stage. Jason raised an eyebrow as he stowed his own weapon, but then turned and headed through the crowd. The wolves parted for them as they made their way to the men at the back of the room. Most of the guards looked angry, but a few looked frightened.

"Once you hand over your weapons, the wolves and I will be leaving the hall. We'd appreciate it if you'd let us go peacefully." My voice was level and steady, full of confidence I didn't feel. It was almost as though I was channeling someone else. *Eve*, I realized. I sounded like Eve.

"And why would we do that?" asked a burly guard who was definitely more angry than frightened. The sleeves of his uniform had been rolled up to his elbows, revealing forearms that were covered in intricate patterns of ink.

"First: we outnumber you by, like, thirty to one. You might tase or shoot a few of us, but you won't get all of us. Second"—and here I glanced at Sinclair—"we have the warden and we won't let her go until we reach the gates. And third: the pack is tearing apart Thornhill as we speak. If you let us go peacefully, they won't have a reason to come inside. Keep us in here, and they'll eventually break down the door."

"Don't listen to her." Sinclair's voice rang out across the hall. "You know the policy: no negotiations with inmates—even in hostage situations."

I raised my voice over hers as she spouted a section from the employee manual. "And if you need a more personal reason: the warden has purposefully been putting every Thornhill staff member at risk. Including each of you."

"She's lying." I could feel the force of Sinclair's glare between my shoulder blades; it was like a dagger buried to the hilt.

"That female wolf who was removed from the hall and the guy who's currently holding your warden hostage? They aren't the only ones the HFDs don't work on. Wolves build up a tolerance. The more they're exposed, the less they're affected—it's why the counselors have HFDs and you don't. Sinclair is trying to limit how often they get hit. Sooner or later, every wolf in this camp could be immune."

Hundreds of wolves stared at me in shock.

"Lies," repeated Sinclair, but the guards weren't listening to her.

"Did you know?" The guard with the tattoos turned to the uniform on his right. The wolves in the hall had fallen so quiet that, even with the noise coming from outside, it was easy to hear the exchange. "You didn't seem surprised when that girl stayed on her feet."

The other guard hesitated, then nodded. "Everyone assigned to duty in the detention block knows. We weren't supposed to tell anyone."

The tattooed guard scowled at the words, then handed Kyle his gun and Jason his Taser. The rest of the guards quickly followed suit.

The boys returned to the dais, arms full, as Sinclair glared at the guards. If anything was left of Thornhill in the morning, I had a feeling each one of them would be getting a pink slip.

"Do we hand them out?" asked Dex as Kyle and Jason climbed onto the stage.

"No." I expected Jason to speak, but the answer came from Kyle. "If you give them weapons, it'll be too big a temptation. Someone will use one. It will just give the guards outside one more reason to shoot." He headed for the far corner of the dais and left the guns hidden in the shadows.

Jason did the same with the Tasers.

"This is ridiculous." Sinclair twisted in Dex's grip. Her voice rose sharply and it was unclear whether she was addressing the guards or the wolves. "This is completely insane. Everything this girl has told you is a lie."

Both groups ignored her.

The guard with the tats strode forward. "How many wolves are out there?"

"Enough," I bluffed. The gunshots outside had almost stopped; I had no idea if that was a good sign or a bad one.

"If we let you leave, will you call off the attack on the other guards?"

I nodded. "Yes. You have my word."

"And the warden?"

"We'll let her go once we're through the gates. Just like I said."

"Conditional on the guards holding their fire," added Kyle, "and provided all of the wolves—including the ones in the detention block—are allowed to leave."

"You can't!" The woman with the glasses pushed forward. One of the program coordinators pulled her back, hissing at her to keep quiet.

The guard stared at us for a long moment, then nodded and pulled a radio from his belt. He tried to raise the guards outside, but all he got was silence.

Hank. His team had succeeded in taking out the communications system. *Please let them also have gotten to the detention block*, I prayed, thinking of Serena. To the guard, I said, "We cut your radios."

He shrugged. "Then you'll have to let me out. I can't make a deal if I can't talk to the men outside."

I hesitated. He had a point, but . . .

"I'll go with him." Jason hopped off the stage. "One of us has to, otherwise someone from the pack will attack him before he gets two words out."

I knew he was right, but I hated splitting up. Still, there wasn't much choice. "Be careful."

He nodded before following the guard to the doors.

"Do you have any idea how valuable the wolves in the detention block are?" Sinclair pulled my attention away from Jason as he exited the auditorium. "Do you have the faintest clue what you'll be jeopardizing if you take them out of here? The work you'll destroy? The lives that could be saved? You think you're helping them, but all you'll do is prolong their suffering."

"Prolong their suffering?" Dex's hand curled around Sinclair's neck. He didn't scratch her or squeeze the breath from her throat, but the muscles in his arm writhed under the surface. "What about Corry? She wasn't suffering before she got here. Did she suffer after you took her? What about the others? They're people, not your personal lab rats."

"They're not," said Sinclair, a note of misery in her voice that took me aback.

"Lab rats?" I asked, confused.

"People." She rushed on. "As long as they can shift, they're a threat that needs to be contained. But they can be disarmed. We're so close."

It was too much for Dex. "That's what you did to Corry? You 'disarmed' her?" His hand tightened around the warden's neck and she struggled for air.

"Dex. . . ." Kyle stepped forward. "Let me take her."

Dex shook his head, the simple movement almost violent. "Did you hear what she said? We're nothing but things to be opened up and tinkered with. That's what she did to

Corry. She opened her up and crossed her wires and when she didn't like the result she threw her away."

"I know," said Kyle, voice soft but firm. Sinclair looked like she might pass out. "Dex, let me have her. You're hurting her."

"Corry's dead because of her."

"Hurting her won't bring Corry back." Kyle took a second step toward him, then a third. "If you hurt her—if you kill her—all anyone will remember about today is that a wolf killed a warden. What happened to Corry—what's been happening to the wolves in the detention block—won't matter because her death will be all anyone will see. We're not bombs or weapons or things that need to be fixed, Dex." Kyle's gaze flicked to me, his eyes so deep and dark that they threatened to pull me under the surface. "But if you hurt her now, no one outside will see that."

Emotions warred over Dex's face, and for a moment I wasn't sure which would win. Then, shaking with the effort it took, he released his hold on Sinclair and pushed her to Kyle. Shoulders hunched and head down, he stepped off the stage and joined the rest of the wolves.

The nearest wolves edged slightly away from him, and my chest ached. Dex had been proven right—something had happened to Corry, wolves had been killed at Thornhill—but it didn't seem to matter.

"Are you okay?"

I glanced at Kyle. He was staring at me over the warden's shoulder. "I think I'm the one who should be asking you that," I said.

"I'll be fine."

He shifted his weight and I caught a glimpse of the bloodstains on his shirt. How could he be strong enough to stand there and touch the woman responsible?

I stared at Sinclair and a wave of hatred swelled in my chest at the thought of all the pain she had caused. She didn't deserve to come out of this unscathed. I wasn't even sure she deserved to come out of this alive. In the end, it didn't matter what her original intention had been, what she had done at Thornhill had been pure evil. It . . .

Before I could finish the thought, the doors at the back of the auditorium swung open with a bang.

Hank strode into the building and across the room. An excited murmur swept the crowd as the Eumon teens recognized him. Every single wolf—whether they knew who he was or not—got out of his way.

A knot that I hadn't been aware of unclenched in my chest. I was oddly . . . relieved to see him. Not just because we needed him to get out of here—though that was part of it—but because I was glad he was all right.

Though he did look decidedly worse for wear. His face was streaked with what looked like ash and his clothes were bloodstained. As he got closer, I noticed several tears in his shirt that looked suspiciously like bullet holes.

He jumped lithely onto the stage and gave me a quick once-over. "You all right?"

I nodded.

Hank hesitated, like he wanted to say or do something else, but then he turned to face the wolves. "Listen up because I won't repeat this: We proceed to the gates en masse. The warden goes last. No one lays a finger on a guard or any reg in camp and no one stops for any reason. No matter what you see, you keep going. Is that clear?"

No one spoke and no one moved.

"Is that clear?" Hank's voice tore through the hall like a thunderbolt.

"Yes!" said the wolves in unison. A few even added "sir" at the end.

"Once you're through the gates, you'll be told where to go and what to do. If something happens and you get separated, just head for the gates."

As soon as he finished speaking, I drew him to the side. "Serena?"

"She's all right. We got them out of the detention block in time."

"In time for what?" I asked, but my father had already turned to confer with Kyle.

Sinclair stared at Hank as though he were a code she could crack. "Do you have any idea how much trouble you'll bring down on yourself and your pack if you go through with this?"

Hank let out a low, dangerous laugh. "Your concern is touching given that you tried to frame me and mine for murder."

Sinclair's hair swished against Kyle's cheek as she shook her head. "After today, there won't be anywhere in the country where you'll be safe. You have to know that. Whatever you think you're accomplishing here, it's not worth it."

Hank took a step toward her. For a moment, he did nothing but stare as a blush darkened the warden's pale cheeks. "That girl you tried to have killed, the one standing a few feet to your left? She's my daughter. You say anything else before we get to the gate and, deal or not, I'll let those kids down there tear you apart."

He stepped off the stage and headed to the door as the wolves in the auditorium fell into a clumsy swarm behind him. "Remember: no stopping, no engaging the regs."

Kyle steered Sinclair to the dais stairs and I followed. "What about the program coordinators and the guards inside?" I asked. My gaze locked on the woman with the glasses. Without entirely realizing it, I curled my hand into a fist.

"We stay here." The guard with the tattoos was back. "A small group will meet you at the gate and take custody of the warden."

Sinclair twisted in Kyle's arms. "None of you have the authority to agree to this." Her ice-cold gaze locked on the guard. "When the LSRB finds out—"

Kyle pushed her forward. "You heard what he said: not a word until the gate. Besides, I think the last thing you want is for the LSRB to find out what's been happening here."

Sinclair looked like she was about to argue, but then thought better of it. It was a good call. Hank didn't make threats unless he was prepared to follow through.

Outside, it was still night, though the spotlights on the building made it as bright as day. The air smelled of smoke and chemicals—probably from the explosion at the gate.

The ring of guards had pulled back. Most had retreated to a nearby strip of grass. Several had been injured and the infirmary doctor moved among them, trying to help them as best he could.

The injured had gotten off lucky.

Bodies littered the ground like broken toy soldiers. Some were Thornhill guards or staff, but most seemed to be wolves who had stormed the camp as part of the second stage of the breakout.

I tried not to stare too long or too hard at the bodies as I followed Kyle and the warden down a paved path, but I couldn't stop checking for familiar faces.

I had wanted the breakout. Had pushed for it. No matter what happened, I was partly responsible. I paused and looked down into the sightless eyes of a woman with graying hair and a plump face that was slack in death. She looked like someone's grandmother. With a pang, I wondered whether or not there was a family waiting for her to come home.

"Casualties were inevitable. We all knew that." I started at the familiar sound of Jason's voice.

"That doesn't make it any better."

"No," he said. "I suppose it doesn't."

"Serena?"

"Hank said she was near the gate with Eve."

I let out a deep, relieved breath. It was almost over.

We fell into silence as we walked through the camp. Ahead, the olive and gray uniforms of the Thornhill wolves were a churning mass. I should have felt ecstatic—after all, we had actually done it, we had liberated an entire camp—but all I felt was a bone-deep longing to go home.

I was so lost in thoughts of Hemlock and Tess and how the hell I was going to tell Trey what had happened to Serena, that I didn't realize Kyle and Sinclair had stopped until I almost collided with them on the edge of the courtyard.

The smell of smoke had been growing steadily stronger and here it became so thick that it coated the back of my throat.

I stared, stunned, as I realized why Kyle had stopped.

The sanatorium was on fire.

Flames stretched out of every window, bathing the courtyard in an orange glow. The roof was completely engulfed. As we watched, part of it caved in, sending a shower of sparks into the night.

I took several steps forward and then tore my gaze away to look at the warden.

A small, satisfied smile tugged at the corner of Sinclair's mouth, but her eyes were those of a woman on the verge of weeping.

Hank made his way back to us.

"What happened?" I asked. "You were supposed to bomb the entrance, not the sanatorium."

I glanced toward the gate to confirm that it was gone and caught sight of a small, dark figure near the admission building. Serena.

Thank God.

She stood in the shadows, but her white tunic and pants made her easy to spot. She seemed completely oblivious to the three hundred wolves streaming out of the camp or the fact that she could join them and walk out of Thornhill. She just stood and watched the sanatorium—watched Willow-grove—burn.

I thought I saw her smile, but I knew it was my imagination: I was too far away to actually see her expression.

"—blew the detention block while we were getting the wolves out." Hank was speaking. Reluctantly, I tore my gaze from Serena. "They were trying to keep us from getting our hands on any of the files or records." His eyes locked on Sinclair and the look in them sent chills down my spine.

The full implication of his words hit. "So any proof of what they were doing? Any notes on how to reverse it . . . ?"

"Gone," said Hank. "The wolves are the only proof we have. We at least managed to get them out."

"So we don't let her go." Jason nodded to Sinclair. "We take her with us and keep her until we get the information we need." He glanced toward the admission building and I knew he had seen Serena. "We hold her until she tells us how to reverse what she did."

"Do that and you're signing your own death warrants," said Sinclair, apparently deciding she'd rather risk Hank's wrath than stay quiet. "Besides, I can't tell you how to reverse it."

"You're lying," said Jason.

When Sinclair didn't immediately reply, Kyle tightened his grip on her arm, digging his fingers in until most people would have cried out.

Sinclair didn't protest or flinch. She didn't take the words back or beg. Her blue eyes met mine and in them I saw a shadow of regret. The same shadow I had seen in her eyes when she told me about her sister.

"She's not lying," I said softly.

Before anyone could respond, six guards approached. The last of the Thornhill wolves had made it through the gate—even Serena seemed to have slipped out—and the guards must have wondered why we had stopped on the edge of the courtyard.

Two of the men had their hands on the butts of their guns. A third man was familiar: Tanner. The light from the fire made his red hair look like it had been set aflame. He didn't show any sign that he knew Hank as he stepped forward. "We held up our end of the deal. You're the only wolves remaining in the camp."

Kyle glanced at Hank. My father nodded, and he let go of the warden. He stepped back and flexed his hands, then wiped them on his pants as though trying to brush away the memory of her skin.

The warden seemed to become smaller as the guards surrounded her protectively. The look on her face was worn and defeated, and she suddenly appeared decades older. It was almost as though she was only just now really accepting that she had lost.

Kyle and Jason waited until the guards began ushering her away and then they started toward the gate. I hesitated, watching the smoke and flames lick the sky as the sanatorium burned. I wanted to believe it was all over—I wanted to go home and put all of this behind us—but it was hard to turn away.

A heavy hand fell on my shoulder. The touch was familiar, but not in the easy, comfortable way Jason's or Kyle's would have been. "You all right, kid?"

I nodded—I might even have said yes—just as a guard shouted.

Everything took on a slow, dreamlike quality as I looked toward the guards. Sinclair had broken away and held a gun—Tanner's, given the expression on his face—in her hand. She aimed it at my chest, and it was as though all trace of the woman I'd seen when I first came to Thornhill had burned along with the sanatorium. "Do you have any idea how long I've worked for this? Do you have any idea what you destroyed? I tried to help you—I tried to help all of them—and you took everything."

The gun was pointed at me but her gaze slid to Hank. Suddenly, I knew I wasn't the one in danger. Everything Sinclair had done had been motivated by the loss of her sister. She wanted to hurt me, and she would do it by taking away the thing she assumed would destroy me most to lose: my family.

Without thinking, I threw myself at my father, trying to knock him out of the way as Sinclair swung the gun and pulled the trigger.

Something slammed through my body, setting it on fire. I fell back—fell so slowly it was like moving through liquid—and just before I hit the ground, I saw a dark shape tackle Sinclair: Serena.

My last thought was that at least she and Kyle would be all right, that Hank and Jason would make sure they both got out. Then the world exploded in a burst of white.

27

"WE REALLY HAVE TO STOP MEETING LIKE THIS." AMY picked up a stone and skipped it over the dark water. We were on the shore—she was standing, I was sitting—but it wasn't the lake near Hemlock. Even though a wall of fog— thick and impenetrable—rose twenty feet out and obscured my view, I had a feeling the water went on forever. There were no waves, and only Amy's stone disturbed the still surface.

She was wearing a familiar white dress—the dress she'd wanted to wear to prom. I glanced down. I was wearing jogging shorts and a T-shirt. Both were too big and both looked suspiciously like they had come from Kyle's closet. I should have been cold, but I wasn't.

"Am I dead?"

Amy looked at me sadly. "Maybe," she admitted. She crossed her arms. "Seriously, I'm beginning to worry you have a death wish. When I wrote 'BFF' in your yearbook, I didn't mean it as a suicide pact."

"Shut up," I muttered as I pulled my knees to my chest

and wrapped my arms around my legs. Secretly, though, I was glad to see her. I didn't want to be alone.

"Amy?"

"Yeah?"

"I don't want to be dead." I felt guilty saying it—she hadn't wanted what had happened to her—but the words slipped out.

"I know." Pebbles rolled under her feet as she crouched next to me and put a hand over mine. Hers was cold to the touch, but for once I didn't mind. "I don't want you to be dead, either," she said.

After a moment, she lifted her hand and sat next to me. She stretched out her legs. She was wearing black tights, but they were ripped in a dozen places, and her pale skin showed through the holes.

"What happens now?"

She pulled at one of the runs in her tights, stretching it out until her whole knee was exposed. "Now, we wait."

"For what?"

"Some sort of resolution." Amy nodded toward the fog. "Everything you left behind is on the other side. That moment when the bullet tore through you? It's still playing out. The universe rolled the dice but they haven't come to rest."

"What happens when they do?"

She shrugged and stared out over the water. "I don't know," she admitted. "I'm still waiting for my moment to play out."

"But you've been dead for months." The words were like

jagged pieces of metal: they sliced my throat on the way out and left the taste of copper in my mouth.

"There's more than one reason people get stuck."

I picked up a handful of gray stones and let them fall through my fingers. "Amy?"

"Yeah?"

"Are you really you, or is this just another dream?"

She smiled her Cheshire cat grin. "Does it matter?"

I opened my mouth to tell her that of course it did, but pain exploded across my chest. Sharp and immediate and ripping me to shreds. Amy and the shore burned away in a flash that was as bright as an atomic bomb, and I fell into nothingness.

It felt as though someone had taken a hot poker and thrust it into my shoulder. I could barely breathe. Barely think. Barely move.

Somehow, I managed to open my eyes. Everything was blurry—like I was underwater—but I could make out an oval of dark skin and a familiar brown gaze.

"Serena?" My voice was the rustle of leaves over pavement.

There was shouting around us—so much shouting—but I couldn't make out any of the words.

Another person—another voice—leaned over me on the other side. "It's all right, Mac." Jason. The words were raw, like he was having a hard time speaking. "Hank went to get a car and Kyle's getting the doctor from the infirmary. You're going to be okay."

Hank was alive, then. *Good.*

There was sudden pressure on the space below my shoulder. The world went dark at the center and too bright at the edges and everything was on fire. I screamed.

"No, Serena!" Jason's voice rose over my own and the pressure fell away.

Darkness threatened to pull me back under and I fought against it even though some distant part of my brain pointed out that the pain would stop if I passed out.

"I was trying to keep it inside," Serena whispered. Her voice was halting, like a child's. She fumbled for my hand and cradled it gently. "You have to cover the red so they can't see it. It makes them so excited."

The red? The hand that held mine was sticky and I struggled to turn it over. Serena's palm was covered with blood.

My eyes sought out Jason.

"She was trying to help." He brushed the hair back from my face, the touch so light it was lost to the pain. "She went crazy when Sinclair shot you. You should have seen what she did to her."

At the mention of the warden, Serena flinched.

It was getting so hard to keep my eyes open. Almost impossible.

Not yet, I thought.

"Bloodlust . . . ?" The word came out a rasp as I fought to hold on.

Jason shook his head. "No. Whatever they did to her, it's not bloodlust."

330

Time twisted and turned. Minutes stretched out and snapped back.

Eve came. Serena left.

Kyle took Jason's place at my side.

A man in a white coat gave me something for the pain.

I began to drift.

Strong arms lifted me. The movement should have hurt, but everything was numb and far away.

"Dad?" The unfamiliar word slipped out as Hank carried me through the gates.

"I'm here, Mackenzie. It's all right." He eased me into the back of a waiting car.

I opened my mouth to ask him not to leave me, but the drugs made it hard to string the words together and the car door slammed shut before I could get them out.

Epilogue

HEMLOCK'S A TYPE OF POISON, YOU KNOW. THE PLANT, NOT the town. Though I guess both are pretty toxic. Amy's words—uttered so long ago that I couldn't remember why or when—drifted through my head as we passed the town limits.

It was strange: Amy had always seen Hemlock as something that was holding her back whereas I had always seen it as a safe harbor—at least until the attacks last year. It was the first and only place that had ever been home.

I glanced at Kyle's profile in the dashboard light. He was a big part of that.

Him. Jason. Tess. Hemlock was home because it was where they were.

I shifted in the passenger seat and sucked in a sharp breath.

"You okay?"

"Yeah. I just moved the wrong way." I slipped a hand under the collar of my shirt and traced the edge of the heavy bandage on my shoulder. I'd been lucky. Way luckier, according to Eve, than I deserved. As soon as I had retained consciousness long enough for a lecture, she had wasted no time in reminding me that a werewolf had much better odds of surviving a gunshot wound than a reg.

I hadn't argued. A few inches in any direction and Sinclair's bullet could have left me with permanent loss of mobility in my arm—that was if it hadn't just killed me outright. Miraculously, it had missed just about everything important. I had spent a few days in bed and would have to undergo some minor physical therapy.

That was it. I was lucky.

The same couldn't be said of Sinclair.

Serena had lost the ability to shift completely—at least temporarily—but she was still able to change the shape and structure of her hands. Eve had hauled her off the warden but not before she had almost ripped the woman to shreds.

Sinclair would live, but she'd be disfigured for life. Not to mention infected. If there was any justice, she'd end up in one of the camps she had worked at, completely at the mercy of the wolves she had once overseen.

Kyle pulled up in front of my apartment building and killed the engine. The familiar street seemed so normal that it almost felt surreal.

He didn't say anything. He'd been unnaturally quiet since we left Colorado, but every time I asked what was wrong, he insisted he was fine.

"Tess is going to kill me."

"Probably," he agreed.

"What are you going to tell your folks?"

"No idea. Not the truth. Maybe I'll just tell them I joined a militant cult. It would at least explain the hair."

"I think Jason's already using that one." Of the four of us, the only person whose family could handle the truth was Serena.

As quickly as that thought came, I blocked it out. The afternoon had been long and painful, full of blame and difficult questions—all of which I deserved, but none of which I felt up to thinking about at the moment.

Instead, I leaned toward Kyle—carefully because of the whole just-being-shot thing—and brushed my lips against his. "In case you get grounded," I murmured, before moving in and kissing him again.

Kyle hesitated—in the days and hours since I'd been shot, he'd treated me as though I were made of glass, barely touching me and only giving me chaste pecks on my forehead or cheek—but then he kissed me back. Tentatively at first and then so hungrily that every nerve in my body sparked.

After a few minutes, I pulled back, breathless. Not because I wanted to, but because I was actually starting to get light-headed.

A light burned at the bottom of Kyle's brown eyes. I half expected him to kiss me again, but he just ran his fingertips along my temple and tucked a strand of hair behind my ear. "I never got the chance to tell you thanks."

The words were soft and serious and seemed out of place with what we'd just been doing. "For what?"

"For coming after me. For risking everything to get me

out." He smiled, but there was something sad and almost uncertain about it. "For knowing what I am and what I've done and not acting like I'm less than human even when it scares you."

I bit my lip. The werewolf thing did scare me. Sometimes. But Kyle was human—more human than most regs. I just didn't know how to make him see that. How did you convince someone of something they didn't want to believe?

"Kyle . . ." I struggled to find the right words.

He shook his head. "It's okay, Mac. Sometimes there isn't anything to say."

. . . there's something I have to tell you.

The words Kyle had said that night in the sanatorium came back to me as he opened his door and climbed out of the car. He pulled my knapsack from the backseat and waited for me before heading up the walkway.

I stopped when we were halfway to the building. "Kyle?"

He paused and turned, my bag held loosely in his hand. "Yeah?"

"Back in Thornhill, you said there was something you had to tell me—something I might not like—and I asked you to wait. . . ."

He didn't say anything for a moment, and I felt my body tense of its own accord, as though bracing for an impact.

Finally, the words so soft I had to strain to hear, he said, "I really never thought you'd come after me. If I had . . ." He set my knapsack down. When he spoke again, his voice was stronger, more certain. "I joined the pack, Mac. The night before I saw you at the club."

I stared at him uncomprehendingly. "Hank's pack?" I said, as though there were dozens of packs Kyle might have gone out and joined.

He nodded.

That's what Hank was talking about, I realized, *back in the trailer park when he said Kyle and I didn't have a future. He knew. Both he and Eve did.*

Hurt, confusion, and anger collided in my chest. Jason and I had risked everything to find him, and Kyle hadn't waited as much as a week before completely turning his back on his old life. On us.

I fought to keep my voice steady. "So tell Hank you've changed your mind."

"It's not that simple." Kyle ran a hand over his face. "Wolf packs are a bit like the mob. Once you're in, it's a lifetime gig. I can leave, but if I do, no other pack will take me once they find out. I'll be blacklisted."

"Would that be such a bad thing?" I stared at Kyle, desperately trying to understand. He was home. He had us. Me. Jason. His family. Why did he need anything else?

"Maybe." He let out a shaky breath. "Those few days with the Eumon? For the first time since I became infected, I didn't have to hide what I was or worry about losing control and hurting someone."

"And that's worth turning your back on your whole life? That's really what you want?" My voice shook as pain spread through my chest. I wanted to ask him if it was worth turning his back on me, but I was too scared of the answer.

"No," said Kyle. "It's not what I want. What I want is

for there to really be a cure—some pill or shot I could take so things could go back to the way they were. But there's not. This is what I am—who I am—and that changes everything." He shook his head. "Could you hide what you were? Every moment of every day, could you pretend to be something else? Someone else? Could you stand spending every day worried that you were going to hurt someone if you knew there was an alternative?"

I remembered the look on Kyle's face the first time he told me he was a monster—how utterly convinced he had been that he needed to turn himself over to the LSRB. How pain and loathing had filled his eyes. Suddenly, I didn't know what was right or what I wanted.

I loved Kyle and he hated himself. Or at least parts of himself. If being in a pack could change that, how could I really ask him to stay?

Tears gathered at the corners of my eyes and I hastily wiped them away with the heel of my hand. "So what happens now? You leave again?"

"I don't know," he admitted. "Your father gave me a few weeks to make my decision and tie things up here. After that, if I don't go back . . ."

"You forfeit the pack."

He nodded.

I forced myself to pull in a deep breath, to be stronger than I felt. "Then I guess you have a lot to think about."

He stepped forward and folded me in a hug. "Thank you." He breathed the words against my hair before stepping back. "Do you want me to come up? Help you talk to Tess?"

"Kyle, if she thinks you're the reason I ran away, she'll chase you out of the apartment with a crowbar."

"Good point. And I've got to deal with my own parents, anyway." He hesitated, like he wasn't sure whether he should kiss or hug me again. In the end, he didn't do either. "I'll call you tomorrow?"

Chest aching, I nodded. I watched him walk to the car and slide behind the wheel. And I fought the urge to call him back, to beg him to stay, as he slid his key into the ignition.

I loved Kyle. More than anything. Maybe enough to want what was best for him—even if what was best would end up hurting me.

And it did hurt. Watching the Honda's taillights disappear into the night and not knowing where Kyle and I stood hurt every bit as badly as the wound in my shoulder.

There was nothing I could do but pick up my knapsack and head inside.

I reached the second-floor landing and tried—unsuccessfully—not to glance toward Ben's old apartment. A few flattened cardboard boxes were leaning against the wall next to his door. It looked like someone had already moved in.

Like Ben had never existed.

If only.

I could hear the faint sounds of a television coming from our apartment when I reached the third floor. I thought about using my key, but I didn't want to walk in as though nothing had happened. I'd run out on Tess when she needed me and left her worrying for weeks. No matter what my reasons, she had every right to be furious with me. Even hate me.

Trying to ignore the way my hand shook, I reached up and knocked on the door.

The TV went silent. The couch springs groaned and the floorboards creaked. There was a long pause and I pictured Tess on the other side of the door, staring through the peephole.

I started counting down the seconds to ease my nerves, tapping them out against my leg as I waited.

One. Two. Three. Three and a half. Four. Five.

The door was flung open.

Tess stared at me. Her hair was the same wild rainbow of pinks and purples it had been when I left, and she was wearing the tatty terrycloth robe that she'd had for as long as I had known her.

I never thought I'd be so glad to see that ugly bathrobe.

"Tess?"

She shook her head, and I had no idea what to say or do. I hadn't even called to tell her I was coming home. Given everything that had happened, I didn't want to get her hopes up until I actually reached Hemlock in one piece.

The longer she went without speaking, the worse I felt, until I wondered if coming back had been a mistake, if maybe, somehow, she didn't want me here anymore.

"Tess, please say something."

She opened her mouth, and I steeled myself for yelling

and cursing. Possibly some shaking.

Instead, she pulled me into a hug, squeezing me so tightly that pain blossomed across my shoulder. But I didn't let go. I didn't let go or ask her to ease up.

"Thank God," she said, voice thick. I realized she was crying. "*Thank God*. Don't EVER do that to me again."

And suddenly I was crying, too. Crying and burying my face in the shoulder of her robe. I'd seen so many horrible things over the past few weeks, but I'd survived. I'd survived and I was home.

For three years, I had hated my father for leaving me, but when he gave me up, he'd given me Tess and my friends.

He had left me in a place where I found people worth caring about. People worth fighting for.

Hank was certain there would be a nationwide backlash against wolves. When it came—if it came—I would be ready.

I would fight for my friends. All of my friends.

They were my family. My home. Maybe I couldn't hold on to them as tightly as I wanted, and maybe I had to let them go when they were ready to leave, but I wouldn't let anyone try to take them from me.

No matter what happened, I would stand by the people I cared about.

Acknowledgments

So many people deserve thanks, but especially:

My agent, Emmanuelle Morgen. Without her, Mac and her story would have ended up in a drawer years ago. I can't imagine taking this journey with anyone else and am so grateful to have her in my corner.

Claudia Gabel and Melissa Miller, my amazing editors, whose patience, guidance, and support made book two possible and who didn't run for the hills when I said things like "werewolf rave" or "zip lines" or "check out this lobotomy documentary."

Katherine Tegen for her continued support and for giving the Hemlock series a home with such an incredible imprint.

Thanks, also, to Editor-in-Chief Kate Jackson and Publisher Susan Katz.

Barbara Fitzsimmons, Amy Ryan, and Tom Forget for making *Thornhill* look every bit as gorgeous as *Hemlock*. Lauren Flower in marketing and the publicity team. Katie Bignell (who should have been thanked in the acknowledgments for book one—so sorry!) and Alexandra Arnold.

And a huge thanks to everyone else at KTB and HCCB who had a hand in getting *Thornhill* into the world and in the hands of readers.

Special thanks, also, to Shannon Parsons, Vikki Vansickle, and the HCC team. And to Whitney Lee for working so hard to get Hemlock published in other countries.

Thanks to Kimberly Derting, Sarah Beth Durst, Sophie Jordan, and Sophie Littlefield for reading the first book and saying such nice things about it.

I often think that I've never been more fortunate than I have been in my friends. Thanks to all of you, but especially: Debra Driza, Jodi Meadows, and Kate Hart for reading chapters and snippets of *Thornhill* and for keeping me from panic attacks once *Hemlock* hit the shelves; Nancy and Chris for supportive late-night phone calls and patiently listening as I tried to work out plot points; Teresa for not kicking me out of her bookstore when I needed to get away from my desk; Peter and Krista for making sure I periodically came out of hiding; and Rob for helping me celebrate my release day in style even though he was halfway across the country.

As always, nothing would be possible without the love and support of my family. Eternal thanks to my parents, whose support, guidance, and love of books set me on the road to writing. And thanks to Sarah, Justin, and Krystle for being far better people than I'll ever be.

Finally, thanks so much to everyone who read book one— especially to all of the wonderful bloggers who reviewed it, posted about it, or even just mentioned it on Twitter. You guys make all of the late nights worthwhile.